Praise for the novels of Victoria Schade

"Pet lovers, eat your heart out."
—*The Boston Globe*

"With huge heart, great tenderness, and plenty of unforgettable moments between dogs and their humans, Victoria Schade reminds readers that sometimes it takes getting away to find out where you are truly meant to be. . . . Add this literary gem to your TBR immediately!"
—Kristy Woodson Harvey, *New York Times* bestselling author of *The Wedding Veil*

"Chock-full of heart and humor, anyone who has ever been redeemed by the love of a dog will treasure this uplifting, big-hearted novel. A treat from start to finish!"
—Lori Nelson Spielman, *New York Times* bestselling author of *The Star-Crossed Sisters of Tuscany*

"A perfect romance—charming characters, amazing chemistry, and a rescue dog that steals your heart!"
—Jennifer Probst, *New York Times* bestselling author of *The Secret Love Letters of Olivia Moretti*

"Charming and heartfelt . . . The perfect book for dog lovers!"
—Chanel Cleeton, *New York Times* bestselling author of *The Cuban Heiress*

"Like the proverbial dog with a bone, I devoured this book in almost one go. It's the adorable tale of a movie star dog at the heart of a rescue doggie custody battle . . . which is actually a love match rescue. Pure delight!"
—Julia London, *New York Times* bestselling author of *It Started with a Dog*

unleashed holiday

VICTORIA SCHADE

BERKLEY ROMANCE
NEW YORK

BERKLEY ROMANCE
Published by Berkley
An imprint of Penguin Random House LLC
penguinrandomhouse.com

Library of Congress Cataloging-in-Publication Data

Names: Schade, Victoria, author.
Title: Unleashed holiday / Victoria Schade.
Description: First Edition. | New York : Berkley Romance, 2023.
Identifiers: LCCN 2023007853 (print) | LCCN 2023007854 (ebook) |
ISBN 9780593437414 (trade paperback) | ISBN 9780593437421 (ebook)
Subjects: LCGFT: Romance fiction. | Novels.
Classification: LCC PS3619.C31265 U55 2023 (print) | LCC PS3619.
C31265 (ebook) | DDC 813/.6—dc23/eng/20230309
LC record available at https://lccn.loc.gov/2023007853
LC ebook record available at https://lccn.loc.gov/2023007854

First Edition: September 2023

Printed in the United States of America
1st Printing

Title page photo by Pixel-Shot / Shutterstock

For Thomas, forever

unleashed holiday

chapter one

W here did you come from, cutie? Where's your person?"
It wasn't a complete shock to discover an adorable white boxer in my parking lot, given I ran the only dog training school in town, but it wasn't exactly normal to have a student try to register for class solo. I scanned the dark lot behind my building, hoping to see someone ready to claim the dog, but the only car left was mine.

"Well, that's not good." He wagged his tail at me. "Let's be friends. C'mere." I smiled as I reached for the dog but he danced a few steps backward, ducking out of my strike zone like he was well versed in sneaky grabs.

I mentally applauded the runaway for opting to swing by a business with an owner who usually worked ten-hour days and always had treats stashed on her. I reached into my back pocket. "Hey, look what I've got."

I held out the chunk of dry biscuit and cursed the fact that it wasn't something meatier. But if the dog was hungry—and it was canon that boxers were *always* hungry—it would do. I squatted and the dog moved closer but then froze, eyes trained on something just beyond me. Then I heard it. Myrtle, the tiger-striped feral parking-lot cat, meowing, daring the dog to come closer like a bewhiskered siren. She loved taunting my canine students on their way into class and had given more than a few curious pups a bloody scratch to the nose.

"Bad idea. She means business. Don't do it."

I was relieved to see that the pup was wearing a collar and I reached for it while the cat sang an off-key aria. My fingers were inches from the black leather strap when the dog rocketed away, intent on getting a mouthful of Myrtle.

"No!"

It wasn't a surprise that the dog didn't even pause when I screamed, but what *was* a shock was that Myrtle opted to run across the empty parking lot instead of retreating into the shadows along the building. Feral cats have to be clever to survive the streets, which made ancient Myrtle a certified genius. So why would she make herself vulnerable by heading into open space?

"Hey! Leave her alone!" I yelled at the dog as I took off after them. "Stop!"

Myrtle finally darted up a twig that passed for a tree and the dog managed to launch himself halfway up the trunk, making a high-pitched yodeling noise. The dog didn't even seem to notice me as I got closer and barely even turned back to look at me when I finally managed to snag his collar.

"Sorry, no cat snacks for you," I said as I pulled the dog away.

He continued to strain toward Myrtle as we started back to my building, him running triple time in place and me hunched over and awkwardly holding on to his collar. It was late and since the shelter was closed my only option was to call the police nonemergency line and hope that they'd be willing to hold him for the night. It wasn't like I could bring him to my place, since my geriatric mutt, Birdie, wasn't a fan of teens without manners.

"I have to send you to jail, buddy," I said to the dog, who was acting like I wasn't even there.

He suddenly switched directions, charging back across the parking lot as if Myrtle was no longer a potential appetizer. I was more focused on keeping hold of the thin collar, cantilevering myself backward against his weight, and didn't notice the huge form that seemed to materialize out of the darkness and was lumbering right for us.

My fight-or-flight switch toggled until I remembered that I was in Wismer, Pennsylvania, where the crime blotter was filled with heinous acts like stolen lawn ornaments and public intoxication. Didn't matter that it was after ten o'clock and I was alone in the dark parking lot, the only thing I needed to watch out for were the raccoons that raided the dumpster after hours.

The dog was practically levitating at the sight of the man. The giant form was backlit by the lights on the building, giving him the perfect horror movie silhouette. But if the runaway boxer belonged to the guy, he couldn't be all bad, right? And if he *was* bad maybe the dog would defend me, and we'd make the front page of the *Wismer Register*?

I leaned over to grip his collar tighter now that he'd kicked into overdrive, and in the split second that I looked down I didn't see the edge of the asphalt, the obnoxious lump of black that ringed the lot that I kept complaining about to my landlord. I wasn't the first person to trip on it, but I *was* the first to swan dive because of it, scraping my knees then landing on my stomach with a muffled "oof" that didn't let on how absolutely agonizing the fall was.

The dog never even paused to check on me as he took off for the guy.

"Shit, are you okay?"

The voice carried over to me as I tried to pinpoint which part of my body hurt the most. My knees were screaming, my palms felt like they were embedded with shards of glass, and my chest and stomach were going concave, but my *wrist*? No words.

Worst of all, I was mortified that someone else had witnessed it. I sat up slowly.

"Looks like that really hurt."

The guy had jogged over and was kneeling next to me while what was unmistakably his dog jumped in circles around us.

"Yeah, I'm fine."

It was a lie and we both knew it. When I finally found the nerve to look at his face I froze.

"You."

"Hey, Chels."

Up until that moment it had been an unseasonably warm September night but a chill rolled through me as I tried to process why Andrew Gibson was squatting next to me in my parking lot.

"What are you doing here?"

I watched his face cycle through a series of emotions, but before he could answer, his dog hunched over and made a deposit just a few feet away from us, buying his person time in the form of three perfectly shaped logs.

The dull pain seeping through my limbs was completely at odds with my reflexive reaction to seeing Andrew. Heartbeat speeding to triple time, the urge to stand a little taller, heat rushing to my face that I hoped he couldn't see in the dim light. It was like every part of me automatically recalibrated to trying to look cute despite my actual feelings for him. I hated my body for betraying me.

Andrew slapped his jacket pockets. "Damn it, I don't have a bag on me. Do you . . ."

"Does the woman who owns a dog training school happen to have an extra poop bag on her?" I winced as my palm rubbed against my back pocket, then handed him the eco-friendly bag. It was just like Andrew to let his dog run wild *and* forget to carry one of the core components of responsible pet parenthood.

I rose to my feet slowly while he picked up the mess.

"That's some quality poop. Nice work," Andrew said to his dog. I saw him flash a thumbs-up and the dog wiggled harder, then jumped up and rebounded off his chest. He barely budged, but then again, it wasn't like a sixty-five-pound dog could have much of an impact on someone as massive as Andrew.

He was big when we were in college, but the Andrew staring me down in my parking lot was certifiably *gigantic*. It seemed like he'd also gained a few inches of height in addition to the muscles he'd packed on, as if his entire body had kept growing well past puberty into this man-shaped mountain. His sandstone Carhartt jacket was unzipped, exposing a simple gray T-shirt that fit like he'd never eaten a carb. It was hard not to gawk at him, despite the fact that when I caught him in profile I noticed a tiny man-bun at the crown of his head.

How did he manage to make it look good?

My best friend, Samantha, had told me during one of our

gossip sessions that he'd moved on from his job as assistant strength coach with the Washington Commanders, but I never asked for follow-up details. There was no reason for me to keep tabs on Andrew Gibson and I was sure he felt the same about me.

"You didn't tell me why you're here," I said.

Andrew tied the poop bag in a tidy knot and launched it in the general direction of the dumpster. I let out an agitated sigh when I heard it hit the ground.

"I hope you're going to put that where it belongs," I said, trying to keep the schoolmarm out of my voice.

A smile played around the corners of his mouth and it was then I realized that he had the beginnings of a beard, a shadow that underscored the cut of his jawline. "Well, you haven't changed a bit."

That grin. I knew what it could do.

"Why are you here?" I punched each word to make it clear that I wasn't going to let him dodge my question again.

"Yeah, sorry, I've been meaning to stop over. We're, uh, we're gonna be neighbors, I guess." He pointed at the modest industrial building behind us. "I just signed the lease today."

No.

Impossible. The taut muscles along the back of my neck cranked tighter at the thought of being forced to deal with him every day. The last tenant in the space had been a T-shirt printing business that kept to themselves and occasionally gave me misprints, like the shirt they did for a local brewery that was supposed to say "Try an ale" but accidentally dropped the "e."

"Doing *what*?"

"I'm finally opening my private gym."

He cracked his knuckles and stared at me as his dog parkoured off of him again.

I wasn't surprised that Andrew was making his dream a reality. He'd always been a doer. Not in the way I was, of course. It wasn't like his major in exercise science was tough, which left him plenty of time to focus on his extracurricular activities. There'd always been something about him that made people want to fall in line behind him. Whether it was rallying the crowd for the next stop of a pub crawl or gathering enough signatures to host a Squats for Tots fundraiser in front of the library, Andrew Gibson got shit done.

"Congrats." The one-word response to what was a huge achievement would have to do. It was all I could muster up since I was still reeling about the fact that he was *right there*.

"Thanks." He reached down to pet his dog. "And sorry about this guy. He's still pretty wild. I've only had him a few weeks and I just found out he's deaf."

Of course. Deafness is common in white boxers. How did I miss that?

"He's cute. What's his name?"

"Dude."

"You named your dog *Dude*?"

Andrew nodded, looking pleased with himself. "Yeah, before I realized he was deaf I thought it would be funny to yell 'Hey, Dude!' when I wanted him to come. It was either that or Mister."

It was just like him to turn his dog's name into a joke. Although, yeah, it was kind of funny.

Not that I'd ever tell him that.

"You ripped your jeans," Andrew said, pointing at my knee. I blushed in the darkness because he'd probably scanned my entire body. The fact that I'd worked a long day was written all over me, from the dusty paw prints tattooed up and down my legs to my two-days-dirty hair shoved into a ponytail. It wasn't fair that he looked like Andrew Gibson Action Figure, now with a dynamic physique for more realistic poses.

"I don't think that's the only thing I ripped." I winced as I tried to roll my wrist. I was exhausted, in pain, and mystified why, of all the places he could've wound up, Andrew had picked the rental next to mine. There was a small commercial cookie baker in between us, but it wasn't enough of a buffer for me. Hell, Pennsylvania to DC hadn't been enough of a buffer. "Anyway, I need to get home. Glad you and Dude are reunited. Good luck with your business. Guess I'll be seeing you."

I realized too late that I'd teed him up for the perfect dad joke, but instead of rattling off the typical response about seeing me first he gave me a curt nod then looked down at his waist.

Andrew fiddled with his belt buckle, then whipped it out of the loops on his jeans with a snap that echoed through the parking lot. I sucked in a breath, trying not to focus on the many ways everything could go south. We'd never been close despite our ties to Samantha and Nolan, but I knew he wasn't the type to make me wish I had the Mace my mom had given me a million years ago. At least back in the day he wasn't. He'd even carried me home from a bar that one time I passed out in a corner booth. I didn't remember much of it aside from how solid he felt as he cavemanned me back to my dorm. I *might* have nestled up against him as he deposited me in my twin bed, but more than likely it was just due to the spins. That night I'd dreamed

Andrew and I were on a roller coaster together, kissing each time it crested a hill, and I woke up the next morning feeling more hungover than usual.

I hadn't talked to Andrew in over five years yet here he was, standing a few feet away from me in the darkness in a deserted parking lot that was a quarter mile away from the next closest building.

Beltless.

I held my breath when he took a few steps toward me, then let it out in an embarrassed whoosh as he reached down to thread it under Dude's collar. Of *course* he didn't have a leash for his dog.

"Anyway, sorry about Dude. We'll both try to stay out of your way. Probably for the best, right?"

I struggled to figure out if he meant because of our history or because of my canine students. I ignored the first option. "Well, yeah, with all the dogs going in and out, he shouldn't be running around unattended. I teach Rowdy Rover classes on Wednesday nights and he'll be sorry if he tries to mess with those dogs. Keep him on a leash."

I cringed. I sounded like the dog police.

"Yup, understood." He saluted me then turned.

I watched him walk away, waiting until he'd disappeared into the building before heading for my car. After an absolutely shitty year, Andrew showing up was undisputable proof that things were *not* going to get better for me.

chapter two

Puppy play group was the highlight of my week.

Sure, I loved all my classes at the School of Frolic, even the Rowdy Rover classes filled with dogs that sounded like they were out for blood if they managed to catch sight of one another (and which I tightly managed to make sure didn't happen), but it was hard to top a roomful of goofy pups learning how to dog.

Even though I spent way more time than I should in the place, I never got tired of being in my building. I'd purposely broken the "it's dogs so make it cutesy" mold and turned the warehouse space into a tasteful oasis, complete with washable navy walls, a high white ceiling that camouflaged the exposed pipes, and a polished concrete floor that looked like weathered barn wood. I always joked that if I aired the place out I could start a side business renting it for small weddings in the spring and summer.

There's a rhythm to my class enrollment, and the back-to-school vibe during the month of September also seemed to apply to dogs. I was booked to capacity with a waiting list for all my offerings, including my always popular puppy classes. As much as I wanted to let every single one of them in and fill the room with little ones, I knew I could only handle eight four-legged clients at a time.

Because along with those adorable, inquisitive pups came the parents. And *they* could be a handful. But I was lucky with my current session. Everyone seemed to know how to follow instructions, and they were genuinely interested in doing what was best for their new best friends. Sadly, that wasn't always the case.

After the forty-five-minute class ended there were always "darters" and "stragglers." The darters zipped out the door the second we wrapped up, but the stragglers hung around, eager to chat and pick my brain for advice on how to handle common challenges like nipping or potty training regressions. Paula Davis was Queen of the Stragglers, often keeping me twenty minutes after class. But she was irresistible, a huggable, squishy senior with a white-blond pixie cut who brought me homemade oatmeal raisin cookies at our second class because her dog Ivan learned how to sit at the first one.

"Did you see how sweet Ivan was tonight?" Paula asked, her little brown and white shih tzu mix clutched under her arm like a pocketbook. "He tried playing with that pop-leon."

I loved the way she managed to mangle every breed name. Even her own dog was a "shit-zoo" mix.

"I did see him getting frisky with Brandy the *papillon*," I said, gently hinting at the correct pronunciation. "He's finally learning how to play well with others."

"Hmph," she snorted with a frown. "Wish I could say the same for Hugh. I swear, he hasn't gotten off his rump in a week straight."

Paula had retired from her forty-year career as a daycare owner two years prior and was still eagerly awaiting her husband, Hugh, to join her in the joys of over-65 life. She'd filled me in during our brief postclass chats that the only thing Hugh wanted to do was sit in his recliner and yell at political programs on the various news channels all day.

"Maybe I should start teaching husband classes?" I joked.

"Oh, you'd make *millions*," Paula cackled. "And I'd be first in line, dragging Hugh here on a leash."

"Whoa, hold on, Paula," I said, holding my hand up. "I don't teach those kinds of classes."

Her face crinkled in confusion, but realization slowly dawned across her face and she laughed even harder. "You are *bad*."

"What's so funny?"

Carly Gorski was another straggler, but she had special dispensation since she was my closest friend in Wismer. As usual she was way more dressed up than she needed to be, perfectly turned out from her perky brown lob to her patent leather loafers. It was a little weird having her in class, especially because she constantly tried to throw me off my game by making faces every time I glanced at her. She considered her adorable taffy-colored terrier mix, Geneva, a milestone in her march toward convincing her husband, Joe, to finally buy a house. The townhouse they'd been renting since they'd moved to Wismer a few years prior didn't have a yard, so she could blame Geneva for "needing" to upgrade to a home with grass.

"Chelsea is making adult jokes," Paula said, slowly bending over to pet Geneva, not noticing that Ivan was turning upside down in her arms as she got lower.

"Paula, watch out for—" I said, gesturing toward Ivan, who was probably punchy and irritable after an extended period of being social. Not that I blamed him. By the time I walked out the door at the end of each day my forced extrovert persona was fraying along the edges.

Ivan erupted in a chorus of barks, causing Paula to jump away with surprising agility.

"Woopsie! I think someone needs to go to bed." She placed a gentle hand on Ivan's head. The little dog was well on his way to living up to his Russian czar namesake.

I nodded. "Class is fun for them, but it can be overstimulating. We want to keep his experiences positive so we should probably wrap up for tonight."

"You're right, as usual." Paula chuckled and headed for the door. "Until next week, my dears!"

The second Paula was out of earshot Carly turned to me with eyes wide. "Um, who's your new neighbor?"

Right. I hadn't told her about Andrew. It had been two days and the only reminders of him were the trash bags piled next to the dumpster. Well, that and the still-aching wrist thanks to Dude. It had taken everything in my power not to march over and tell him to use his massive shoulders to lift his trash *into* the thing, but I opted to give him a little grace since he was just moving in.

If they were still there by Friday I'd have no choice but to say something.

Carly was studying me like she was waiting for gossip. I waved my hand as if the fact that Andrew had moved in was no big deal, when it was, in fact, the biggest of deals.

"His name is Andrew. I used to know him at school, sort of.

You know my friend Samantha I always talk about? Andrew and her husband, Nolan, were roommates, so we were forced to hang out in college. He moved here and he's opening a gym or something."

"Is he single?" Carly cocked her head at me and wiggled her eyebrows. She knew that I was in no mind to even consider dating, yet she never stopped trying in a good-natured, pushy, I'm-doing-this-for-your-own-good kind of way.

"Don't know, don't care. He was a bit of a meathead."

"*Wow*, judge much?"

It was just like Carly to call me on my b.s., but she didn't understand my history with Andrew. Sure, I'd always been quick to try to knock him down a few pegs, not because I wanted to, but because I *had* to. With Andrew, I had no choice but to be on the defensive. I'd always forced myself to ignore my embarrassing involuntary response to him—that seasick, racing heartbeat, shaky hands feeling—because whenever we were together his "jokes" didn't stop, and I was his favorite target.

"It's a long story," I replied.

"And what's wrong with being a meathead?" Carly asked. "Because have you seen him?"

I didn't want to admit that, yeah, I'd seen him plenty. Not around the building, but in my dreams, when I was powerless to resist him. The one where all my teeth fell out and landed in his open palm had me especially freaked out.

"Trust me, I'm *so* not his type. Not that I'd want to be," I hastened to add. "And I have nothing in common with him."

I also had nothing in common with the type of no-beauty-filter-necessary women he usually went for.

"That's not always a bad thing," she mused as she gave Geneva a treat. "Opposites attract, you know."

"We're not opposites, we're . . . I don't know, I can't explain it." I huffed. I was too tired to get into all of the Andrew Gibson red flags. I knew I'd eventually be forced to tell Carly about how he'd always made me feel like I was an alien specimen he was studying under a microscope.

Except for that night, the one glaring exception in the Gibson/Higgins war.

Carly opened her mouth to be her contrary self but we were interrupted.

"Excuse me, do you have a minute?"

I turned to find class wallflowers David Taplin and his dog, Edith the Boston terrier, standing a few feet behind us. David kept to himself during class while tiny Edith opted to sit beneath his chair the whole time. I could tell she wasn't scared, but she had no desire to join the mosh pit with the rest of the pups, and that was perfectly fine. If anyone understood the need to hold back and analyze a scenario it was me, so I never forced any of my students to make friends if they weren't feeling it. I knew that Edith was learning plenty just observing the melee. And the fact was, most shy pups eventually found their way out onto the dance floor by the time our classes ended. Sniffed a few butts, popped a few play bows, and then went on to become perfectly well-adjusted adult dogs.

"I'm gonna run," Carly said, glancing at David, then widening her eyes at me. She scooped Geneva up off the floor. "Text me later."

I knew I had to wait at least until the next day to reach out to avoid a continuation of the Andrew inquisition.

When the door shut behind her I gave David my full attention. "What's going on?"

He shuffled his feet and crossed his arms. David was one of those clients who seemed to have a wall up, and no matter how hard I tried I knew I'd never truly connect with him. Carly had joked that he looked like a police sketch of a window peeper, complete with a not ironic Members Only jacket and oversized square glasses. I was happy that he kept showing up to class despite the fact that neither he nor his dog seemed particularly excited to be there. His face was normally expressionless, like he was bored, but now I could see that something was brewing in his eyes. After six years dealing with new-puppy crises I felt confident that I could help him weather whatever it was that had him tracking me down at the end of class. Especially because Edith was the cutest Boston I'd ever seen and she deserved every chance to live her best life.

"So, uh . . ." David glanced around the room again to make sure everyone else had left. He took a deep breath. "I just got a new job and I'm moving and I don't think I can take Edith with me."

It came out in a stream of words, like he'd rehearsed it a few times before actually saying it to me.

"Wow, okay. Congrats on the job. And don't worry, I might be able to help out so you can keep Edith. Where are you headed?"

"Florida."

He didn't seem happy about it, but then again, I wouldn't be eager to relocate from bucolic Wismer to always hot Florida either.

"So is it a matter of your living space not allowing dogs? Or do you think your job will keep you away from her for too long during the day? Which is your bigger concern?"

"Um, both."

His eyes darted down to Edith and she glanced up at him, a shared moment of connection. When he'd filled out the class paperwork he'd written that he'd gotten Edith at "a breeder in Lancaster," which I knew was code for a puppy mill. While Edith looked perfectly perfect now, I was all too aware of the hidden health concerns that could crop up due to her sketchy origin as she got older.

"Okay, so have you checked with your building or landlord to see if there's a size limit? Some apartments allow smaller dogs even though they might advertise no dogs. And as far as leaving her alone all day, I can refer you to a pet sitter organization that has a search by zip—"

"That's not going to work."

He was antsier now, shifting his weight and running his hand through his shaggy hair over and over.

"Are you locked into your new place?" I asked gently, because he looked like he was ready to run away from me. "Because maybe you could—"

"It's *rehab*!" he yelled at me, clearly frustrated with my inability to take a hint. "I'm going to rehab, okay? She can't come with me." His shout echoed around the room.

I froze. Now I got it. The disconnection, the wall. David had been fighting a battle and we'd never had a clue.

"Oh."

He stared at me, which I took as an invitation to babble.

"I'm, uh, I'm sorry to hear it. Or maybe I should say good for you, because that's . . . that's a big step. It's going to be tough, but you're doing the right thing. Hope is the only thing stronger than fear, you know? You've *got* this."

Everything I said sounded stupid, like I'd cribbed it off a "You're strong af" inspirational wooden wall hanging from Marshalls. I had no clue what to say to someone in David's position and the more I talked the more obvious it became. David only nodded his head in response, looking uncomfortable that he'd had to tell me, a stranger who couldn't shut up.

"I need to do something with her." He nodded toward Edith. "Find her a new home."

Ah. And there it was.

"Any family . . . ?" I trailed off. If he had family he would've asked them first. I didn't need to ask about friends because he probably would've exhausted that option as well.

"I put some pictures of her up on Facebook and said I was looking for a good home for her, and I got, like, two hundred responses, but I don't have the time to go through all of them."

"When do you head out?"

"Tomorrow."

The word hung in the air, and suddenly I understood why he'd seemed so nervous. It wasn't just that he was uprooting his life to try to heal himself, it was because he was desperate to find a home for Edith. And the clock had essentially wound all the way down.

"Would you . . . would you want to take her?" David asked, his hope and desperation clear. "Could you?"

A *puppy*? Now?

As much as I adored them I knew firsthand how much work they were. There was a reason why my dog, Birdie, had been approaching middle age when I'd brought her home from the shelter in Philly. The silver on her face and paws seemed to be doubling every year, but I appreciated her slow-lane approach to life. It was exactly what I needed as I'd grown the School of Frolic. At the end of the day I didn't have the bandwidth to manage potty training challenges, needle-sharp teeth, and the adolescent temper tantrums that followed.

But what David was asking of me was different. This wasn't me making a choice, it was an emergency. And while Birdie didn't like teen dogs, for some reason she could tolerate pups. Usually all it took was a single correction and they bowed to the queen.

I realized that the only thing standing between a dodgy Facebook adoption and a home that could help Edith reach her potential was one simple word.

So I said it.

"Yes."

chapter three

Nothing was going the way I would've wanted, but this was one scenario I couldn't micromanage into submission. I trudged up the stairs to my apartment with my work bag slung across my back messenger-style, Edith's trash bag of stuff from David clutched under one arm and the trembling puppy under the other. My wrist was still sore from the fall and being weighed down wasn't helping matters.

I could've sworn I saw tears in David's eyes when I said I'd take her, which made *me* weepy. When it came to dogs it didn't take much to turn on my waterworks. Everything else in my life? Mojave-dry. Or at least it felt that way lately.

We'd both sniffled and looked away to hide the fact that the spur-of-the-moment handoff was hitting both of us *way* harder than we were willing to admit. But when David knelt down and kissed his dog on the top of the head? That's when I shifted into full-on, don't-try-to-hide-it, ugly-face bawling. He'd placed his forehead against Edith's and when she licked his cheeks I was convinced she was helping him hide his tears. I was so overwrought by what was going down that when he asked me to keep her *no matter what* I'd stupidly agreed to it. I probably would've promised him my firstborn in that moment.

"Honey, we're home," I said under my breath when I reached my door. I rearranged the puppy and tried to dig through my jacket pockets for my keys. Edith looked up at me and trembled so hard that the tips of her ears vibrated. "Aw, little baby, you're *okay*! You're going to be fine!"

I realized that I was moving way too fast for her liking so I slid down to the ground in the hallway and took her onto my lap. She stood on my legs awkwardly, one paw raised like she was impersonating a pointer.

"Listen, Edith, you're about to meet Birdie. She might be bitchy at first but that's her right. She's old, and you don't know how to dog yet, so prepare for an education. But you two will figure it out. I hope."

I watched her looking around and realized that I'd just been emotionally manipulated into a decision I would normally need a month and several Excel spreadsheets to justify. A puppy, right as the holiday season was about to kick off. And this was going to be year two of me faking it. It took almost all my energy to put on my happy face so the rest of the world thought I was normal and that I enjoyed the stretch of forced gaiety from early November through December.

I used to enjoy it. A *lot*. I had the boxes of decorations packed away at Frolic to prove it. But then my dad had the nerve to die in early October nearly two years prior, forever yoking the unimaginable loss to the orgy of familial celebrations. The holidays with just my mom, my sister, Taylor, and her husband, Ryan, felt like a half-finished puzzle.

I cleared my throat, startling Edith. "Let's get this over with. You ready?"

She gave me a tentative wag, as if to tell me that she would soldier on and do her very best, which almost set off the tears again.

Birdie wasn't known for her watchdog abilities thanks to her failing hearing so I knew she wouldn't greet us at the door. It gave me a chance to put my stuff down, grab a baby gate stashed in the hall closet, and plop Edith down in the kitchen behind it. The high ceilings and tall windows in the ad for my apartment in this old building had camouflaged the fact that the entire place could be crossed in a dozen steps.

My old lady came strolling out of my bedroom and shook off, still unaware that there was a ridiculously adorable trespasser just a few feet away from her. Again, not a watchdog. I took a few minutes to say hi to her, stroking down her chestnut fur then rubbing the black patch on her forehead until she closed her eyes. Birdie looked like a tan Belgian Malinois who hadn't gotten the memo about needing to come across as intimidating. Her pointy ears were a touch too short, her eyes a little too soft, her mouth a little too smiley. Add in the gray muzzle and she was the picture of a sweet, mellow senior. I peeked over at Edith, who seemed *very* aware that she was about to meet someone new. Her head was tipped back and her tiny nose was working overtime.

"Hey, Bird. I have some news for you . . ."

I trailed off as she investigated my hands. She was used to the smells of my students lingering on me, but she seemed to understand that what she was detecting was actually coming from inside the house, like a phone call in a horror movie. Birdie finally darted past me and right up to the gate, her tail high and quivering.

"Bird, be nice," I cautioned. "She's been through a lot."

If I hadn't seen it with my own eyes I never would've believed what happened next. Instead of being blustery Birdie, or grumpy Birdie, or my least favorite, asshole Birdie, she dropped into a down in front of Edith. The little dog went into the world's fastest play bow then hopped a few times.

"Oh, that's good," I said softly.

Birdie lowered her head so that it rested on top of her paws. Her tail wagged slowly, and she couldn't take her eyes off the puppy. Then it hit me. She hadn't seen a puppy this small in ages, and never in her own home.

My tough old girl Birdie was going into momma-mode.

"Are we okay to try this?" I asked, placing my hand on the gate and glancing between them. "You ready, Edith?"

I slid the gate to the side and Edith stepped out of the kitchen all stiff-legged and confident, like she *wasn't* the puppy who hid under the chair at every class. Birdie slapped the floor with her front paws like she couldn't believe the new BFF strutting toward her, and the room went still as they brought their noses together.

Edith stood still and allowed Birdie to check her out, but whipped around to prevent her from doing a full inventory of her rear end. It was surprisingly ballsy, but Bird rolled with it.

After a quick walk around the block with the two of them I changed out of my work clothes and into leggings and my dad's oversized Nantucket hoodie. It had taken me a year to wear it and now it was my go-to comfort outfit. I was finally at the point where the faded pinkish-red thing felt like a hug instead of a reminder of all we'd lost. After I washed my face I stuck on two shiny charcoal under-eye patches that Taylor had given me. Thanks to the freebies she scored through her job I was well versed in self-care.

Edith was asleep on her feet after all the upheaval so I settled on the couch and pulled her onto my lap. Birdie hopped up beside us, still wagging at the puppy like she couldn't believe her luck.

I grabbed my laptop and navigated to my schedule, finally allowing the stress I'd been ignoring to wash over me. How was I going to juggle this new, very adorable problem that had just been dropped in my lap? Sure, I had friends with a doggy daycare business, but as much as I loved and trusted them, I didn't want to risk a *thing* about Edith's new life. If she was going to be mine her critical socialization period had to be perfect, without any chance of a negative situation shaking her already dicey foundation.

My phone rang and when I saw my landlord's number my heart dropped. Mike only called me when there was a problem, like the time the heater broke in January, or when the pipes burst in the bakery and a film of flour-infused water seeped into my space. And then there was the ticklish alarm system that tripped if you looked back at the building after locking up but *didn't* alert when I accidentally left the back door propped open.

"Hey, Mike, what's up?"

Edith shifted in my lap at the sound of my voice. I placed my hand on her body and was reminded how tiny she was.

"Hey, the alarm is going off in your place. I'm in the city and I sent someone to check it out, but he can't get over there for forty minutes at least. Can you go turn it off?"

There was a slight chance that someone had broken in and was trying to find anything worth stealing among the dog paraphernalia, but we both knew it was more likely due to the shoddy wiring job his friend had done when he installed the alarm system. I sighed, glancing down at the puppy curled on my lap and the senior with her big head resting on my thigh, her nose inches from Edith. It was after nine and the last thing I wanted to do was leave my couch because of my landlord's inability to invest in the property.

"Yup, I can head over and turn it off. But can we talk about getting it fixed? This is like the fourth time it's happened this year."

"Um-hm," he said. I could hear him exhaling smoke and pictured the inch-long ash dangling from his cigarette. "I'll add that to your list of requests."

You mean my list of demands.

After we hung up I ran down to my car, brought Edith's crate to my apartment while ignoring the daggers shooting in my wrist, then got the puppy settled inside. I kissed Birdie on her head. "Watch out for her, okay?"

My black-and-white-striped home-socks were too thick to fit in my sneakers so I slipped on an old pair of Birkenstocks instead. I looked more like my mom in the getup than I wanted to admit, although she'd be sporting elastic-waist jeans instead of paint-spattered leggings. Frolic was only a seven-minute drive from my house so I planned to be back on the couch in fifteen, unseen by anyone.

I parked on the back side of the industrial building and glanced at the time. Eight minutes down. I hopped out of my car and started to shuffle-jog toward the door in my Birks when I noticed that it was *open*. The screaming alarm and flashing lights inside added to the something's-different-and-very-wrong vibe.

I froze. This wasn't a drill, someone was inside my building! Anger-spiked adrenaline flooded through me. What kind of idiot breaks into a dog training school? My business did okay, but it wasn't like I had a big safe stuffed with cash in my office. I crept closer, my back against the outside wall, intending to peek inside to see if I could spot the person dumb enough to do it before calling the police. I leaned toward the open door slowly, inch by inch, until . . .

"Don't be scared . . ." a deep voice said as a figure emerged from the shadows.

I jumped backward with a shriek, clawing and smacking the air as if I had the strength to fight off the giant heading for me.

Until I realized that it was none other than Andrew Gibson, emerging from the darkness to torture me yet again.

chapter four

I bent over and clutched my heart, gasping from the shock.

"Whoa, sorry. Didn't mean to scare you," Andrew said, barely hiding his laughter.

I glared at him. "Oh, this is *funny*?"

"No, not at all. I take alarms very seriously. I think you need some self-defense lessons is all. Those haymakers were sad."

I narrowed my eyes at him until they were almost closed. "What were you doing in there?"

"Yeah, that's my fault." Andrew pointed to the building looking slightly embarrassed.

"How?" I rubbed my wrist, which was starting to smart now that the adrenaline was draining out of me.

He frowned. "Your back door was propped open with a little rock. I looked in to see if you were still there since all the lights were off in the front and the second my head crossed the threshold the alarm went off."

It was just like him to insert himself into a situation where he wasn't needed. Yeah, I'd accidentally left my back door propped open all night a few times, and sure, sometimes I'd come back in the morning to evidence that the trash pandas had pried their way in and raided the treats in the storeroom, but that was the extent of it. I didn't need him to swoop in and play savior.

"Why are you wearing eye black?" He scowled like he'd tasted something sour and gestured to his cheeks. "You look like one of my quarterbacks."

"What?" I reached up to touch my face and realized that I'd left my charcoal under-eye patches on. I pulled them off quickly and tried not to wince because they felt like they were super-glued to my skin after staying on for so long. I rolled them up into little rubbery balls and tucked them in my sleeve. "It's nothing."

I couldn't decide if I was more angry at Andrew for barging into my building or for commenting on my appearance, because I still had baggage about all the stuff he used to say back in the day. The guy noticed *everything* about me. Like, if I happened to wear a nice sweater to class instead of my usual hoodie and leggings he'd ask who I was trying to impress. When I got some ill-advised highlights he'd accused me of wanting to be a blonde, then said my hair looked better before. I'd finally started firing back at him, making jabs about his easy course load and tendency to skip class, hoping he'd leave me alone. I never *really* believed that he was brainless. It was just the easiest way to make him back off a little.

Of course I looked like Edie Beale and he was even hotter than the last time I saw him. The scruff I'd noticed the other night was a little thicker now, not quite a full beard but defin-itely headed in that direction. Figures he could go from nearly clean-shaved to half mountain man in just a few days. It was like his testosterone couldn't be tamed. And the stupid man-bun was still there but a few strands had escaped, the messiness somehow artful and deliberate looking, like a stylist had pulled them out so he didn't look *too* coiffed.

"Are you gonna..." He trailed off and pointed inside to where the siren was still wailing.

I stormed past him without replying.

It took me three attempts to get the damn thing to stop, partly because the touchpad was more of a punchpad and partly because I was still furious and shaky that Andrew had caused the problem in the first place.

"Nice space. A little bigger than mine, I'm jealous." I heard his voice echo behind me, which meant that he'd let himself in *again*.

"Can you please leave?" I turned around to where he was peering at photos of recent graduates that lined the wall. "I'm trying to reset the alarm," I lied. It was going to stay off until Mike fixed it once and for all.

The space was dark and I didn't like being in the stillness with him. I didn't like being *anywhere* with him. The forced civility between us was making me feel unbalanced and I wasn't prepared to fake it with him any more than I had to.

"Okay, sorry," he said. "I'll wait in the parking lot."

"You don't have to wait for—"

The door slammed shut behind him and I followed shortly after without setting the alarm.

"All good?" Andrew was leaning up against the wall with his arms crossed when I came out, looking around like he was doing surveillance or something. Why couldn't he understand that I didn't need him to do anything for me?

"It's fine. It happens all the time, not a big deal."

I fished my keys out of my pocket with my good arm and jangled them so he'd get the hint that I was ready to leave.

"Well, seems like it would be pretty annoying to me, getting dragged out at night in your pajamas," Andrew said, pointing at my outfit and lingering on the Birkenstocks and socks part of it. I braced myself for a comment that thankfully didn't come. "Is the landlord an asshole? He seemed okay the few times I met him."

I sighed, remembering that Andrew was never one to take a hint. "He's pretty absentminded. Cuts corners. Raises the rent every year. The usual commercial landlord stuff." I took a step toward my car to make it even more obvious that I wanted to leave.

"Got it." He nodded. "I'm sure you heard that Nolan and Samantha will be back for Christmas. Obviously they're bringing Mia too."

The news hit me like an unexpected dropkick. I *hadn't* heard that my best friend, her husband, and their two-year-old were coming home from his assignment in Tokyo for Christmas because I hadn't connected with her in weeks. Maybe months. I could blame the time zone difference for not picking up her calls. And she was busy with her toddler half a world away, so it was no wonder she was slow to respond to my texts. There were perfectly good reasons why I wasn't the first person she told about the trip.

"Yeah, it's great," I answered vaguely, unwilling to give him a window into the way I was really feeling about it. "It'll be good to see them. And little Mia."

"You and Sam still talk a lot? Me and Nolan are in a Call of Duty league so it feels like he's still around, you know?"

I felt a twinge of envy. "We connect when we can."

"Maybe the four of us can hang out—"

It finally broke me. The fakeness. I couldn't keep pretending that I was okay with him trying to take up space in my life after what had happened between us.

"Why are you here, Andrew?" I'd wanted to sound confident but my voice came out thin, almost whiny.

A shadow of confusion crossed his face as he pointed over his shoulder. "Unloading. Setting up. I still have a ton to do before I open."

"No. Why are you *here*?" I flicked my good hand to the ground beneath my feet emphatically, and I was tempted to stomp my foot like a child. "Of all the places you could've set up your business why did you have to choose right *here*? This is *my* spot."

"Oh, okay." He closed his eyes, tilted his head back, and swiped his hands over his face. "So we're going to do this now?"

"Yes, now. Because I'm very confused by your choices, Andrew."

He fixed his black eyes on me with a glare that sent a shiver along my skin. The man had the most expressive eyebrows even when he wasn't using them to furrow at me, with an arch that looked like it had been expertly threaded. Between the brows and the laser crosshairs of the Gibson Glare I felt paralyzed. I folded my arms over my chest and stood my ground.

"Not that I owe you an explanation," he said, refusing to break off eye contact in his annoyingly intense way, "but after I left the Commanders I looked around for the right place to open my space. DC and northern Virginia were out because they're too expensive and already packed with gyms, so I looked to come back north. Obviously the 'ville wasn't an option."

Andrew's hometown was thirty minutes away and still mainly farmland.

"And I've always loved hanging out with Nolan around here," he continued. "I've been searching for a while but nothing was quite right, until this space opened up. It's perfect for me."

"Well, it's not perfect for me." My voice cracked a little and I quickly cleared my throat to try to cover it.

Andrew took a deep breath, then let it out slowly, a long sigh that to me sounded like he was about to try to reason with a toddler. Which made me even angrier.

"The truth is I'm not happy about it either, Higs."

I bristled at him using my nickname. It was a throwback from college and no one called me that now.

"The last thing I want to do is bicker with you every day," he continued. "Because God knows that's the only way we can communicate."

I thought about the pub trivia nights we'd been dragged to and how many times we'd go head-to-head about an answer, arguing until we almost missed the cutoff buzzer. The number of times he was right was too embarrassing for me to admit, because I'd always told myself that *I* was the smart one, and *he* was the hot one. Deep down I had a feeling that there was more to him than just his good-time persona, but it wasn't like he shared that side with me, and what other weapon did I have against someone who seemed flawless in every other way? I'd quickly learned that one dig about his intelligence was usually enough to short-circuit his commentary about my jeans being too baggy.

I stared at the mountain in front of me and realized that the real Andrew was back, without any of the fake friendliness he'd been deploying so far. It was the version of him that used to watch me with that judgy expression, like he smelled something unpleasant. Sometimes I swore I caught him rolling his eyes at me, like when I talked about my workload. To him, school was a cakewalk of sports and parties.

And girls. Couldn't forget about that part.

It was pointless to revisit any of the past with him so I switched gears to the very shitty here and now.

"There's no reason for us to pretend like we're friends and we both know it," I said plainly.

"Exactly, agreed," he responded, almost too quickly. "So I'll stick to my side of the building and you stick to yours. Does that work for you?"

"Yeah, if you stop leaving your trash on the ground," I said in a Gretchen Wieners you-can't-sit-with-us voice that made me cringe. "The raccoons get into everything."

He clenched his jaw, Gibson Glaring at me. "Any other rules I should know about, Miss Higgins?"

I had a list of them I could rattle off, but opted to go with the most pressing one. Andrew took a few steps closer, probably hoping that looming over me would intimidate me.

"Yes. You have to stick to the assigned parking spaces," I said, standing up straighter and pointing to what had to be his Jeep parked in one of my reserved spots.

He made a sharp, exasperated noise. "Jesus, Chels, I was literally pulling out when I saw that your door was open and parked there because I was trying to help you! And for fuck's sake, it's after hours so not like you're using it."

"How was barging into my building helping me? You're the one who set off the alarm!"

"Oh, you've *got* to be fucking kidding me, Chelsea," he said in a low voice, nostrils flaring.

We stared at each other as buried hurts from our past zombie-clawed their way into the present. I drew myself to my full, admittedly unimpressive, height and met his glower with my own furrowed intimidation, unwilling to back down even though my heart was galloping from the nearness of him.

My breathing went shallow as his eyes tracked all over my face. I had a flashback to him doing the same thing all those years ago, which I'd always chalked up to him trying to figure out if I was in the same species as the sorority girls he was trying to get into bed. I fought the urge to smooth my hand along my cheek to check if there was any charcoal patch left as his gaze bounced from my eyes to my mouth and then back to my eyes again.

Being this close to him after not seeing him for so long, and being *studied* by him again from beneath that perma-arched brow, left me feeling as unstable and woozy as that night on the boat. Only this time I couldn't chalk up the feeling to copious amounts of champagne and my tendency toward motion sickness.

It was because of the force field he had around him. That magnetic pull to watch him that no one could avoid. He'd caught me getting sucked into it a few times, the most embarrassing being that early spring day when everyone was spread out on the lawn pretending the late April sun was actually the beginning of summer. Andrew had peeled off his shirt in slow motion and I, like every other red-blooded woman in the area, had watched him. I didn't *want* to look, but the moment was almost cinematic, lit by the sun and choreographed. As he flicked his shirt to the ground it was *my* gaze he caught, leaving me to wish I could slap the smug smile of victory off his face.

"Listen, we both agree that this situation sucks," I said. "You could've avoided it by choosing a different space—"

Andrew opened his mouth, but I flashed my hand at him so I could continue uninterrupted.

"But you're here and there's nothing either one of us can do about it until your lease is up."

He snorted. "That's funny, you're assuming that I'm going to leave when my lease ends."

I ignored him. "The only way this is going to work out is if we agree to more rules: keep Dude leashed, maintain the common areas, only park where you're supposed to, and don't enter my building unless I ask you to."

"Ah, so you're relegating me to vampire status."

I furrowed at him in confusion.

"I can't go into your home unless you invite me."

"It's not my home," I scoffed.

"That's not what Nolan says," Andrew muttered.

"*Excuse* me?" The fact that he and Nolan talked about me raised my hackles.

"Nothing. So what about my rules for this arrangement? Am I allowed to have any?"

I finally took a step away from him and gestured dramatically. "Please, feel free to lay yours out as well."

Andrew finally looked away from my face and it was only when I saw his puffs of breath in the air that I realized how cold it was. My white-hot anger had been doing a fine job keeping me warm.

His frown deepened. "Okay, I don't have any yet. It's too early to know exactly how you're going to drive me insane. But I'll be sure to keep you posted."

"Yeah, you do that," I snarked back, wrinkling my nose at him for emphasis.

Andrew had the nerve to shake his head at me. "I forgot what a pain in the ass you are."

"Oh, trust me," I shot back, "I could *never* forget how annoying you are."

"Huh." Andrew tilted his head as the corner of his mouth turned up. "Guess that means you think of me."

I wanted to scream at his presumption.

I spun on my heel to speed-walk back to my car, my face burning with the realization that Andrew Gibson had won again.

chapter five

A new puppy? Oh, Chels, that's great! When can I meet him? Maybe I can stop over later? I'm going to be in town after my book club this afternoon—"

I cut my mom off before she could get too deep into her planning. "I've got a couple of back-to-school pop-up classes today that I need to prep for. You know how busy September is for me."

"I do, I do," she answered quickly. "You work so hard. Too hard, sweetheart."

The conversation was about to unfold like we were following a map. My mom telling me I needed to hire someone to help me so I could get away from Frolic more often, and complaining that she didn't get to see me enough. Inviting me over for dinner in the hopes that we could go over "a few loose ends" that felt more like leaden anchors.

The window ledge was an uncomfortable perch, but I wasn't about to settle on the couch. I didn't have time for a long chat with my mom, and I liked looking out the window as we talked, listening to her cheerful chatter as I watched the world go by. Three stories above the main intersection in town meant that I could see eight sidewalks and all of the dramas that played out on them.

"It's a girl, by the way," I said, leaning my head against the glass and watching as a guy in a suit tripped, then looked around like he'd been pushed. "Edith."

"What is?"

"The puppy is a girl," I said, glancing back at where she was pouncing on Birdie's gently wagging tail. "You called her a boy. I'll send you a picture. She's perfect."

"A new granddog!" she trilled.

At the rate I was going it was the only type of "grand" she'd ever get out of me. Thankfully Taylor would be giving her a human one, a boy, in January, to welcome the new year with hope for the future. That baby was about to be loved harder and better than any child in history. I couldn't wait to be an aunt.

"How are you going to handle Edith with work?" she continued. "Do you need my help? I could watch her if you like."

It was a tempting offer. My mom had given me my early education with our family dogs. She'd never taken classes; it was just her tendency for kindness and patience with every living thing that made her shockingly good at puppy rearing and training.

"No, I should be okay," I lied. I still wasn't sure how I was going to juggle a roomful of people and dogs with a puppy who seemed to think that being in a crate necessitated a nonstop loop of editorial barking. I'd spent my two days off working on crate training to get her ready to go to school with me, but our progress was depressing for someone who was supposed to have all the answers.

"Hey, I was going through closets and I found some photos I

thought you might like to see. Want me to leave them in an envelope in your mailbox?"

"I'll swing by at some point and check them out," I replied quickly, because I knew that they had to be photos of Dad.

I closed my eyes. When would I stop being such a jerk?

Normal people would welcome the chance to reminisce about a lost loved one. Me? I still couldn't get past the choices he'd made as the end came rushing toward him. When I thought about my dad my anger somehow eclipsed my grief, and I knew that it was the wrong emotion. No one could figure out what to do with it, or me, so I buried my feelings to seem like I was processing the loss the proper way. People understood sadness when dealing with death. They knew which platitudes to say back to a weepy mourner. But my reaction to the loss of my father didn't make sense to anyone else, so I kept it to myself.

Because I wasn't sure if I'd ever be okay with the fact that he'd stopped fighting.

"Have we talked about Thanksgiving yet?" my mom asked, a welcome distraction from where my thoughts were heading.

It was still over two months away but she was a planner at heart. Another trait I'd inherited from her.

"Nope." I sighed. How could the family holidays be cranking up already? The only one in my sight lines was Halloween.

"Well, Taylor said she'd be happy to host, but I'm not sure I want to put that pressure on her, being pregnant and all. Maybe I should just have it at our place?"

Our. The word hung in the air. It was her place now, there was no "ours" for my mom.

"We could help her," I answered quickly before she could

correct herself. "Potluck-style. And it's not like she'd need to make a huge turkey since Ryan and I don't eat it."

My brother-in-law and I had bonded early over our vegetarian status in a family of meat eaters.

"Hm. I don't know . . ."

"No, Mom, it would be great to let her do it," I said, amping up my enthusiasm. "She's been offering for years. And you know she wants to show off the kitchen renovation."

"That's true. Ryan's parents haven't seen it yet and she could invite them too."

"Exactly!" I enthused, almost a little too over the top. But I wasn't faking it. Thanksgiving at my sister's could be a great new tradition. A fresh start.

A way to not focus on how different things felt now.

"Okay, I'll talk to her about it. Maybe you two could stop by for coffee and we could plan . . ."

"Yup, definitely soon. I have to run, Edith is sniffing the ground," I lied. "Love you, 'bye!"

I pushed disconnect as my mom was probably offering to build a guest wing at her house for Edith so she could watch her. The fact that the woman's generosity knew no bounds made me feel like that much more of an asshole.

"C'mon, you two lovebirds, let's go for a walk."

Birdie hopped up immediately, or as immediately as her old bones would allow, and Edith followed right behind her. I smiled when Bird turned to make sure that the puppy was close.

Our walk was a painful reminder that my wrist was still a mess even though I could use a spiderweb to walk Bird and it wouldn't pull taut. Normally navigating a trainee dog and a tenured professor at the same time was a no-go, but I was allowed to break my own rules when I was short on time. I kept my eye on the puppy, taking in her quirks. There were many. Rather than walking forward, her technique was to pause, wait until she was nearly the full leash length behind us, then run up behind Birdie and try to get tangled in her legs.

"You're making me look bad, kid," I joked as I tried to straighten out the puppy's leash. Birdie gave me a ridiculous wide-mouth pant that made her look like she was having the time of her life and I laughed at her. Even though I never would've picked a puppy at this stage in my life, it wasn't like I had a choice. She needed me. *Us.* I felt fortunate that Edith had both me and my seen-it-all senior to help show her the ropes.

Twenty minutes later Edith and I arrived at Frolic to find my work neighbor Roz loading her signature yellow bakery boxes into her minivan. What had started out as a weekend side hustle in Rozalynn Thompson's kitchen had grown into a full-time business called Auntie Roz's Smart Cookies, with flavors that ranged from lemon shortbread bars to sweet potato sugar cookies. Her signature braids, oversized glasses, and equally big smile were incorporated into her logo, and she was now getting recognized in public because of her cartoon avatar.

"Hey, Roz, you look busy," I called to her as I unbuckled Edith from her seat belt.

She waved to me. "Hey, Chels. Yeah, I'm booked and blessed. Who's that little cutie?"

"Meet your new neighbor—Edith. I just adopted her, sort of," I said as we walked over. "It's a long story."

Roz squatted down to pet her and the puppy immediately rolled onto her back and exposed her stomach. "Aw, I love her."

She scratched her gently. "Hey, speaking of neighbors, I've been meaning to come over to chat with you. Do you have a sec?"

The bands across my shoulders wrenched a centimeter tighter when I realized that she probably wanted to talk about Andrew. "Yeah, everything okay?"

"Yes and no." She stood up and her face looked more "no" than "yes." "I wanted to let you know that I'm moving out."

"Roz! That is the worst news *ever*," I exclaimed so loudly that Edith jumped.

There was no better neighbor than Roz. She was funny and kind, and generous with her almost-perfects, which meant that I often found bags of broken cookies hanging from my door-knob. And sometimes she cooked up batches of cheese biscuits for my students. In return I helped her load boxes when she was short-staffed, and had even done a few delivery runs for her.

She laughed. "That's actually the good news. I need to scale up to a bigger space."

"Congrats on the growth." I rolled my eyes and she swatted at me. "When are you leaving?"

"End of the month."

"Is Mike already showing your space?"

Her face twisted into a frown. "Well, that's the bad news part. I think he's up to something weird. He was here super early yesterday with some guy and they were walking all around the building. I thought for sure he was going to bring him in to show him my space, but he didn't."

"Maybe he's finally getting someone to fix the alarm system?"

"It didn't look like it to me. I don't know what's going on, but you should probably keep your eyes open. That man is shifty."

Our landlord was another aspect of industrial park life that we commiserated over. It killed me that Roz was leaving. Our building wasn't exactly in a prime real estate location, which meant that I probably wouldn't get lucky enough to have a neighbor like her again. Definitely no retail, maybe another food-related business. Or worse, something like auto parts or construction. I was probably going to wind up outmanned.

"Do you need any help moving? Packing, or eating your overruns to reduce the weight limit in your moving truck?"

Roz laughed. "Don't you worry, I'm only going to Hastings. You can still get your fill of Smart Cookies anytime you want to make the drive."

"I hate this." I pouted, pretending to kick a rock on the ground, which caused Edith to chase my shoelace.

"I don't know," Roz said. "You keep talking about how crowded your classes are getting. Maybe me leaving is a good thing for both of us. You could expand."

It was something I'd been considering for ages, in theory because I never thought that Roz would leave. But taking over her space would enable me to add new services, and allow me to bring on employees as well. A healthy expansion, which, based on my spreadsheets, was the only way I could hit my long-term financial goals.

"Hey, if you don't want my space maybe you'll get another hottie in my spot." She pointed to the cursed portion of the building. "I met the new guy. What's his name again? Alex?"

"Andrew." I frowned as I said it.

Roz immediately picked up on my displeasure. "What? You've got a problem with him already?"

There wasn't enough time to explain who'd fired the first shot in our little war. "Not sure yet."

"Well, I think he seems like a sweetie. I ran into him a few days ago. Great smile. I gave him a little welcome box and he said my oatmeal raisin were the best he'd ever tasted."

Andrew eats *cookies* now?

"Gotta watch him with his garbage, though," Roz continued. "He keeps stacking it next to the bin."

"I *know*, right?"

"If that's the worst thing he does you'll be fine. He seems like a genuinely good guy."

And that was Roz's first mistake when it came to Andrew Gibson. Believing the hype.

chapter six

Andrew was a walking cliché.

It wasn't even nine a.m. and I could hear the hardest of hard rock seeping through the ceiling. I hadn't seen his Jeep in the lot when I'd arrived so I wasn't sure why I was being subjected to metal in the morning. I couldn't identify the artist screaming away in my HVAC but I could tell it was eighties rock. I squeezed my hands into fists until the fire shooting from my left wrist reminded me that Andrew had been causing me pain since the first night he'd arrived.

I was used to silence from my neighbors. Even when Roz blasted Prince right next door I could barely hear it. What quirk of architecture was turning his stereo system into my surround sound? And how long was I going to let him get away with it? To keep from freaking out I tried to identify what he was listening to. One of my useless party tricks was being able to name almost any song within a few notes. I cocked my head like a dog hearing a siren in the distance. Ozzy? Judas Priest?

"Whatever it is, it's too damn loud," I said to Edith, who was happily chewing on a bully stick on her bed beneath my desk.

She paused, then went back to gnawing on the thing that now resembled a wad of wet paper towel.

In the three weeks since he'd arrived, we'd both been making good on our promise to stay away from each other. I'd expected to run into him in the parking lot at least, but he'd managed to work out a schedule that was the exact opposite of mine. At times I doubted he was really moving in, but then I'd see the telltale garbage bags stacked *next to* the dumpster and the nightmare would be real again. Plus, Roz mentioned that he'd invited her into his space for a crack-of-dawn tea break after he finished unloading various weight machines from a moving van, so there were sightings.

And of course, now there was glam rock keening through the vents. So it was definitely real.

I looked down at the stack of paperwork on my desk and realized that I'd left the rest of my handouts in my car. As much as I wanted to get rid of homework sheets, I'd learned the hard way that emailed homework tended to be ignored. Handing out something tangible at the end of class, with measurable progress listed for each exercise, was like a paper guilt trip that no email could match. I slid a baby gate in front of my desk, effectively trapping Edith beneath it for the three minutes I'd be gone, and jogged to the door.

When I stepped out into the chilly air I wished I'd grabbed my jacket. The change of seasons in Pennsylvania was unpredictable, so one day you'd be enduring a blistering summer redux in September and the next you'd need a hat and gloves for a we're-not-ready winter surprise. I booked it across the lot, not only because I was cold but because I didn't want to run into *him*. I'd been trying to look a little tidier than normal, just because, but today I'd resorted to a braid and Birkenstocks combination that had me shuffling to my car with my head bowed in shame.

There was one other car in the lot, which I didn't recognize, and when I got closer I realized that a woman was on her hands and knees trying to fish something out from beneath it. I squinted and saw that there were oranges scattered all around her.

"Do you need help?" I asked, slowing down.

She turned to look at me. "Oh, hello! Yes, I do. My arms are too short to reach the ones under my car and I'm afraid if I move it I'll squish some of them. They're too gorgeous to waste."

The woman was in the typical age range of many of my clients, and because people often dropped in to chat with me or check out the property before committing to classes I figured she was on-site for a tour. She looked to be in her early sixties and was wearing cold-weather coastal grandmother attire, in an oversized butter-yellow knit turtleneck, slim khakis, and clogs. She had a blond chin-length bob, arresting blue eyes, and the kind of bone structure that would keep her striking as her hair faded to white. Her vibe was "favorite librarian" so I immediately felt a kinship with her.

"No problem," I said, dropping to my knees next to her Volvo.

I reached under and felt the telltale twinge in my wrist, which reminded me that I probably needed to go to the doctor. I wondered if I could bill Andrew for it.

I finally snagged the half dozen runaway citrus and handed them to her.

"Thank you so much! I'm guessing you're Chelsea the dog trainer?"

We stood up and I brushed off my knees. "I am indeed. Chelsea Higgins, nice to meet you. Welcome to the School of Frolic. Did you want to come in and take a peek around?"

"I'm Patricia." She reached out to shake my hand, clutching the torn bag of oranges in the other. "Do you allow goats?"

"Uh . . ." I frowned, trying not to let my confusion register on my face. I was used to all sorts of strange questions, like if letting your dog watch you pick up their poo gave them a power trip, or if two male dogs humping one another meant they were gay.

"It's just that my dog, Murray, doesn't need training, he's the best little guy. But I recently added three new goats to our farmette that are downright unruly. Rude, unlike anything I've ever experienced. And trust me, this isn't my first goat rodeo." She chuckled.

Unruly goats? I was intrigued. I knew that positive reinforcement training could work on any organism with a brain stem and a desire to eat, from dogs to devil rays to rats to elephants. I'd honed my skills in clicker training on a chicken and I knew just how transformative the science-based training could be. And I *loved* a challenge, especially one that came with witchy eyes and a tendency to herkie like a cheerleader for no reason.

"Are you serious about wanting to train your goats?" I asked, hoping that she was.

She paused and I watched possibility register on her face. "Well . . . yes, I guess I am."

"Maybe I could help out. Do you live close?"

"About twenty-five minutes, give or take."

"Okay." I nodded. "That's doable. And what sorts of things would you want them to learn?"

I realized that I had no idea what she was about to say because the only goat education I had came from cute social media videos. I knew nothing about goat behavior.

Patricia frowned. "The new ones have split personalities. They act like mean girls to my two resident goats, but they're terrified of me. I can't approach them. They haven't accepted me as their caretaker, so I'm on eggshells around them. And I've tried all of my usual tricks but everything is backfiring."

I'd worked with plenty of nervous dogs. Hell, I now owned one, so overcoming fearfulness was a way of life. But could I do it with goats?

"I'd love to try. This would be a first time for me so I can't guarantee anything. But I'm really curious so I'd be willing to give it a shot. I won't charge you, of course."

"Nonsense," she scoffed. "If you're coming all the way out to my place I'm going to pay you. I'm happy you want to try. Can't hurt, right?"

"Can't hurt," I agreed, meeting her smile with my own. "And I'll give you the friends and family rate. Let's pick a time." I pulled out my phone and we settled on Friday afternoon since my classes ended early. We were just about done when I saw Andrew's Jeep pulling into his spot, which was my cue to shuffle away as quickly as possible.

"It was nice to meet you," I said as I backed up.

Patricia was focused on Andrew's car as he parked. "Finally," she muttered.

I froze. Wait . . . what?

Patricia was there to see *me*, to talk about goat training, right? So why was she staring at *him*?

Andrew flipped his seat up and Dude hopped out of the back. The dog scanned the parking lot, then greyhounded right for us. No surprise, he was unleashed.

"Careful, his dog is a little wild," I said. I moved toward Patricia to body-block her so she wouldn't get knocked off her feet by the incoming canine missile.

Dude spun in a few circles as he got closer, then came to a stop right in front of Patricia, wagging and panting with excitement.

"Aww, there he is," she cooed and petted him with her free hand. "Hello, baby!"

The level of familiarity between them seemed to be more than just a dog lover meeting an overly friendly pup. I felt panic rising inside of me as I tried to piece together what was happening.

Andrew walked over to us with no leash in sight, clearly forgetting my first rule. Despite the fact that it was visible-breath weather he was in a sleeveless white T-shirt and a black down vest, the dumbest combination of clothing I'd ever seen. Was I always going to be subjected to his body? Were his biceps so huge that no sleeves could contain them?

"No leash?" I asked, stating the obvious. "You should know that some of my clients get nervous around big dogs."

"Ah, you mean people who have those little rat dogs, right?" He chuckled. Andrew leaned over and gave Patricia a kiss on the cheek. "Thanks for bringing the oranges."

No, no, no, *no*. It couldn't be.

He turned to me. "I see you two met."

Patricia beamed at us. "Chelsea is going to help me train the Mean Girls."

Andrew froze, and not because he was exhibiting his right to bare arms in forty-degree weather.

My brain was still scrambling to catch up with what was unfolding in front of me even though I knew on a cellular level exactly what was going on. It didn't matter that their coloring was totally different, the eyebrows were the same. And the cheekbones. It was like a photograph of the same person except Patricia was the highlights and Andrew was the shadows.

"Hold on, Mom. You asked her to help with the goats?"

I felt a furnace kick on inside my face as Andrew confirmed that I'd just agreed to provide aid behind enemy lines.

"Yup! And I guess you two will be there at the same time," Patricia said, not realizing that she was dousing the fire with gasoline. "You're helping your father clear the leaves out of the gutters on Friday, right?"

Andrew took a step backward as his eyes flicked toward me. "Uh . . . I might have to reschedule because—"

"No," Patricia interrupted, shaking her head. "If you can't do it Friday then he's going to do it himself, because he's got that fishing trip this weekend and he wants it done. And you know how much I worry when he's up on that ladder alone. I guess *I* could hold it steady for him, but my balance can be funny sometimes . . ." She trailed off and gave Andrew an innocent look.

I could tell the glower on his face was all for me and not the fact that he'd been roped into chores on a Friday afternoon. "Fine, yeah, I'll be there."

He shot me a withering look then turned to go, with Patricia trailing behind them.

"See you Friday, Chelsea," she called out, walking backward and waving at me. "Can't wait!"

I managed a convincing smile as I tried to decide how I was going to lie my way out of it.

chapter seven

I couldn't remember the last time my sister and I had gone out for coffee together, although it wasn't for her lack of trying. We were finally sitting outside the Basic Bean in the shockingly mild October sunlight, Edith dozing in my lap, stealing a few minutes before Taylor set off for the day. She lived in Philly, in a gorgeous renovated brownstone in Fishtown, but she was in my neck of the woods for a store visit.

My sister had the coolest job in the world and it was literally written all over her face. Taylor Higgins Engelman was a divisional merchandise manager for Anthropologie in the beauty category, which meant that she had access to every cutting-edge, froufrou moondust elixir available. Between her proximity to a limitless supply of clean beauty products, the pregnancy glow, and a wardrobe filled with Anthro-designed jewel-tone velvets and cashmeres, my sister looked absolutely radiant. As usual.

Luckily she shared her loot with me, always giving me bags of goodies that never seemed to shine me up the same way they did for her. But between our similar hair color (though hers skewed more strawberry blond than auburn like mine) and the impressive "fivehead" that we both worked hard to camouflage, it was easy to tell that we were sisters. Taylor took after our blue-eyed, fine-featured mother, while I repped our Irish peasant lineage, with dark brown eyes that were a touch too far apart for my liking and a square jaw. During my awkward stage, when all of my features seemed like thrown-together pieces from mismatched puzzles, kids used to tease me and say I looked like a mix between a cat and an alien. But once the growth spurts ended and everything settled into place I came to like the way I looked.

It had taken me years to realize that it was because I took after my handsome father.

"So, Thanksgiving at my place is a go," Taylor said, taking a sip of her green tea. She pointed at Edith. "Bring that little one."

"Are you sure you want to host?" I countered. "I know I was pushing for it with Mom, but it is a lot of work. I hope you don't feel like you have to."

"No, we're excited to do it. New tradition, you know?"

She gave me *the look* after she said it. The appraising, vibe-check glance that only I could pick up on. But it was always there anytime she even alluded to the way things used to be, before Dad died.

"Yup," I agreed, brushing the scone crumbs off the table with the back of my hand, hoping the local birds would enjoy the feast. "That's exactly what I said to Mom."

"She thinks you're mad at her," Taylor volunteered, getting to the heart of the issue, as always.

"Oh, come on," I scoffed. "I'm *busy*! She knows that."

"She just misses you." Taylor locked on to me with the big-sister guilt trip that had stopped working when we were in college but she still occasionally deployed. "You should go visit her."

I fiddled with the handle of my mug, feeling scrutinized. "Tay, you know what happens every time we go over there."

"Yeah, and it's normal for her to want to talk about Dad. It's healthy. I don't understand why you refuse to."

"I don't *refuse*." I accidentally spat the word at her. "But what's left to say? Talking about him just makes me—"

"Angry. Yeah, we know." Taylor glanced around the patio to see if anyone was listening to us. "You need to deal with that. Talk to a therapist or something, Chels. You keep saying you will, but . . ."

"I don't need to. I'm fine," I insisted as a stone rattled around in my chest.

Taylor frowned at me.

"This time of year is just hard for me, okay?" I examined Edith's tiny paw so Taylor wouldn't see my watery eyes.

"It's hard for all of us, but it would be a lot easier if we could actually reminisce about him with you."

I doubted it. Talking about the wonderful memories made his absence that much harder for me to bear. Anytime I was at the house I half expected him to sweep into the room and wrap me in one of his bone-crushing bear hugs. The fact that it would never happen again gutted me.

"If you can't do it for yourself, do it for Mom," Taylor continued. "Just let her talk. Listen to her."

I sniffled and finally met her stare. "Okay, I'll try. She needs to meet Edith anyway."

"That'll be a good distraction for both of you," Taylor agreed as she leaned back in her chair, the worry not quite erased from her face. "She's a good puppy."

We went quiet, not sure what topic was safe other than pets or skin care trends. I adored my sister but we'd had a tough time finding our way back to one another after the upside-downness of losing our father. I was half convinced her baby was conceived in grief, as a way for all of us to recalibrate and focus on the joy of new life instead of the hole in our hearts from the one we'd lost. And the truth was, a baby on the way was sort of working. We all had something beautiful and perfect to look forward to.

"I should go," Taylor said, glancing at her phone. She reached into her purse and plopped an iridescent shopping bag on the table between us. "There's some good stuff in there. Lip stain, a retinol sleep mask, a shimmer lotion, and some gel under-eye patches."

I was reminded of my charcoal under-eye patch run-in with Andrew. It was Thursday and I still hadn't come up with a way to get out of goat training. But the truth was, I didn't want him thinking that he'd scared me off. His mom needed help and I was going to do my best to provide it.

Plus, I *really* wanted to hang out with goats.

I had a vision of Andrew helping his dad and accidentally falling off the ladder, clinging to the gutter with his legs dangling like in the movies. I stifled a gleeful giggle at the thought.

"What are you laughing at?"

I hadn't told her about Andrew moving in next door to Frolic. She'd met him once and I wasn't in the mood to get into the inevitable twenty questions that would follow.

"Nothing," I said, reaching into the bag as Edith tried to nose her way into it as well. "Just something ridiculous."

Or *someone* ridiculous.

"Oh, hold up," Taylor said before I could pull my hand out of the bag, glancing around at the other tables. "I probably should tell you there's something a little . . . *extra* in there."

I peeked inside and saw a thin white box that looked like it contained a high-tech product nestled among the beauty supplies.

"What is that?" I asked with narrowed eyes.

"It's a wand massager called Le Rush," she said innocently. "I thought you could use some tension relief."

I dropped my head to the table and it hit with a thunk. "You seriously gave me a *vibrator*?"

"What? Everyone is raving about this one, we can't keep it in stock. Take control of your pleasure!"

"With a vibrator from my *sister*?" I hissed. I finally picked my head up from the table and looked at her. "That's so creepy!"

"Chels, I just thought maybe you're a little lonely. It's been a long time since you were with someone."

Sure, it had been a while since I'd been in a relationship, but it wasn't like I was sexless. In the two years since my boyfriend Jake Monahan had cheated on me with my friend Lauren I'd gone out on a few dates. Even hooked up with a couple of guys. And it wasn't like Jake had been the great love of my life; we'd only been dating for four months when it happened. Lauren wasn't a close friend, but we'd hung out enough to have a bunch of photos of us together at parties and restaurants. Despite my nonchalance about it, the whole thing left me feeling pretty raw about relationships. For now, I was happier on my own.

"I'm fine," I said a little too loudly.

"I know you are, but Le Rush can help you be even finer. Trust me." Taylor winked.

"Ugh, this conversation is over, thank you," I said, crumpling the top of the bag down and shoving it in my backpack.

We walked out side by side, nearly the same height thanks to Taylor's footwear. She hadn't surrendered to the sensible, pregnancy-swollen feet shoes yet but at least she was out of her usual heels, opting instead for a platform boot that gave her a good three inches.

Taylor drew me into a tight hug once by our cars. "Go see Mom. Let her talk," she said into my ear.

I closed my eyes and hugged her back, letting my head rest on her camel cashmere shoulder. "I will."

We pulled apart and Taylor shivered, drawing her coat closed over her belly. "We're in for a long winter."

"Bring it on," I cheered. It was another way we differed. Taylor was a summer girl and I thrived in the dark of the cold seasons. It was better for snuggling up on the couch, with a dog or two nestled close and a good book for company.

"Hey, love you," she said over her shoulder. "And Chels?"

"Yeah?"

"Take Le Rush for a test drive soon, okay?"

I felt my face go hot. "We're never talking about that again, got it?"

Taylor laughed and waved as she climbed into her car, making it clear that I wasn't going to hear the end of it.

chapter eight

I was still coming to terms with the fact that I was on enemy turf as I pulled up Patricia Gibson's driveway. It was tucked away on a twisty Bucks County road, so camouflaged by trees that I passed it twice.

The house was up a gentle rise, a typical stone farmhouse that looked like it hadn't changed in over a hundred years. Not the sort of genteel spot I imagined Andrew growing up in, but then again, I wasn't sure exactly what sort of home life could've created him, other than a frat house.

Patricia came out waving both hands at me and looking overjoyed, in a navy beanie and oversized khaki farm jacket. She pointed to a parking spot near the garage and as I eased to a stop I took a quick look around to make sure Andrew hadn't arrived. There was no sign of his Jeep, which meant there was a chance that I could complete my mission without running into him. My hands shook a little as I grabbed my stuff and I blamed the tremor on goat-related stress.

"Welcome," Patricia called to me as I headed toward her. "We are *so* thrilled you're here."

I was sure there was one Gibson who wasn't.

"I'm excited to give this a try," I said as I climbed the porch steps. I touched the black treat bag clipped to my jeans. "I did my research so I have some animal crackers and tortilla chips ready to go. I know they're not super-healthy options, but I figured I needed to bring my A game the first time I'm meeting them."

"Ooh, they are going to *love* you." Patricia beamed at me. "Why don't we chat for a few minutes before I bring you back to meet them? Let's sit on the porch, it's not too chilly today. I made some hot chocolate for us."

The way she said it left no doubt that I was about to have hot chocolate whether I wanted it or not. Which of course I did, though I felt weird about delaying the work I was there to do. My goal was to avoid any unnecessary time behind enemy lines, but I could already tell that Patricia was going to make my mission impossible.

I sat on one of the black slat rockers and picked up the hardcover book on the table next to it. *Frankenstein*? We were certainly heading into the right season for it. My annual Howl-o-Ween bash was just a few weeks off.

Patricia hustled out carrying two steaming mugs as I placed the book back on the table.

"I just finished reading *A Vindication of the Rights of Woman* by Mary Wollstonecraft." She nodded toward the book as she handed me a mug. "I wanted to see if the mother of feminism impacted her own daughter's work."

I thought I knew a lot about books, but I was stumped. My expression must have made it clear.

"Mary Shelley was Mary Wollstonecraft's daughter."

"Right, right, of course," I said once she'd connected the dots for me. I filed the fact away for future trivia use. "So what did you discover? I haven't read *Frankenstein* in forever."

Patricia considered the question as she blew on her mug. "I wouldn't call it an outwardly feminist book. But the 'birth' of the monster is interesting when viewed through a feminist lens. Victor Frankenstein subverted the laws of nature in several ways, including male maternity."

I took a gulp of the still-hot cocoa and winced. How was it possible that I was sitting on Andrew Gibson's front porch talking about feminism with his mother? And how had this lovely, clearly brilliant woman given birth to a man who was famous for using his double-header beer bong to attract women?

"Pat?" A deep voice echoed through the storm door. "Where's Drew?"

"Honey, he'll be here in a bit," Patricia yelled back.

So it was going to be a family affair. I tried to visualize Andrew's father before I saw him and conjured up a bear of a man, a little soft in the middle but still fit for his age, wearing an Eagles baseball cap. The man who appeared looked like he could be the accountant for the man I'd imagined.

"Oh, hello," he said when he saw me, bobbing his head in my direction with a grin. "I forgot you were coming. I'm Gerard."

A British accent? Andrew's father was *English*?

He had to be adopted.

There was no other explanation as to how these two people could've created Andrew. His father was tall and reedy, a gray-haired professor of a man with the hint of a white beard and round arty glasses with thick gray rims. Even though he was about to do yard work he was dressed in pressed jeans and a striped button-down shirt.

"Nice to meet you. I'm Chelsea," I said, standing up to shake his hand.

"Ah, my favorite footballers," he said as he clasped my hand with both of his. "Lovely to meet you. Here's hoping you can work your magic with the girls. Andrew tells us you're quite gifted."

I froze. Andrew talked about me to his parents?

The crunching of tires on the driveway made us all turn to watch as the man of the hour rolled in.

"There he is," Gerard muttered. "Late."

A dog inside the house started barking as Andrew got out of the car. He pulled back the seat and Dude came barreling out.

"Why did he bring the dog?" Gerard grumbled. "We never get anything done when Dude is here. It's nonstop refereeing with him and Murray."

"Stop," Patricia chastised softly. "He's young, he needs exercise, it's good for him to be here."

The boxer raced to the porch and cleared the three steps in a single leap, then nearly took my knees out. I glanced at Andrew to see if he noticed that his dog was accosting me, but he was too busy unloading tools from his Jeep. At least he was dressed appropriately for the cool weather, without a bicep or pec in sight beneath his black hoodie.

When he turned to head toward us it felt like he fixed me in a tractor beam of hate. He glared at me, unblinking, as he strode closer. I swear I felt the ground rumbling with each step, like he was a giant who was angry about the trespasser on his beanstalk.

So why did my stomach do a little flip-flop?

"Hey," he said as a general greeting. "Sorry I'm a little late."

"More than a little," his father corrected. "Off we go."

"Can you let Murray out for Dude?" Andrew finally acknowledged that his dog needed a distraction other than trying to chew his way through my treat bag.

"Drew, if these two run off again I swear I won't be wasting a second chasing them down," Gerard scolded. "We have work to do, and you know they always come back."

Patricia wordlessly moved to the door and let a big-eared, spotty white and black cattle dog mix out to greet his boxer nephew. They tackled one another and took off into the yard.

I glanced between Gerard and Andrew and felt like I was in the middle of a grudge match. It felt sort of familiar, the clipped shorthand born from a thousand little and not-so-little disagreements that eventually lit the fuse to the crackling tension in the air. Gerard was fixed on his son and Andrew was staring off in the direction the dogs had run.

"You certainly are grumbly today," Patricia said under her breath as she brushed by her husband.

"We're behind!" Gerard exclaimed. "We have a lot to accomplish before the sun goes down."

"Dad, I'm literally ten minutes late, and I work fast. You know that. Is the ladder in the shed?"

"No, I've already set it up out back. Let's go."

The two men set off wearing twin frowns as the sound of canine wrestling echoed from somewhere in the distance.

"Well!" Patricia said, turning to me with a slightly embarrassed smile. "They're so similar, those two."

I tried to hide my disbelief that the mountain and the gentleman had anything in common other than blood.

"Shall we go meet the girls now?"

"Of course!" I answered a little too quickly. But I was eager to get to the reason I was there: three temperamental goats that needed to learn how to be part of a family.

"I think that's all I should try for today," I said, snapping my nearly empty treat bag shut to the dismay of the three Nigerian dwarf goats watching me from twelve feet away. "I don't want to push too much."

The trio, one black with gray ears, one camel-colored with a white belly, and one that was brown with dramatic gray accents, had shifted from sprinting away every time I moved to holding still to wait for goodies. They were still maintaining a huge buffer from me, but I considered their eventual lack of scatter a step in the right direction.

"I think you made fantastic progress!" Patricia called from the other side of the fence. Because she had an accidentally negative history with the trio she'd opted to let me work alone, calling out advice from the sidelines if she noticed me doing anything that might set them off. "They've never gotten that close to me."

She'd told me that the three teenage goats had been rescued from a bad situation, where the only handling they'd had was being chased down by their prior owner to tag their ears. They were as skittish as deer in a field and didn't trust anyone on two legs, even kindly Patricia, who told me that her two resident goats, Rainbow and Happy, adored her. Her goals were modest: to help Darling, Petunia, and Thistle understand that humans weren't the enemy, to get them to stop headbutting her when her back was turned, and eventually, to enjoy handling.

"I think they're going to come along nicely," I said, taking a few steps toward the gate door, then pausing to glance back at my students. They opted to watch me instead of sprinting away, so I tossed them the last handful of broken-up animal crackers. I speed-walked out of the pen as they bent their heads to scoop up the goodies.

"So simple, yet I never considered it," Patricia marveled.

That was the beauty of the first lesson, where all I had to do was teach the goats how damn easy it was to get paid. I'd make them work a little harder in each successive class, but for now all I wanted them to understand was that I was a treat floozy.

"I have a feeling we're going to have some very eager students next time." I paused. "That is, if you want a next time."

I wondered if Andrew was going to get to her and tell her how truly horrible I was.

"Are you kidding me? Of course I want you to come back! Let me get my calendar and my checkbook." She frowned and squinted into the distance. "But where *is* my checkbook?"

"Oh, you don't have to pay me," I said, jogging a few steps to reach her. "This is fun for me. Keeps me sharp."

"No, ma'am," she answered quickly, shaking her head. "This is a huge help so you're definitely getting paid. Just give me a few minutes to find my things. Now that I think about it, I haven't seen my checkbook in weeks. Are you okay to stay for a few minutes longer?"

"No problem." I'd run home after my last class to take care of Edith and Birdie before coming so I was fine to wait. And it wasn't like I had plans.

Patricia headed for the house so I shoved my chilled hands in my jacket pockets and took a few minutes to survey the land.

It was a beautiful spot, with rolling hills dotted by gigantic orange-and-yellow-clad trees. It was the kind of property that had something new and beautiful to offer with each season, from the leaf-peeping fall splendor we were in now, to slopes perfect for sledding once the snow came, to the honeybees and blossoms of spring, to a swimming hole and tire swing come summer. It wasn't unlike where I'd grown up, give or take a few acres.

The sun was dipping lower and the temperature was dropping just as quickly. I was happy to be done for the day. I was looking forward to heading home for an evening of Netflix and canine chill.

Just like every Friday night.

chapter nine

I turned back toward the Gibsons' house just as a figure crested over the roof, the buffest Santa to ever live. I pivoted on my heel and pretended like I hadn't seen him.

"*Damn* it," I heard Andrew exclaim.

I looked over my shoulder at him to make sure he wasn't dangling from the gutter, but he was gingerly pacing along the edge of the sloped roof, peering at the ground below. He slapped his back pockets and let out a frustrated grunt.

It was clear something was wrong and I was the only one within grunting distance. "You okay?"

"Yeah. I mean, no. My dad forgot that I was on the other side of the roof patching a hole and brought the ladder back to the barn. My phone is on the ground so I can't call him."

I hid an evil grin. "Um, I hate to break it to you, but I just saw your dad pulling down the driveway."

"Are you kidding me?" Andrew bent over in exasperation, his hands on his thighs. "He did this on purpose. I *told* him I'd come back tomorrow with the brackets we need and install them myself, but he must've decided to go to the hardware store now."

"And he left you up there," I mused, slowly realizing the full extent of Andrew's predicament. I walked closer so I'd be able to see his face as he begged for my help.

"I could jump," he said, leaning over the edge and eyeing the patio at least sixteen feet below him.

"You could," I agreed. Even though he was a brunet Thor, I didn't want to encourage him to drop off the roof into a super-hero pose on the flagstone. "Or you could tell me where the ladder is and I could bring it to you."

He dismissed me with a smirk and wave. "It's too heavy for you. I can wait. He won't be that long."

I ignored his insult and squinted up at the sky. "The forecast calls for rain. Starting soon."

Mother Nature kicked up the wind and spit out a few rain-drops to prove that I was right and I relished my power position. Maybe I could let him get a *little* wet before I rescued him.

"Have you seen Dude?" Andrew asked, peering into the distance.

I shook my head. "No, but I was focused on my students."

"Damn it, I need to chase him down before the rain." Andrew sighed. "Okay, fine. It would be great if you could grab the ladder for me. See that barn?" He pointed to a small stone and slat building down the lane. "It's probably on the far side of it, on the ground."

"Okay." I bobbed my head. "Be right back." I paused and smiled sweetly. "Or not."

"Hey, that's fine," he shot back, clearly not enjoying my power play. "Do whatever you want, I'm totally content."

"Maybe you can spot Murray and Dude from up there," I mused.

"Exactly," he said, still not looking at me. Andrew cupped his hand around his mouth. "Murray!" He clapped his hands, hoping that the one dog with hearing would respond.

It hit me that I was sort of being an asshole. "I'm going, I'm going. Back in a sec." I set off at a trot.

"Be careful, it's heavy," he yelled after me. "It's okay if you can't manage it. Don't be a hero."

I snorted over my shoulder at him. "Give me some credit, Gibson. I'm strong like ox." I flexed my arms like an old-timey muscleman.

Or I *thought* I was strong until I tried lifting the damn thing. Not only was the giant metal ladder heavy, it was almost impossible to find a comfortable spot to grab. I finally managed to grasp it in a way that would allow me to drag it and was reminded of the pain in my wrist. How was it possible that Andrew kept injuring me over and over without even getting close to me?

I dragged the ladder gracelessly until I reached the spot in the yard where he'd be able to see me, at which point I repositioned myself in the middle of it and hoisted the entire thing up on my shoulder so that I was the fulcrum in the world's stupidest teeter-totter. I took a deep breath and started moving with purpose toward him, ignoring the way the metal cut into my shoulder.

I half expected him to clap or hoot as I rounded the corner supporting the full weight of the ladder, but he just watched me make my way closer, squatting and silent like a gargoyle.

An incredibly attractive gargoyle. If you went for that sort of thing, which I didn't.

I put the ladder down with a clatter and "wunf" but tried to pretend that it was no big deal.

"Nice," Andrew said and it felt like the most appreciation I'd get out of him. "Okay, first you need to find a level spot," he directed. "We set it up right there, by the flowerpots." He pointed below and to the left of where he was perched.

I took a deep breath and shook my hands in the air to try to get feeling back in them.

"You got this, Higs," he said, pulling my nickname out of his back pocket. "Feel it." Andrew clapped like he was rallying a football huddle.

I nodded and tried not to be obvious that my shoulders were already screaming from the weight of the thing. I moved to the correct spot on the patio and managed to get the ladder above my head, but I couldn't find the gear to give it the final push so it would fall into position against the gutter. I stood there, the ladder hovering in the air, frozen.

"C'mon, Higs, you *got* this!" Andrew clapped louder.

I felt heat spread to my cheeks. Suddenly I didn't want to disappoint him. Andrew had never cheered me on and I sort of liked what it was doing to me. I felt a little . . . invincible. I took a deep breath and mustered the strength to walk my hands up one more rung.

"Ow, ow, ow," I let out before I could stop myself.

Andrew scooted closer along the roof to where I was struggling to keep the ladder up.

"So close, don't stop now. Can you boost it like another three inches?"

I could barely keep it in the air let alone get it any higher. My arms were starting to shudder from the weight and pain in my wrist, but I wasn't about to let Andrew see me fail. I adjusted my grip on the ladder and inched toward where he was leaning out to grab it.

"Careful," I managed to squeak out when I looked up and saw how unstable he was as he leaned out to try to reach the ladder. I didn't want to be the reason why he fell off the roof.

"Almost," he said. "Reach down deep and *push*. Come on!"

I giggled despite the struggle. "You sound like a Lamaze coach."

"Quit playing and *do it, Higgins*! I know you can!"

His gravelly voice came from somewhere prehistoric, a cave-man sound that set off something inside of me. Suddenly, I found myself engaging the muscles in my back instead of my shoulders and managed to lift the ladder high enough for Andrew to finally reach out and grab it.

"Got it," he yelled. "Nice work!"

I fought the urge to bask in the compliment and focused on the pain in the wrist instead.

"Can you check if it's level for me?" Andrew asked. "Make sure the feet are flipped out."

I cradled my arm against my chest and peered at the base of the ladder. "They are."

"Perfect." He looked down on me like Zeus himself. "Thanks for the muscles. I just need one last thing: can you put your weight on the bottom rung? Just step on it. Coming down can be a little dicey."

"Yup." I positioned myself at the bottom of the ladder and propped my foot on the rung, then glanced up at him at the absolute worst moment.

Because Andrew had swung himself around the ladder so

that his ass was directly above me in all its splendor. The ass that had earned him the nickname "Volleyball Butt." So perfectly round that it was impossible not to at least glance at it, which was exactly what I'd managed to *not* do until that very moment.

He came down slowly and I was mesmerized by the thing. Why did he have to wear jeans that showed it off like that? Maybe wearing butt-flattering jeans was a way of advertising that he knew what he was doing in the gym? Like, was his ass an actual business asset?

I was so busy considering if Andrew's butt was a write-off that I failed to notice that his vantage point above me gave him a perfect view of my line of sight. I glanced up and saw his bemused smile through the rungs. I coughed and looked away.

The sound of jingling dog tags gave us both something else to focus on when he finally hit the ground. Dude and Murray rounded the corner with muddy paws and covered in burrs, panting and happy.

Dude ran over and rebounded off of me, knocking me back a few steps because I still had my wrist cradled to my chest.

"What's up with your arm?" Andrew asked, nodding toward it.

"It's my wrist, from the night I met Dude," I admitted. "When I fell."

"And it's *still* bothering you?" Andrew took a few steps closer, his gaze fixed on my arm.

"A little."

"Let me see it." He reached out toward me.

I flinched like his fingers might be hot to the touch, but he was so focused on diagnosing me that he didn't seem to notice.

His forehead was creased in concentration as he grasped me. My jacket was the only thing between his fingertips and the sensitive skin of my wrist, a berm between the ceasefire we'd agreed to and the sexy, angry heat we'd made together so many years ago.

"Does this hurt?" he asked as he placed his thumb and pointer finger on either side of my still-sleeved wrist and squeezed.

My wince was the only answer he needed.

"Sorry. Make a fist," he ordered.

I complied and he wrapped his massive hand around it, swallowing it completely. The warmth of his palm against my knuckles made me want to take a few steps closer to him, to absorb some of the heat he seemed to give off in spades. I glanced at his face, but he was deep in diagnostic mode.

I hadn't been this close to him since . . . well, since that night. I took the opportunity to study Andrew as he examined my arm. Same aquiline nose, same black-brown eyes beneath the dramatic, envy-inducing brows, same lashes so long that they looked fake, same fat bottom lip. The only thing different about him was the mess on his head and the additional bulk. He had the vibe of someone who didn't have the time or inclination to bother with grooming, but he somehow made the shoved-back bun look better than all of the perfectly coiffed guys I came across on dating apps.

He slowly rolled my fist in a circle, gentle but appraising.

Damn it. I remembered those hands.

The way they fumbled with the buttons on the front of my dress, finally resorting to popping a few off in our frenzy to get the thing off of me. How they burned into the bare skin of my waist as he lifted me on top of him. The way his fingertips traced a gentle trail from my lips, down my neck, to the peak of each breast, teasing downward until he hit—

"Range of motion is okay," Andrew said, releasing me from his grip. "Describe the pain for me."

"Um." I wobbled a little when he let go of me, like he was a kickstand that had been flicked away. "It feels like it's always there. Sort of like a bruise."

Andrew nodded. "Because that's what it is. A strain." He paused and finally looked away from my arm and up to my eyes. "I could help you with that."

"Huh?"

Up close, the Gibson Glare was lethal. I slapped my mouth shut and exhaled through my nose, willing my body to un-clench.

"A little rehab, a little strengthening." He softened and gave me a half smile. "I know a place that's convenient for you."

Andrew wanted to *train* me? That went against every rule I'd outlined the night we'd crashed back into one another. And there was no way I wanted to be indebted to him.

But . . . I also wanted to make him pay for what he'd done. Although Andrew probably wouldn't consider it payback. He'd use training me as an opportunity to show off, to wow me with his gym prowess. Find a way to preen so I'd be forced to ad-mire him.

Well, two could play that game.

"Only if you let me train Dude," I shot back before I could think better of it. "Or, let me train *you* to train him."

If I didn't know better I would've sworn the boxer heard his name and decided to seal the deal by running past us and donkey-kicking against my legs midstride, knocking me backward again.

I pointed after the retreating dog as evidence. "I mean . . ."

Andrew fixed those damn black eyes on me and fired off another half smile, making me wait a full uncomfortable five seconds under the heat of his gaze before finally nodding slowly.

"Yeah, that works."

"Three for three," I suggested quickly. "Three sessions with you and the same with me."

I wasn't sure I could tolerate him for my standard six sessions.

"Okay." He nodded. "Three for three."

The silence stretched on until it became uncomfortable, but neither one of us seemed willing to walk away. Despite everything we'd been through, in this moment it felt like there was something invisible tethering us together.

"Chelsea!" Patricia's voice echoed through the yard. "Where are you? I finally found my checkbook."

"She's over here," Andrew said, still staring at me from close range.

I crossed my arms and stared back until Patricia rounded the corner, holding the checkbook up victoriously.

"The first of many more sessions to come," she proclaimed as Andrew and I locked eyes again.

chapter ten

I didn't like the looks of the guy skulking around the building.

Edith and I had arrived just before eight and I was giving her a quick potty break in the grass beyond the parking lot when I spotted him. He was walking around the building and taking pictures. Edith locked on to him and let out an adorably squeaky bark.

"I know," I said to her in a low voice. "I don't trust him either."

I looked at the door to Roz's now empty space. Mike still hadn't hung a For Rent sign in her window, but it was possible the guy was an early bird scoping it out. I scanned him to try to figure out what sort of business he could be affiliated with. He actually looked sort of fancy for the location, in dark dress pants and a checkered shirt with the sleeves rolled up.

I was feeling as territorial as Edith yet I'd done nothing to claim the vacant space. I'd run the numbers a few billion times and expanding made sense. I knew I could handle the financial aspects of an expansion, and even though I didn't love the idea of dealing with construction, I could appreciate how amazing it would be once Frolic had more room. Now was my moment, to swoop in and grab it before anyone else could.

The problem was I no longer had my business adviser to sign off on the whole thing.

My dad was a corporate man, but he loved my entrepreneurial spirit. His advice ranged from practical, like helping me negotiate parts of my lease before I opened Frolic, to a little woo-woo, like encouraging me to listen to my gut if I couldn't make up my mind on something. His advice was the reason why I closed early on Fridays and took Sundays off. Even though all signs pointed to expansion, I still felt paralyzed since I couldn't get his blessing on it.

The guy finally noticed me shooting darts at him from across the parking lot and watched us for a few beats longer than I liked. Maybe he was a Boston terrier fan and he was admiring Edith, or maybe he was trying to figure out if he could chloroform me and get me into his BMW before anyone showed up. I glanced toward Andrew's building. Of course today was the day he wasn't around.

Edith finally found the perfect place to squat. "Good girl. All done? Let's go."

I squared my shoulders and headed for the building right as Andrew's Jeep turned into the lot. Why did relief spread through me at the sight of it? I didn't need him to rescue me from Creepy Beemer Guy. In fact, he'd been the trapped party in need of rescuing lately.

I swear, his damn car was so loud that it made me want to cover my ears as he pulled in. I squinted as he got out of it to see if Dude had come with him, but he was solo for the day. Andrew noticed the interloper guy and gave him a wave, but he hurried to get into his car and leave.

"See?" I muttered to Edith. "Suspicious behavior."

Andrew was so focused on unloading boxes from his Jeep that he didn't notice me walking up behind him.

"Hey," I said. Edith was doing her little "I'm nervous but curious" dance of scenting the air while pulling away, attempting to put distance between her and Andrew while at the same time trying to figure him out.

Andrew turned quickly. "Oh, hey," he said. His eyes immediately dropped to Edith. "Well, good morning, little pup!" His voice went higher than I thought was physically possible for him. "Is your mom finally going to let me meet you? Huh? I've been admiring you, but she never lets you come over to say hi to me!"

It was true. I didn't want Edith to decide that she liked him and then force me to interact with him when we were in common spaces. But now it was too late. She was marching in place, her head bobbing up and down as her little stump of a tail fanned the air, her entire body wiggling in excitement.

Edith was under his spell and he didn't even have to use treats to bribe her.

"She can be a little skittish," I said even though she was acting like a well-adjusted, outgoing puppy. "Men sort of freak her out."

It was a bald-faced lie. Her original anchor human had been a man.

"Well, then let me change her mind about my kind," Andrew said, setting down the boxes he was carrying. He folded his massive body in half, plopped to the ground, and crossed his legs. Edith kept high-stepping.

"If your mom doesn't tell me your name soon I'm going to give you one," he singsonged, lowering himself even more and beaming at the puppy. "You look like a 'Bug' to me."

"Edith," I said quickly. "Her name is Edith."

"Ed-i-i-i-ith." He drew it out in a low, goofy voice. "Will you come say hello to me?"

She marched in place but still didn't move.

"What if I do *this*?" Andrew flowed from crisscross applesauce into push-up position and held it for a second like he was trying to prove that he also did yoga and was king of Chaturanga pose, then dropped to his stomach on the asphalt. "Now, come give me a kiss."

The weaponized charm. I knew it wasn't directed at me but damn it if his sweet talking didn't tempt me to take a half step closer too.

Seeing the giant brought down to her level was more than the puppy could take. Edith lowered herself into a play bow and wiggled over to him, then rolled on her back right in front of his face.

"Aww, there's a good girl!" Andrew said, reaching out to gently rub her belly. "See? I'm nice. Don't listen to what your mom says about me. And wait till you meet Dude. He's going to love you."

I cleared my throat, about to remind him to keep Dude on leash, but I managed to shut myself up and let the moment unfold. Andrew's hand seemed impossibly gentle on Edith even though it was bigger than she was. He trailed his fingertips on her belly with one hand and cradled her with the other, cooing to her softly. This giant of a man was reduced to a baby-talking dork and didn't seem to care if anyone pulled in and saw him.

But then again, Andrew always seemed to understand that he was hot enough to get away with nearly anything. I never allowed his looks to work on *me*, at least not usually, but the rest of the world gave him a Get Out of Jail Free card no matter what he did.

"She's amazing," he said, glancing up at me.

His smile was so warm, so genuine that I found myself incapable of not smiling back, as hard as I tried to avoid it. He held my gaze a few beats longer than necessary, sending a wave of heat to my face. I looked away and felt his eyes linger before he turned his attention back to Edith. He cradled her head and kissed her on the nose, then set her back on her feet.

"Who was that guy?" he asked, finally standing back up.

I tried not to notice as he brushed off the front of his gray workout pants. They weren't sweatpants exactly, they were more fitted at the bottom and were a little looser toward the waist. But not so loose that it left any mystery as to what he had going on downstairs. I remembered. I'd seen it firsthand. I looked away quickly.

"I'm not sure, I think he might be interested in seeing Roz's space."

We both glanced at the building.

"I'd love to check it out now that it's empty," Andrew mused, rocking back and forth on his feet.

"I still have a key, and knowing Mike, he hasn't changed the locks yet." I'd wanted it to come across like I was connected and knew more than he did, but I realized too late that it actually sounded like an invitation.

He raised an eyebrow at me. "Well, then it's not breaking and entering. Let's go."

Edith took off after Andrew despite the fact that I was offering her a piece of freeze-dried liver to ignore him, making me realize that I was going to have to work hard to sever the bond he'd just magically grown with her. I couldn't have my new puppy mooning over the enemy.

Andrew leaned up against the doorframe of the empty space and grinned at me. "I hope she doesn't have an alarm in there. I don't want you getting all flustered again."

I frowned as I sorted through my key chain, refusing to look at him. "Flustered? What made you think I was *flustered*?"

He shrugged then squatted to pet Edith again. "It's sort of your general aura, you know? Always tense. It's that big brain of yours, overthinking stuff."

How was it possible that the man could insult me and compliment me in the same breath?

"Well, you clearly don't know how to read me. I was angry." I met his eyes. "At you. Remember?"

That axis-tipping devilish grin again. "Honestly, I haven't given that night another thought. Sorta busy setting up my empire, you know?"

I gritted my teeth and pushed past him into the dark warehouse. This was going to be quick or I might wind up making some content for a true crime podcast about women driven to murder by annoyingly egotistical men.

The more time I spent with Andrew the more obvious it became that I wasn't going to be able to navigate the ridiculous training swap we'd agreed to. I was now convinced that I'd been flooded with ladder-lifting endorphins when we'd agreed to it and I wasn't thinking like my normal, rational self. It was the only explanation why I'd willingly subject myself to him.

Because I couldn't just *be* with Andrew.

There was still too much between us that would never be resolved. I wasn't sure how he could ignore it, because I felt like our history was an open, festering wound, too far gone to heal without surgical intervention.

Andrew turned in a circle, taking in the space that was almost as familiar to me as mine. Seeing it empty made me sad that Roz was gone but excited for what I could do with it.

"Roz seemed great, but I have to admit that I'm glad she's gone," Andrew said, walking around and staring up at the skylights. "I tried her cookies and I don't know if I would've been able to resist them."

"She told me. I'm in shock that you eat cookies now."

"People change."

I dropped Edith's leash then jogged to the light switches, ignoring the comment. People might make surface changes, like packing on enough muscle to be a Marvel stunt double, but the core of a person never really does. Eating a few cookies didn't mean that the Andrew prowling through the building was any different from the one who used to prowl the bars. And just because he was being friendly didn't mean he was my friend.

I flicked on the lights and he let out a whistle.

"Whoa, the things I could *do* in here."

He was striding around the space like it was already part of his kingdom. If anyone was going to make something of the place it was going to be me, he just didn't know it yet.

"How so?" I wanted to let him talk, to reveal his plans so I could be ready for whatever he was going to try. I hadn't read *The Art of War* for nothing.

"I have a feeling I'm going to outgrow my space pretty quickly," Andrew said, walking along the wall that separated his unit from the one we were in. He knocked on it. "I bet this could come down really easily."

I bristled that he assumed he could just waltz in and start demolition before the ink was dry on his current lease, but I wasn't ready to show my hand yet. The more I pulled out of him the more prepared I'd be in battle. "You're not even open—how can you tell it's not big enough for you?"

"Prebooking," Andrew said, crossing his arms and eyeing me like he could tell what I was up to.

I leaned over and pretended to adjust Edith's harness so he wouldn't see my surprise. "You mean you've got people willing to sign with you sight unseen?"

"You know it," he answered, miming swishing a basketball. "The artist's rendering of the space on my website was a big help." He paused. "Oh, and the Twitter shout-out from the Commanders' starting lineup helped too." He winked at me. "ESPN retweeted it."

Of course he was going to succeed. Andrew *always* won.

But who wouldn't want to train with someone who helped keep professional football players in shape? Especially if he looked like one himself.

"So when are you finally going to open? You've been prepping long enough." I couldn't resist the dig.

"Yeah, I should show you what I did to the place." He stalked across the room toward me. How could someone that bulky be so graceful? "Got a minute?"

I shook my head and pulled my phone out of my pocket to pretend to check the time. "Busy day. So when are you opening?"

I wanted to prepare for the influx of parking spot thieves in the lot. And I still needed to address the music situation.

"Soon. I'm throwing a grand opening–slash–Halloween party. I'm calling it Swole-o-Ween."

I rolled my eyes. My puns were a thousand times better.

"What's the exact date? Because my annual Howl-o-Ween party is coming up and there's no way they can be on the same night. It's one of my most popular events."

"Thursday the twenty-seventh."

I closed my eyes and saw visions of bros doing keg stands in the parking lot while my sweet clients and their dogs hurried past.

"Nope. Absolutely not," I finally managed. "Looks like you're going to be changing it, because that's *my* date."

chapter eleven

Funny how easy it was for us to slip back into our old patterns, despite everything that had changed.

I'd finally made time to bring Edith and Birdie to my mom's house for a visit (it still hurt not to say "parents' house") and the first thing we did was head out for a walk in the fall sun. We used to spend plenty of time outside together, strolling with Birdie on the paths my dad had carved out in the woods. Now we did it as a warm-up before going inside, to help me get ready to be around all the reminders of him. His glasses still nestled in the remote control caddy in the family room, the last biography he was reading tucked back in the bookshelf, but with the blue tassel of his bookmark trailing from it.

Sure, the property had my dad's fingerprints all over it as well, but for some reason it was easier for me to deal with him not being around when I was outside. Maybe because he lived on in the dogwood and red maple trees he'd planted when he and my mom had bought the place over thirty years ago. They'd transformed the run-down stone farmhouse and surrounding five acres into something out of a fairy tale. It was a home that managed to be cozy in the fall and winter thanks to the over-sized fireplace in the great room and breezy during the warmer months, which were spent out on the covered porch. Going home was my favorite journey, and it only took me twenty minutes to get there.

"She's perfect, you know," my mom said, pausing to lean down and pet Edith. "You were meant to have her. Might not make sense now, but there's a reason why she's here with you."

I watched the little dog melt into my mom's capable, tender hands, then roll onto her back in the dappled fall sun. I could see the top of my mom's head as she petted Edith and the only hint that she was pushing sixty-five was the tiny line of white hair creeping along her scalp. As soon as she started getting grays she'd found a hairstylist who matched her auburn hair so expertly that you couldn't tell it was dyed. Her face was almost completely wrinkle free thanks to the curse of fair skin and a lifetime of hiding from the sun, and her eyes were always smiling. I felt lucky to have her blood in my veins.

"Edith is really great," I agreed, laughing at the way the puppy kept trying to nibble on my mom's fingers. "Not what I needed right now, but we're making it work. And Birdie is being patient with her."

My senior paused at the mention of her name, then trotted back to us, her tail wagging low and slow. She pushed in next to my mom's knees, demanding her own pats.

"Birdie, I love you too, you know that." She laughed at the dog's blatant jealousy, giving her a kiss on the top of the head. "You were my first granddog and you're a certified good old girl."

My mom was one of her favorite people, to the point where I used "Nana!" as my go-to word to ensure a cute expression and head tilt when I snapped a photo. It was obvious by the way she was clamoring for attention that Birdie missed her.

And I did too.

I took a deep breath and wished I could bottle the moment. That familiar, comforting scent of fall leaves, a breeze that was cool enough to make you wish you'd worn a hoodie even though it was still warm in the sunshine, and two dogs reveling in the freedom of sniffing whatever they wanted to. After sweating it out all summer, autumn always used to make me feel excited for the cozy sweaters and hot beverages to come. I loved the anticipation of the approaching holidays. Now, though, it felt like everything was a reminder that he wouldn't be around to share them with us.

"I feel like we haven't talked like this in forever," my mom said as she straightened up slowly. She glanced at me and waited for me to meet her eyes. "I'm glad you're here."

I fought off the stab of guilt at the reminder that I hadn't been around much. "Me too."

We kept walking on the carpet of fallen leaves, watching Edith try to keep up with Birdie. "Did I tell you your aunt Helen is coming to Thanksgiving too?"

"You mean she's not off in Qatar buying rugs or something?"

Aunt Helen was my dad's sister and she and my mom had been best friends since the day they met at a family barbecue, back when she was just a girlfriend. Aunt Helen had never married or had children, instead choosing to devote herself to a life of her own making, including plenty of adventures traveling to stock her antiques business.

"Nope, she's stateside through the holidays. I'm looking forward to seeing her."

We passed the rock garden where my dad used to create little balance sculptures that lasted until the elements or gravity decided to reclaim them. I looked away quickly.

"Tell me about you, sweetheart," my mom said, looping her arm through mine and giving it a squeeze. "What's happening in your world?"

"Roz moved out," I said, happy to be able to focus on something safe. Or, safe-ish, considering how much I still needed to do now that the space was mine for the taking.

"So have you spoken to Mike about taking it over yet?"

I felt a ball of nervous energy form in my gut at the thought of finally committing to the decision. As much as I wanted to expand, the truth was it felt overwhelming. It made sense and all my projections backed it up, but taking on the extra space meant demolition, and dealing with contractors, and leaping from the predictable I needed to something unknowable, at least for a little while. But my spreadsheets didn't lie. If I wanted to keep growing I needed to stake my claim and go for it.

"I haven't spoken to him yet. But I will, and soon, because there's this guy . . ." I stopped. I didn't want to give Andrew any more airtime than he deserved.

"What guy?"

I sighed. She was going to find out about him moving in eventually, might as well tell her now. "Remember Nolan's roommate at school? You met him once, I think, when we were carpooling back. His name was Andrew. *Is* Andrew."

She nodded slowly. "Of course. Very handsome guy. Seemed sweet."

Even my own *mom*? Damn him.

"Trust me, he's not. Anyway, he moved into the warehouse

where the T-shirt guys were, and he wants to expand into Roz's space too. He literally just moved in!"

"Doing what?"

"Gym stuff." I thought about the double-booked Halloween party night and felt nauseous about all the ways it was going to go wrong since he'd refused to change his date.

"Well, that's nice," she said as if she couldn't hear the disdain in my voice. "Seems like a good fit for your complex."

"It's *so* not," I shouted, causing Birdie to pause and look back at me. "He acts like he owns the place already; the last thing I need is him taking more real estate. And his clientele is going to be obnoxious, I can guarantee it. Gym dudes are the worst."

"Not all gym patrons are men," she scolded. "Women go to the gym. *I* go to the gym."

It was one of the many changes she'd made in the past year and it had been good for her. But the place she went to was a gym for normal people, with little pink three-pound weights, and Zumba and SilverSneakers programs, not some airless box filled with bros working on their "gains."

"You're right, you're right," I admitted. "But still, he doesn't deserve the extra space. I'm a legacy tenant, it should be mine."

"So talk to Mike," my mom said with her usual common sense that didn't take ancillary details into account. "Tell him you want it. Won't that be enough?"

"It should. I'll do it." I paused. "Tomorrow."

"There's the spirit." My mom squeezed my arm. "Chels, I know you don't like talking about it, but you have the financial—"

"It's not necessary, Mom." I cut her off quickly as my heart-beat triple-timed. The visit had been so nice and I didn't want her to ruin it. "My finances are fine. I can handle it."

"Okay, well, it's there when you're ready."

"Um-hm." I nodded, pretending to look around for the dogs when I knew they were six feet ahead of us, nosing in the tall grass by the goldenrod.

"You look tired," my mom said, drawing back to take me in. "I can tell you're overdoing it when your eyebrows seem pale."

"Gee, thanks!" I laughed at her perceptiveness. "And I was just about to say that you look great."

"You think so?" she asked and ran her hand down the back of her hair. "I've been keeping up with that yoga class *at the gym*"—she gave me a pointed look—"and I really think it's helping."

I loved that she kept discovering new ways to stay busy. She was a homebody for years, content to stick around the house with Dad, reading books and gardening. Now her social life was busier than mine.

But that was true of most people these days.

"Looks like it suits you," I said, glancing at her out of the corner of my eye. "You seem . . . good."

It was the closest I was willing to get to the sleeping tiger between us and she seemed to understand.

She bumped her shoulder against mine. "I am, all things considered. I'm doing okay these days, Chels. And I hope you are too."

I nodded too quickly.

"But I still miss him every day," she continued. Her voice wasn't sad, it was wistful. Like she was talking about a wonderful place she'd visited long ago, or a beautiful dream she'd had but could barely remember.

"Same."

It came out in a shaky whisper.

"Why don't we go inside and sort through some of the things he—"

"No time today," I said quickly. "Sorry."

We both fell silent except for the whooshing sound of our feet sweeping through the leaves and the distant jingle of dog tags.

"Thanksgiving is going to be wonderful," she said, reorienting the conversation to something safer. "I can't wait to use Taylor's new kitchen."

"I hope that means you're assisting her with the food." Taylor was many things but a chef was not one of them. I was the only Higgins daughter who had a clue how to cook. "I mean, I'll obviously be there as sous chef, but we still need you to take the lead."

"Happy to!" She beamed. If there was one thing my mother wanted, it was to help and be helpful. She was the most giving person I'd ever met. "I'll even show you the secret to my prize-winning corn bread."

"You mean Greek yogurt?"

She jerked back. "Darn, did I already tell you that?"

I laughed. "You did."

"Well, don't tell your sister. It'll be our secret."

I circled my arm around her shoulder and leaned over to give her a kiss, knowing that my sister was already in possession of the secret as well. "I won't, I promise."

We rounded the final turn on the path and the house came into view in the distance, as welcoming as ever.

"Hold on, where's Bird and Edith?" I stopped and looked around for real. I'd been so caught up in the conversation that the dogs had run off somewhere out of sight. "Birdie!" I let out the shrill whistle that worked for quieting chatty humans in class and recalling wayward dogs.

I heard the jingle of their tags before I saw them. "Good girls!" I cheered as they ran closer. "Good work!"

They arrived at our feet panting and with mud on their necks and faces. I gave them each a little treat for their responsiveness.

"Dirty girls! Looks like someone got into . . ." I paused when I realized. "*Nooo*, Bird!" I looked closer at the puppy. "And you too?"

"Deer poop," my mom said. "I can smell it from here. C'mon, let's go get them in the bath."

We trudged back to the house while I fussed at the dogs, even though deep down I was happy that they gave me an excuse to stay a little longer.

chapter twelve

Why did I feel nervous?

If I looked at the facts it was just a dog training client coming in at the end of the day for a private session with me, and even though the dog in question was deaf, it wasn't like the pup was my first nonhearing student. I'd trained *dozens* of deaf dogs. I could train deaf dogs in my sleep.

But I couldn't just look at the facts because the person who was going to be handling the other end of the leash was none other than Andrew. *He* was my real student, and even though it pained me to admit it, it freaked me out, big-time. I wasn't looking forward to the Gibson Glare tracking me while I tried to work.

I ran to the bathroom to make sure that I didn't have any bats in the cave or food in my teeth. It was a basic hygiene check that I did before meeting with any new clients, but I also grabbed the tube of nude "pout gloss" Taylor had given me and slicked it across my lips.

Because they felt dry. *Not* because I was trying to look cute. And I was wearing my "going out" jeans that just happened to highlight my ass because all my others were in the laundry, which I had conveniently forgotten to do.

I checked my phone. He was due in five minutes. It had been a week since I told my mom I was going to call Mike and I'd finally done it today knowing that Andrew was probably going to try to rile me up by talking about how big my space was compared to his. We had a week until the Howl/Swole parties and he swore up and down that none of his guests would get in the way of mine, but it wasn't just his clients I was worried about. The parking lot was going to be a *nightmare*. I needed to convince him to get his bros to park their monster trucks on the grass, so my clientele could walk their dogs right in.

Mike was always slow to return calls, but I assumed the promise of easy money from a trustworthy tenant would guarantee a quick response. I automatically started stressing that Andrew had gotten to him first. *Why* had I waited to make the call? And what was I going to do if Andrew beat me?

"Incoming!"

I heard the telltale jingle and before I could brace myself I was on the receiving end of four airborne paws to the stomach.

Andrew walked toward me smiling like what he'd just witnessed was adorable. He was actually wearing appropriate clothing for the cool October evening without a single muscle on display, in a distressed army green jacket, black T-shirt, and yet another version of those damn not-quite-sweatpants, also in black. His hair was slicked back like he'd just gotten out of the shower, which immediately made me think of Andrew taking a shower, which was my cue to refocus on my student.

"Dude, hello," I said, trying to grab the leash that he was technically wearing but that wasn't being put to use by his person. I finally managed to snag it and step on the midpoint of it, so Dude could stand and walk a few steps but couldn't execute a full frontal assault on me.

"That's a cool technique," Andrew said, gesturing to the leash. "I'll have to try it."

"Yeah, but it requires that you actually hold the leash and that's something you don't seem to be able to do," I said before I could stop myself. It had to be my last insult of the session since he was on my turf and I needed to be at least passably cordial to him.

"I do seem to have a problem with that." He grinned at me, oblivious. "So what are we doing first?"

He crossed his arms and leaned against the wall, then began the glare thing, but it didn't have the intended effect because I was too focused on my canine client. I was going to train the hell out of his dog and prove that there was no excuse for Dude's lawlessness.

"Couple of quick questions first. Have you taught him anything yet?" I already knew the answer to the question, but that was part of my plan. To point out that Dude's pushy behavior was directly correlated to his lack of effort.

"Uh-huh." Andrew nodded. "Check this out."

He stomped the ground once and Dude immediately turned to him, grinning in that goofy boxer way. *Damn it.* Andrew had good instincts since he knew that the vibration would travel to where Dude was standing and he'd look to the source. I dropped the leash and moved my foot off so Dude could walk over to Andrew to collect a treat.

"He knows 'sit.'" Andrew lowered his hand in front of Dude to just a few inches above the ground with his palm facing up, which caused Dude to lower his head to sniff and lick it. I kept my face neutral at the exaggerated cue. Andrew raised his hand slowly until it was about hip height. The dog remained standing.

Andrew repeated the motion a few times, then looked at me frowning. "He does it at home, I swear."

"Hey, it's normal for dogs to not respond in new environments. Don't feel too bad about it," I said. "So you're obviously using hand signals, which is great. Now we just need to anchor the behavior to the cue. How do you let him know when he's done the right thing, since you can't use verbal praise?"

"I give him a thumbs-up," Andrew said, then demonstrated, which caused Dude to wiggle and grin at him. He gave Dude a treat.

"Nice. So you did a little research?" I asked.

"Yeah, I watched a couple of YouTube videos. But honestly, I've been so busy that I've been slacking. Clearly." He gestured to Dude, who was straining to sniff something just out of reach.

"Well, everything is about to change. For both of you. Let's get started."

I led them toward the open area in the center of the space as the nervousness drained away and my focus returned. It didn't matter how I felt about Andrew, my job was to get through to Dude.

"You brought a bunch of treats with you?" I asked him.

"You know it. I read every word of the preclass paperwork you sent." He patted his hip. "Cheese and hot dogs."

"In your *pocket*?"

He shrugged. "I go through pants pretty quickly, it's a sweaty job. A little hot dog juice ain't going to hurt."

I tried to scrub the image of a sweaty, pants-less Andrew

from my brain as it struck me that I hadn't once seen any evidence of Andrew actually working out. For someone who looked like, well . . . *that*, I imagined that lifting cartoon-sized dumbbells would be his full-time job.

"Okay," I said, straightening my back and summoning my teacher voice. "The first thing I want you to know is that we're not going to be doing anything different with Dude than I do with the rest of my students. He's a dog before he's a deaf dog, with the same drives and desires as any other pup." It was my normal speech for deaf-dog parents, but usually the phrase "drives and desires" didn't have a double meaning. I hoped that he didn't notice, but I saw the corner of his mouth kick up.

Despite that hiccup the rest of the session went shockingly well. Dude was a genius on four legs, and Andrew's instincts were even better than I'd initially realized. I'd envisioned him joking his way through the class, but he seemed eager to absorb everything I said and was open to my gentle corrections to his technique. It took a while, but I got used to being Andrew's teacher, and by the end of the session I managed to forget our history and just hang with him.

And I *liked* it.

We both seemed to, since the hour stretched to an hour and a half while we basked in the afterglow of a great class.

"So it's my turn to train you next," Andrew said, flashing his new and improved "sit" cue at Dude, who tucked into the position lightning fast. "You're finally going to step into the Gib Zone."

I twisted my wrist reflexively and was about to tell him that it was actually back to normal, and that I didn't want his help after all. It was going to be a one-sided training scenario where

I would train Dude without expecting anything in return. The fact was, I didn't want to wear Lycra around him, or sweat in his presence, or be subjected to the boot camp screaming I was sure he did, but when I tried to open my mouth to back out, I couldn't.

"You still good for tomorrow?" he asked, his expression so hopeful that my heart tripped out of rhythm for a second. "Because I have a lot of cool stuff I want to do with you."

It was the second double entendre of the night, making us even.

"Yup, I'll be there." I nodded, swallowing all of my objections. Did I even own a sports bra that wasn't stained and gross?

My back door swung open suddenly and Andrew and I jumped at the unexpected interruption. Dude realized there were interlopers after a few seconds of delay, then barked at Mike and a guy I didn't recognize.

"Oh, you're still here," Mike said in shock, frozen in place. "You're *both* here. It's late."

"What the hell?" I said under my breath.

The tall bald guy who was with him stood off to the side looking around the room.

"Yeah, and you just walked in your tenant's back door without even knocking," Andrew said, taking a step in front of me. "Is that, like, common practice for you? I just want to level-set myself as a new tenant if you do surprise drop-ins."

I recognized that voice. It was Charming Andrew, which worked on women *and* men. Even though his back was to me I could hear the smile, which was at odds with what Andrew was actually saying to Mike.

"No, uh, I don't. Ask her." Mike nodded toward me, then said something to the guy he was with in a low voice, which caused him to walk out of the building. "Listen, I need to talk to the two of you."

Andrew shot me a look and I felt worry start to claw away inside me. We were going to talk about Roz's space. Now. *Together.*

Mike headed for us, pulling his hand through his spiky black hair, making it stand straight up. He looked guiltier than normal, and I could tell he wished he was actually smoking the cigarette tucked behind his ear. Dude tried to jump up and greet him, but Andrew managed to capture his dog's focus with a small piece of hot dog.

"You've probably noticed people walking around the property lately," Mike said, his eyes darting between us. "That's because I'm selling the building."

It didn't compute for a second. Mike had been my landlord since I opened the School of Frolic and he'd told me a few times, when he was a six-pack into his evening, that the building was an easy moneymaker. And I knew that everyone who'd rented from him had been great tenants, so he didn't have issues collecting money.

"Your current leases will transfer to whoever buys it," Mike continued. "They have to honor them."

Andrew shifted but said nothing.

"Is anyone interested?" I asked, trying to hide the fact that there was a tiny chance that I might be.

Mike glanced back at the door and shrugged. "Dunno. Maybe. Anyways, I'll, uh, I'll keep you posted."

Andrew seemed to crank back to life when he realized that Mike was heading out. "Hey, I just want to confirm that you won't be bringing potential buyers through during business hours. I have some clients who need complete privacy when they train, and I'm sure Chelsea doesn't want her dog students getting all fired up by people nosing around."

Charming Andrew was gone, replaced by No Bullshit Andrew. I sort of liked being on his team.

"Yep," Mike said with a nod as he backed away, already reaching for his cigarette. "You got it, chief." The door slammed shut behind him.

"Fuck."

I glanced at Andrew and he was staring at the ground, petting Dude absentmindedly. "What's wrong?"

His face was pale when he finally met my eyes. "I signed a fucking month-to-month lease. Whoever buys this building can kick me out on my ass before I even get a chance to start paying off my loan."

And with that admission I realized that it *was* possible to feel bad for Andrew Gibson.

chapter thirteen

I stepped into Andrew's gym expecting a no-frills box, but the guy had either hired someone to help him or he had better interior design instincts than I realized. The place looked like a high-end city gym, where bottles of water cost eight dollars and the bathroom soap dispensers squirted out Molton Brown.

The ceiling, walls, and rubber flooring were all black, with the only spot of color a runner of Astroturf along the wall, striped and numbered like a football field. Everywhere I looked, mirrors. If I wanted to check out my spandex-clad ass from sixteen different vantage points it was totally doable. I'd worn an extra-long T-shirt to cover it, but I had a feeling there was probably a mirror angle *somewhere* that managed to show it anyway.

I shouldn't have been shocked that he'd built something this impressive. The fact that it could all be pulled out from under him when the building sold sent an unexpected surge of sympathy through me. Mike had known exactly what he was doing when he let Andrew sign on for a month-to-month lease, but he clearly didn't care. He saw the opportunity to make a quick buck and didn't even consider the potential casualty.

"Hey! Welcome to Crush." Andrew's voice echoed through the place.

And here I thought he'd name it after himself. I swallowed hard and tried to fight off the free-falling sensation in my gut as he stalked toward me. Hair scraped back in that stupid-handsome bun, his scruff trimmed to perfection. He was in a slim-fitting spotless white T-shirt and navy shorts, and when I glanced down I was able to quickly confirm that the man never skipped leg day.

"Crush?" I finally managed.

"It's cool, right? The name is a vibe. There's a bunch of different meanings. Crush your doubts, your limitations, your fears." He pointed to a pyramid of dumbbells. "Crush those weights. Crush a smoothie after you're done."

Crush your frustration at your ridiculously attractive neighbor.

"What do you think?" He gestured around the room proudly. He was fishing for compliments, but the truth was, he deserved them.

"I'm sort of in awe," I admitted. "I can't believe this is the same spot that used to turn out Wismer Bank and Trust T-shirts."

He puffed up his chest. "Thanks. I'm waiting on one more thing." He pointed to an open area above the mirrors. "I've got a Philly street artist named Vasquez coming in to write 'crush' up there. He does everything freehand, but it's so perfect it looks like he uses a stencil. Gonna have a few little drips coming off it, a few paint splatters. Subtle. It'll be done before the party for sure."

He was talking about the space like the future of it wasn't hanging in the balance. I took advantage of the natural segue.

"Yeah, speaking of the *parties*"—stressing the plural to remind him about mine—"I was hoping that we could discuss—"

Andrew folded his hands in prayer pose and held them in front of his mouth. "Can we just please focus on your workout? I need you to forget about everything else and gimme this hour. Please?"

Forget about everything else? It was a big ask, considering the things I could never forget every time I looked at Andrew. But I had to agree. He'd been on his best behavior while I worked with Dude, allowing me to run the class like he was any other client and not a fellow combatant in a decade-long grudge match.

"Okay, fine, you got it," I said. "But before we start I need to come clean about something. My wrist is better now. Look." I held it up and swiveled it. "Zero pain."

He narrowed his eyes at the offending appendage then glanced at me. "You're not just saying that?"

"I swear I'm not. I mean, maybe we should just skip all of this?"

As I admitted it I felt exposed. I was there because I was nosy and I wanted to gloat about what I thought I was going to see, not because I actually needed his help. Andrew had agreed to the swap to help me rehab an injury that had eventually healed on its own, which meant I didn't need him. And it wasn't like I had any desire to take up lifting. I ran occasionally, did yoga now and then, hiked with Birdie, and that was more than enough for me. There was no #gymlife in my future, even if I could spit at one from my front door.

"No, we're not skipping it. Absolutely not." Andrew's expression shifted as a storm cloud passed over his features. "I still want to make good on our agreement, it's only fair. And besides, I want to help your left side get stronger and less susceptible to injury. It's your nondominant side so it's always gonna be weaker."

Andrew wanting to help me was an entirely new concept. Andrew wanting to antagonize me? Poke fun at me? Par for the course. But *help*? Not the man I knew at all.

"How do you know I'm right-handed?" I demanded.

"I'm observant. It's part of my job." His eyes dragged over me in a way that I wanted to chalk up to professional scrutiny but actually felt more like appreciation. "Last night, when you were training Dude I watched the way you worked with him. It was obvious you're right-handed."

I felt heat rush to my face. The Gibson Glare included *intel* too?

I coughed and turned in a circle like I was chasing an invisible tail. "So, uh, what first?" I looked away from Andrew but could still see him reflected back at me from every angle around the room.

"I've been watching you," he said, his genial tone taking the stalker vibes out of the words. "The way you move, how you walk, your posture."

My skin prickled at the reminder of Andrew scrutinizing me without me even realizing it. I braced for the veiled insults.

"I think you're going to do great. You have phenomenal spatial awareness. You move well, you're graceful. We just need to add a little strength to the equation, and that's where I come in."

Graceful? Me?

"I have a bunch of ideas about what I want to cram into these three sessions, but for today we're starting nice and easy. This way." He hooked his hand then headed to a far corner, away from the heavy machinery.

Nice and easy? I bristled. I mean, I wasn't all 'roided up like the rest of his clientele, but I wasn't exactly a weakling. After all, I could walk a sled-dogging eighty-pound Rottweiler with one hand.

He stopped in a corner and pulled out a cut-off broomstick with a two-foot rope tied in the center that was attached to a flat two-pound weight. Of all the sophisticated-looking equipment in the place he was making me use something that seemed better suited for senior citizen rehab?

"This one is great. Let me demonstrate."

Andrew grasped the stick at each end and held it away from his body at shoulder height with the weight dangling down in the middle. In a flash the air around him seemed to shift as he switched on his focus. He adjusted his stance, straightening his back so that each vertebra seemed to snap into place, giving him what looked like an extra three inches of height. He took an intentional breath, let it out slowly, then paused, like he was an actor getting ready to take the stage.

Seeing him give the puny weight that level of preparation was *way* sexier than it should've been. I swallowed hard, trying to focus on his face and not the forearms flexing just a few feet away from me.

"Ready?" he asked, locking on to me to make sure I was paying attention. "Watch me."

I nodded stupidly. As if there were any options *other* than watching him.

"Just like this, see? It's good for the flexors and extensors in the forearms."

He rolled the stick with each hand in a smooth, rhythmic motion so that the rope coiled around it and the weight rose. Andrew was so focused that if I didn't see the tiny two-pound weight myself I would've sworn that he was lifting something gigantic. There was no tough-guy posturing or laughing off the simple exercise that he probably could've performed with his pinkie. He demonstrated the move with what I was sure was perfect form, giving it the same care and attention he probably used when heaving up what amounted to his own body weight.

"Okay, your turn."

Andrew offered the stick to me and I realized that not only was the Gibson Glare about to take me in, it was also going to *professionally* judge me. Correct me. Point out all the things I was doing wrong. I'd always known that was what he was doing in his head anyway, but now I was going to be subjected to it out loud.

I took the stick and did my best to mimic Andrew's pose, flicking my eyes at my reflection then back to him with a questioning look.

"Perfect," he said with a nod.

I tried not to grin at the compliment.

"Let's see what you got," he encouraged.

I rolled the stick up, approximating what he'd shown me, and was surprised to feel the slightest twinge in my wrist. It didn't hurt, it was more a reminder of the fall. Maybe a little attention to it was a good thing after all?

We went through the exercise twice, taking one-minute breaks in between each set. I was a little embarrassed to admit that the tiny weight made my shoulders burn too. Andrew was in his element, explaining all the ways the simple exercise could improve everything from my grip strength to my flexibility.

I finished the final set and handed the stick back to him, shocked that he hadn't found anything in my performance to criticize.

"What did you think about that exercise?" he asked, a smile playing at his lips. "Too easy? Are you ready for a little more?"

"I mean . . ." I flexed my arms, which were hidden under an XL long-sleeve T-shirt I'd gotten from a dog food manufacturer. "Strong like ox, remember?"

He chuckled at me. "How could I forget. Higs to the rescue. Okay, let's go."

I followed him to a contraption that took up much of the center of the room and had various pulleys, bars, and handles suspended from it. Andrew leaned over a low seat on one side of it to adjust the weights, then turned to me so quickly that I had to look at the ground to avoid being caught staring at his ass again.

"This is a simple pull-down that works the back. The goal here is to keep tension out of your neck, so make sure that your shoulders are down as you flow through the movement. You should feel this in your lats." Andrew said this as if I would know what a "lat" was. He grasped the handles suspended over his head then lowered himself on the seat. The weird air shift happened again as he paused to orient himself on the chair and to the handles he was gripping over his head. "Pull down nice and smooth and turn your hands in at the end of the movement."

Andrew took a deep breath then flowed through the exercise with the grace of a dancer. There was no huffing and puffing even though I could tell by the way his back shifted under his T-shirt that the weight was heavy for him. Every segment of the exercise was deliberate, elegant, and without a single wasted movement.

"You're up," he said, rising from the seat after six repetitions. He adjusted the weight to a quarter of what he'd been hoisting. "You got this."

I knew that his encouragement was probably rote, the exact same things he said to all his clients as they got ready to throw heavy things around their bodies. But damn it if it didn't do something to me. The more he urged me on, the more I wanted to prove that, yeah, I *could* do it.

I wanted Andrew to be proud of me.

I looked at the machine and realized that we'd leveled up from the baby-stick stuff. My palms went clammy, nerves for what I was about to attempt. I fanned myself. "Do you keep it warm in here on purpose? Like hot yoga or something?"

"You're *hot*?" He tipped his head at me, wearing a dubious expression. "I was going to grab a hoodie."

"I am working out . . ."

He let out a joyful, rumbly laugh. "Oh, Higs, you're just getting started. Wait till we get to squats."

I could feel sweat beading along my hairline before I even started. Either I was coming down with the flu or I was way more out of shape than I realized.

Or I was melting under the unflinching Gibson Glare.

I remembered that I was wearing an old black tank top under the T-shirt so I whipped it over my head and tied it around my waist quickly, before Andrew had a chance to look at my butt. I grabbed the handles and lowered myself to the seat.

"Is it too heavy?" Andrew's voice came from behind me. "There's no shame in making it lighter."

I shook my head and pulled the handles down toward my shoulders, which was *way* harder than Andrew made it look. I felt uncoordinated, like my hands were moving at different speeds as he counted through the repetitions. My arms actually started visibly trembling.

"Two more," Andrew said encouragingly. "Looking fantastic, nice work."

There it was again, the *praise*. I knew how important it was from working with my own clients, but being on the receiving end was something new for me. I was embarrassed at the way I lapped it up. I finished the set and let out a long exhale, my muscles fizzy from the exertion.

"Excellent work. Really, really strong start. Couple of things I want you to try on the next set." Andrew paused. "Can I touch you?"

The question sent a seismic rumble through me. It wasn't the first time Andrew had asked it, but the circumstances couldn't have been more different. I debated between making a joke and answering like a normal person who wasn't having naked flashbacks. I couldn't find any suitable words to respond to the question that had changed everything between us all those years ago.

Instead, I stared at him stupidly.

"Hey, no problem, it's okay to say no," he said quickly, clearly not catching the subtext of what he'd asked me. "Some people don't appreciate touch during a workout, which is why I ask first. I just want you to be aware—"

"No," I interjected quickly. "It's . . . it's okay. You can touch me." The last two words of the sentence practically squeaked out of me.

My entire body went hot and I was convinced that I was glowing red, like an iron just pulled from a flame. I glanced at my reflection and realized that I was hunched over with my arms crossed over my chest. I looked out of place in the clean, bright room.

"Great," he said, clearly ignoring how far from great I actually was. "Grab the handles and sit back down." He pointed at the machine.

I did as I was told.

"Now, start the movement."

I began pulling the handles down and suddenly his fingertips were pressed on my back where my rib cage flared, a butterfly touch that I wasn't even sure was real.

"*This* is where you should be feeling it," he said. "Not up here." His fingertips migrated to my bare shoulders at the base of my neck, where my skin was a little sweaty. "Switch your focus. Be intentional with the movement."

It was solid advice and I would've followed it if I could think about anything other than the way he was searing my skin. The only thing intentional in my mind as I attempted to pull the handles down was the memory of our bodies crashing into one another. How could he not remember it, or at least elements of it if the details were blurred from the alcohol? I felt my left arm start to give out.

"Don't worry, I got you," Andrew said, grabbing on to the handle so his palm covered my hand to keep it from slipping out of my grip. "You're done."

I hopped out of the seat and practically ran for my water bottle, putting distance between us in a way that I hoped wasn't too obvious. I hated that he could still knock me off steady ground with just a touch. But it was obviously one-sided. The man who'd gone from a night of drunken fumbling with me to dating a literal swimsuit model probably wasn't turned on by what he was seeing. The unanswered text was all the proof I'd needed that I was his mistake.

"Hey, don't feel bad," Andrew was saying when I finally managed to focus on him again. "It's a journey. I think you might have a couple of mental blocks we need to get past and that's the reason why you faltered on that last rep. You're strong, and you move really well."

More compliments. This wasn't the Andrew I knew. He was toying with me. My head felt like it was stuffed with cotton, dulling my senses.

"You know what?" I bent over, my hands clutching my hips. "I'm not feeling great. I think I need to finish for today."

"Hold on, are you okay?" I couldn't look at him, but I felt the weight of his eyes, studying me. "Did you hurt yourself?"

"No." I waved my hand at him as I walked in small circles like I'd just finished running a marathon. "Not at all, just a, uh, headache. I'll catch up with you later, okay?"

"Are you sure you're all right?" Andrew's voice echoed behind me as I headed for the door.

"I'm okay. Thanks again." I sliced the air over my head in a version of a wave but refused to turn around to look at him. I was convinced that if I did he'd be able to see what I'd been desperate to hide from him since the first time we met.

chapter fourteen

I couldn't shake the queasy feeling until long after I was home, showered, and snuggled on the couch under a blanket with Birdie at my feet and Edith on my lap. The puppy was still punchy despite our long walk, so I entertained her with a mellow game of tug as I tried to make sense of the weirdness I'd just experienced.

I was tempted to reach out to Samantha, to get her read on what seemed like a new and improved Andrew. But we hadn't talked in forever, and using him as the reason for reaching out gave the scenario more weight than it deserved. Plus, she'd always been his fan. And even worse, she *loved* the incomprehensible idea of us together. She'd said as much to me that night when she held my hair back while I puked my guts up.

I closed my eyes at the reflexive flood of embarrassment. Every time I thought about that night I cycled through a cringe and shame spiral that made me wish I could scrub it from my memory banks, *Eternal Sunshine*-style.

"It's stupid, right? Forever ago," I said to Edith, and she

moved her mouth off the tug toy and onto my hands as her answer. "I need to get over it."

As if I could.

Parts of that night, Samantha and Nolan's coed bachelor/
bachelorette party, were seared into my brain despite the copious amounts of alcohol I drank. (And later vomited up.) It
didn't help matters that we were on a yacht in New York harbor
for five hours, where thirty-five people got increasingly drunk
and horny as the night wore on, resulting in absolute de-
bauchery by the time we docked. Or so I heard, since I passed
out before the end of it.

It had started off innocently enough, with the guys playing
drinking games clustered around Nolan and the girls toasting
Samantha with bottomless champagne. But as the sun went
down and the DJ pumped up, we all started acting stupid on
the dance floor. I have vague memories of twerking so hard that
my dress flipped up, and I didn't even care.

I usually wasn't the center of attention, but that night I
drank it up, literally and metaphorically. Maybe it was the happiness of everyone being together again to celebrate our friends,
or because I was wearing a pretty dress and felt four-glasses-in
invincible on a rented yacht, or maybe it was because I could
sense Andrew's eyes resting on me over and over again
throughout the night. In retrospect I knew that half the reason
I put on such a show was because I *liked* the idea of him staring
at me again. I felt beautiful, and I wanted him to know it.

I squeezed my eyes shut when I thought about what happened later that night.

Bored by my lack of interaction, Edith moved off of me and

down toward where Birdie was coiled in a tight circle sound asleep. She watched her adopted big sister for a moment, then leaned down to chomp on her tail, eliciting a shocked yelp from Birdie.

"*Excuse* me!" I scolded. "That was not nice, young lady. That's not how we roll in this household."

Edith parried at Birdie again, getting a low growl from her. I expected it to be enough to get the puppy to stand down, but Edith shocked us both and let out a surprisingly unpuppylike growl back.

"Whoa, absolutely not. Nope! Let's go."

I stood up and moved Edith off the couch, then leaned over to give Birdie a quick conciliatory kiss. "Sorry about her."

I felt the smallest flicker of concern over the behavior. Edith was supposed to be my wallflower, my in-need-of-support puppy who would look to her elder for life lessons. What I'd just seen on the couch was an inappropriate response to a totally normal correction from Bird. Most puppies would offer a deferential reaction when scolded that way, but Edith had doubled down. I needed to keep an eye on it.

"Let's give you something to do," I said to her as she battled the hem of my sweatpants.

I walked to the freezer, where I had a supply of peanut butter–stuffed rubber toys ready for her. We were heading into teething season, which meant I needed an arsenal to keep her from chewing up the house. Birdie was the rare dog who didn't like peanut butter so I never had to worry about accidental skirmishes between them over the toys, but then again, now that I was seeing this new side of Edith, who knew what was in store?

She got to work on it with a velociraptor's intensity so I re-joined Bird on the couch, curling myself around her body.

"Sorry about that," I murmured, pressing a kiss on the top of her head. "She'll figure it out."

I hoped.

I sat up and refocused on my laptop. The Howl-o-Ween party RSVPs were still pouring in thanks to an old-school ad in the *Wismer Register* and an Insta shout-out from a former client who'd gone on to become a doggy influencer. It was going to be my biggest event yet.

Was I an asshole because I'd rented traffic cones to cordon off my section of the parking lot? Maybe. But I wasn't about to let Andrew's crowd take over my precious spaces.

Deep down I knew that I could change the power dynamic with the flick of a pen on a contract. Of course, I refused to think about the logistics required to flick that pen, but still. The idea that I *could* buy the whole damn building if I wanted to comforted me a little.

The hurdles necessary to make that happen? Impossible to clear.

My dad had left money for us because of course he would. Keeping us safe and secure was what he did. My mom kept pushing to finalize the details with me, but I preferred to ignore it. I didn't want assets, I wanted *him*. I pretended like his "legacy" for me didn't exist.

In the meantime I needed to focus on securing Roz's space.

I sniffed back a painful prickle in my nose and tallied my attendees again. Twenty-five definites, six maybes. Twelve parking spaces.

If I was honest with myself I could admit that it wasn't about parking. My clients could park along the street if they had to. The point was they *shouldn't* have to. After-hours had always belonged to me, ever since I launched Frolic. Now Andrew had moved in and taken over, before he even opened his doors.

My phone pinged with a text. Of all people it was Patricia, as if she could tell I was thinking negative thoughts about her son, asking if it was okay to call me. It's too much to write, said her text.

My phone rang seconds after I said she could.

"I'm so sorry to call you after hours, but we've had an incident. Darling knocked me over today."

Darling was the queen of the Mean Girl goats, the bravest of the three, which wasn't saying much.

"Oh no! Are you okay?"

"Just a little sore, that's all. The leaves and mud cushioned my fall. But it wasn't pretty."

"I'm so sorry to hear it," I replied, envisioning poor Patricia fighting her way out of the mud. "Has she been regressing?"

"No, we were making a little progress, but something got into her and she's been nastier than ever. Maybe it's the turn in the weather?"

"Yeah, the cold snap came out of nowhere." I pulled the blanket tighter around my body. "Is everyone else doing okay?"

"They are. Darling is the problem. Can you come back and help us again? That is, if you're not scared off."

I laughed. I'd done time with snarling, snapping, muscle-bound leash-reactive dogs, so a bossy old goat with devil eyes was nothing.

"Not at all, I'd be happy to help."

As long as your son isn't around.

"Thank you so much, Chelsea. I'll make it work whenever you can fit me in."

We figured out a mutually agreeable time and I found myself wishing that I could introduce Pat to my mom. They reminded me of one another.

"Maybe I'll run into you at the party?" Patricia said hopefully. "Andrew tells me that you both have events scheduled for the same night. He's disappointed because he said he wanted to bring Dude to your costume contest. But he's been working on his launch for so long and he's really excited for it. Maybe you can pop over after yours ends? I'm sure we'll be there late into the evening. He's got quite a crowd coming."

I sighed. Of course he did.

"I'll definitely try," I replied, not sure if it was a lie or not. Part of me wanted to observe the spectacle of his grand opening. To reacquaint myself with "party Andrew." It pained me to admit that I sort of enjoyed watching him amp people up, because he made it look effortless. And maybe it actually was for him? I had to command crowds as well, to encourage distracted clients and busy dogs to stay focused on me in a noisy room. I'd worked at developing the ability. Andrew seemed to have been born with it.

"Wonderful! Thank you so much, Chelsea. We all really appreciate your help."

I wondered if the "all" included her son.

"Andrew loved what you did with Dude at his first session. And he said he was impressed with how you did at Crush. Sounds like you two are going to be great neighbors!"

She really had no clue. Andrew hadn't filled her in about our history.

"Thanks, I'm doing my best," I managed to respond before we hung up.

It wasn't easy, being so close to him on a daily basis. I didn't see him around much, but there were always reminders that he was existing just beyond the empty space in between us. The occasional garbage bags that still managed to land outside the bin and wound up ripped open by the raccoon posse. His Jeep parked haphazardly. Teeth-rattling blasts of Metallica through the vent when he didn't realize that I was in my building.

I clutched my phone to my chest and watched Edith go to town on the rubber toy. The only consolation to being forced to work near him was the knowledge that there was clearly no way he remembered that night. There wasn't even a *hint* that it had an impact on him. Because if he did remember I'd expect some sort of jokey acknowledgment of how drunk he'd been. Too much alcohol was the only reason why he ever would've traded down to me.

But that night? I didn't recognize him, because it felt like he adored me. He couldn't stop kissing me and his hands were gentle and wild all over my body, like he was desperate to touch every inch of me. In the heat of the moment I didn't care how drunk he was. I just wanted him to keep going.

The next morning I was horrified to realize that I'd sent him a text after I was done throwing up but before I'd passed out. I squeezed my eyes shut and tried to block out the few words I still remembered, like "obsessed" and "forever" and "girlfriend." It wasn't like me to be so forward with Andrew, but I'd still been on the high of everything he'd said to me while we were twisted around each other in that room. That I was beautiful. How he'd always wanted to kiss me. That I scared him and he liked it. Promises that this would be the first of many nights together.

When I'd woken up I was alone, curled up under Nolan's blazer on a hard bench, and my phone was nowhere to be found.

Andrew had left a reminder of what we'd done, the tiniest love bite at the base of my neck, which was too close to the exact spot where he'd placed his fingertips during our workout at Crush. It didn't matter that the rest of the night was muted and hazy, everything we'd done in that cramped space was seared in my mind forever.

It had started with a kiss that was meant to be a joke. A dare. "I bet you won't kiss me," I'd taunted, leaning close to him, hoping that the front of my dress was slipping down enough to tempt him. I was prepared to keep at it, to goad him into doing it, but he'd shocked me and pushed me up against the wall the second the words were out of my mouth.

"Oh yeah?" I remember the scent of mint on his breath, like he'd prepared for exactly this. "What do I win if you lose the bet?"

The logistics were beyond me so I'd come back with "Then you get to kiss me!"

His lips were on mine in a flash, hungry, soft, and more delicious than I'd ever imagined.

He'd pulled away and I remembered pouting, but then his hand had trailed up my bare legs while he held my gaze in the world's sexiest game of chicken. He was daring me to stop him, to move out of his reach, but there was no way I could. I wanted it, wanted *him*, and he knew it. My breath hitched as his hand skimmed higher, spreading out on my thigh to claim more of the bare skin beneath my dress. He teased goose bumps everywhere he touched, then he gently raised the hem of my dress, bent over, and softly kissed the tops of my thighs to warm me.

As if I needed more heat. I was kindling, smoldering, ready

to burst into flames. And he was just inches from striking the match.

Keep going, keep going. It had been a chant as he teased me, a prayer. I was desperate for more.

But he'd stopped right before his fingertips grazed the silk of my thong and I wanted to scream from frustration. Because deep down, as much as I'd lied to myself about how much I despised everything about Andrew Gibson, I knew I'd *always* wanted this moment.

I remember looking down at him, because Andrew was on his knees in front of me in that cramped closet with his hands pressed against my thighs. Then he'd said it.

"Can I touch you?"

I couldn't respond, partly because I was afraid to break the spell but mainly because I knew I'd sound desperate if I opened my mouth. I nodded, then let my head fall back as Andrew finally put me out of my misery and reached my heat. Then it was a tangle of fingertips, mouth, tongue, and me doing everything in my power to keep from screaming out. It didn't end there. The snapshot images of me on my knees in front of him, making *him* beg, made me feel like I'd won the bet in more ways than one.

I was back in that small room for the millionth time, reliving every detail of the way we'd made each other feel. Even now, my breathing was shallow and I could feel a familiar heat coursing through my body.

I got up off the couch slowly to keep from waking the dogs, then headed down the short hallway to my bedroom.

It was time to give *Le Rush* a test drive.

chapter fifteen

D amn, you look hot! Killer smoky eye." Little Red Riding Hood Carly gave me an appreciative whistle as she looked me up and down. "I have to admit that the costume is a little creepy, though."

Carly, her husband, Joe, and Geneva had shown up thirty minutes early to see if I needed any last-minute help setting up for my Howl-o-Ween party, but I'd been ready for hours.

"No, it's *funny*. Ironic," I insisted, smoothing down the front of my black dress. "Right?"

"I mean, yeah, if you think making puppies into a coat is funny, then sure."

I'd planned to wear my usual dog warden costume to the party, which consisted of khaki shorts and a matching shirt, a name badge, and a net, but something made me switch to Cruella de Vil. Maybe I wanted to channel her bitchy energy when I had to deal with the muscleheads about to gather next door.

Or maybe I just wanted to look sexy for a change.

"Is the wig too much?" I tugged at the bangs. The black and

white wig was necessary to complete the look but was scratchy as hell.

Carly shook her head and picked up Geneva, who was dressed as the cutest Big Bad Wolf ever. "Absolutely not. You look amazing. We should go out after the party is over."

"Where are we going after?" Joe asked as he strolled up to us, completing the family costume theme dressed as granny with a beard. "And can I come?"

"I'm not going anywhere—this party wipes me out," I said, adjusting my white faux fur coat, which I'd painted with black dots to resemble dalmatian spots. "Rain check."

"Okay, but I'm holding you to that." Carly wagged a finger at me. "We're going to go bob for bones and wait for more people to show up."

I looked around the room for the millionth time to make sure everything was ready. Realistic spiderwebs and black crepe paper hung out of reach of curious mouths? Check. Piles of tennis balls that looked like jack-o'-lanterns? Check. Hay bales and pumpkins for photo ops? Check. Candy for the humans and treats for the pups? Check. There were a bunch of activities for both ends of the leash, and of course I'd set up a makeshift stage for the costume contest. My clients took that part seriously, which meant that judging was impossible. How could I choose between a hot dog dachshund and her person dressed as a bottle of ketchup competing with a crusty old white dog dressed as a sparkly Cinderella with her person in a Prince Charming costume? I couldn't, which was why I had a winner for every conceivable category and tons of prizes.

My phone pinged with a text message and I felt a tremor roll through me when I saw that it was from Andrew. There was no message history between us since I'd swapped phones a few times over the years, but I knew that the last message I'd sent him was the one he'd ignored.

> About to do ribbon cutting. Going to be loud.
> Come over if you want.

I sighed. Of *course* it was going to be loud. I wouldn't expect anything less. But it was nice of him to give me a heads-up about it. And I did sort of want to watch the spectacle unfold, from a safe distance away.

"You guys want to walk next door and see the ribbon cutting at that new gym?" I shouted to Carly and Joe, who were across the room wrist-deep in water trying to help Geneva grab a dog biscuit. I now sort of wished I'd given Carly more backstory about my history with Andrew because I was dreading her inevitable matchmaking attempts.

"Oh yeah," Joe called back. "I've seen that guy all over social media. I think I want to start working out there."

I sighed. No one was immune to Andrew, even a guy who'd once said that golf required too much exertion.

I could hear the buzz of people before we were even out the door. My side of the parking lot was still mercifully empty thanks to the traffic cones, but every inch of his side was packed with cars and trucks. The group of people gathered outside his door were decked out in costumes and I strained to find Andrew among them. I spotted a bunch of people I knew from town, including the sole intrepid reporter from the *Wismer Register* and Mayor Wilson, who'd dressed up for the occasion in a red clown nose and top hat.

I pulled my fur coat tighter across my chest. Second summer was long gone, replaced by the biting cold of fall, so I hoped he'd be quick. I stood on my tiptoes looking for Andrew, trying to imagine which superhero he'd picked for his costume.

"Let's get a little closer, I can't see anything," Carly said, grabbing my arm and dragging me toward the front of the crowd. As much as I wanted to stick to the shadows I was curious about how Andrew was going to handle his grand opening. Why did he make a point to say that it was going to be noisy? I glanced at Geneva nestled in Carly's arms and felt an anticipatory frown spread across my face. Better not be fireworks.

Carly bulldozed her way to the front and came to a stop right by the building, a few feet away from where a black ribbon had been strung across the door.

"Crush," Joe muttered, reading the sign. "I like it."

I turned to survey the crowd behind us. There were clusters of young guys dressed as memes that I was shocked I recognized, a football player, an incredibly fit Tinker Bell who *had* to be freezing in her tiny green dress, a few zombies, an Edward Scissorhands with killer biceps, a bald circus strongman complete with fake dumbbell, the Sanderson sisters from *Hocus Pocus*, and more.

"He really knows how to draw a crowd," Carly said, glancing around. "What's he like?"

I was deciding between "self-absorbed" and "shallow" when Andrew came strolling around the corner clutching a pair of giant scissors, grinning and waving at the crowd like he was a celebrity.

My breath caught. His hair was down, and the Andrew I knew had been transformed into something wilder, like the sexiest dirtbag in a biker gang. The rogue pirate with a heart of gold. The dashing rake who couldn't be tamed. The smoldering vampire you'd gladly welcome inside. I was desperate to try to hate this side of him, but my body seemed to have other ideas about the way he looked.

"Oof," Carly said, her eyes widening at the sight of him. *"Hello."*

Andrew's costume didn't register at first because he was in a black leather vest and tank top paired with jeans. But then I saw the fake fish scale tattoos running down both his arms and the jade pendant hanging from a leather strap around his neck.

"Street wear Aquaman," I muttered as I realized for the first time just how much he now resembled the superhero. His low-key costume made my tight dress and wig seem silly. I should've been dressed to work, like him, not to show off.

"Well, I feel like a dork now," Joe said, plucking at his blue floral nightgown then glancing back at Andrew.

"Yeah, you should *definitely* start training with him," Carly said, reaching back to smack her husband's midsection without looking away from Andrew.

"Hey, folks, we're going to get started," Mayor Wilson repeated a few times, clapping his hands and trying to get the crowd's attention. When everyone finally settled he continued. "I'm excited to welcome all of you to the launch celebration for Wismer's newest business, Crush."

A few people hooted and clapped.

"Crush's owner, Andrew Gibson, is going to say a few words, then we'll cut the ribbon and begin the party."

"Thank you, Mayor Wilson." Andrew shook the mayor's hand, then stepped into the spotlight. "Hey, everybody!"

His voice rang out strong and clear, like someone had plugged in a microphone to make the crowd stop chattering and take note. The change from the mayor's low-key vibe to Andrew's upbeat energy seemed to electrify everyone.

"I can't tell you how *pumped* I am that you're here with me tonight!"

This time everyone broke into wild applause and cheering.

"I see friends who made the drive up from DC ..." He glanced around the crowd. "I see new friends that I've made here in Wismer as I got set up ..." He scanned everyone until his eyes landed on me and I could've sworn he staggered a half step as his eyes raked up my body. It was a moment of connection that sent warmth to my cheeks that I was sure everyone would notice. "Uh, I see, uh ... old friends ..." He cleared his throat and composed himself. "And monsters and zombies and all sorts of other scary stuff. Huge thanks for being here with me to celebrate, I appreciate each and every one of you. Now let's cut this ribbon and have some fun!"

I glanced at Carly and Joe and they were both clapping like their candidate had won on election night. Andrew maneuvered behind the ribbon and held the scissors over it, smiling as people snapped photos.

"How is he not freezing?" I asked, trying not to notice the way his arms flexed as he pretended to cut.

"Yeah, it's not like he has any body fat to keep him warm," Joe said with awe in his voice.

Carly and I exchanged a glance.

"Looks like I have some competition," she deadpanned.

Joe met her laughter with a puzzled expression.

"Gimme a countdown," Andrew yelled at the crowd. "Five . . . four . . ."

"Three . . . two . . ." everyone joined in.

"One!"

The second the scissors cut through the ribbon the low rumble of drums sounded out as the entire Wismer High School marching band rounded the corner playing a fight riff loudly enough to be heard by the rival school in the next county.

I glanced at Carly and saw Geneva looking panicked in her arms, trying to scale up her body.

"She's scared, you should get her inside," I told her, scowling at the noise. "I need to find out how long this is going to last."

Carly nodded and she and Joe backtracked to my end of the building as I scanned the crowd to try to find Andrew. It was hard to be angry listening to a bunch of high schoolers killing a rendition of "Thriller," but I knew how traumatic it would be for many of my students to have to walk past the sounds of drums and horns. I pulled out my phone and realized that my party was set to begin in twenty minutes.

Someone tapped my shoulder and I spun around to find Patricia grinning at me.

"Hi, there," I said. "Looks like I found you." I shouted over the noise and pointed to her telltale red-and-white-striped shirt, red cap, and black-rimmed glasses. "You make a great Waldo."

"And you are a *devastating* Cruella," she laughed and leaned closer to me so we could hear one another. "You look gorgeous!"

"Stop," I said, fanning away the compliment. "Is Gerard a Waldo as well?" I glanced around, looking for another red-striped shirt.

Her smile faltered for a moment. "No, he couldn't be here tonight, he's not feeling well. But isn't this wonderful?" She gestured around to the band and the crowd streaming into Crush.

"It's . . . something else," I managed, making a mental note that Andrew's father wasn't at his launch party. My dad had left a business trip in California to make it back in time for my grand opening. "Speaking of, do you happen to know how long the band will be playing?"

"Oh, not long," Pat answered, glancing over at them. "Andrew is training a few of the football guys and they arranged the band as a favor for him. I think they're only here for a few songs."

I tried to keep my face neutral as they shifted into a shrieking, trumpet-filled rendition of "Crazy Train" by Ozzy Osbourne. "Oh, okay. Great."

"What a fun little block party tonight! Is yours starting soon?"

"Yup." I bobbed my head and held back from saying that it had been *my* party night for the past six years and Andrew was ruining it. "I should get back there."

"Have fun! And do stop by after your event ends, I'm sure we're going to run late," she said, pointing at Crush. "My son likes to have a good time."

Understatement of the century.

"I'll try," I said. "Please tell Darling I'm looking forward to seeing her."

But Patricia had her back to me and was bouncing along off tempo to the marching band. I glanced inside Crush as I headed back to my side of the building.

Despite the crowd my eye was drawn to Andrew in the center of the room talking to a woman I could only see from the back dressed as a sexy ladybug. I froze.

Dark hair, perfect legs, tan skin . . . hold on, was it *Zadie*?

Andrew hadn't mentioned her name the few times we'd hung out, but why would he talk about his girlfriend with me? There was absolutely no need for the two of us to discuss the flawless woman he'd dated for . . . well, I wasn't sure, but it seemed like forever. His personal life was none of my business. I'd assumed that he was single, but maybe they were dating long-distance?

It wasn't like I cared one way or the other.

Of course, I used to. Sam and I had dissected Zadie endlessly in the aftermath of her wedding. That she'd looked incredible in her clingy pink dress but that it wasn't quite appropriate for the event. That nearly every single man and a few married ones had hit on her throughout the night despite the fact that she was Nolan's work friend's plus-one. That she'd dragged Andrew onto the dance floor when "I Gotta Feeling" came on, and how tacky it was for her to be such a blatant flirt while her date was passed out in a corner.

After all of the wedding hubbub had died down and she'd returned from her honeymoon Sam had offered to run front for me to talk to Andrew about what had happened on the boat, but it was too late. He'd blown off my text message, and he and Zadie had graduated to posting cute selfies together on social media within two short weeks.

It was all the proof I needed to figure out that I'd been his mistake.

chapter sixteen

A re you sure you don't want my help cleaning up?" Paula asked, turning around to survey the room. She was dressed as a giant magnifying glass, in a silver sweatsuit with a circle of cardboard "glass" on her head. Sherlock Holmes Ivan was eyeing the door and I could tell that he was as ready to go home as I was.

"You're too kind to offer, but I've got it down to a science. I'll be finished in twenty minutes tops. I need to get out of this costume."

As much as I wanted to pull off the wig I knew my hair was a matted, sweaty mess beneath it. The outfit might have looked cool, but I was self-conscious and itchy the whole night. My life was soft pants and sneakers, not hoochie dresses and heels.

Paula frowned at me. "I wish you'd hire a helper. You do too much."

"You sound like my mom," I laughed.

I didn't talk about it often, but part of my big expansion plan was bringing not one but two part-time people on board. Expanding into Roz's empty space would give me the flexibility to provide additional services, like all-day training packages. But the sale of the building put everything at risk.

"We had a wonderful time tonight, thank you for our prize. Best Literary Costume, what an honor!" Paula said. She stooped to pick Ivan up and he jogged just out of reach. "C'mere, you."

"I bet he's okay to walk to your car," I offered. I'd reminded Paula time and again that Ivan was perfectly capable of walking, but it was one lesson she couldn't retain.

She peeked out the door. "I don't know, there are a bunch of big guys hanging around outside by that gym place. *I'm* scared of them so I'm sure he will be too."

I'd hoped the Crush crowd would die down, but the party was still going strong.

"Okay, then maybe it's fine to carry him this time. But make it worth his while rather than chasing him. Squat down, let him approach you at his own pace, give him a treat, tell him what you're about to do, *then* pick him up. Like this."

I kneeled and Ivan toddled over to check me out. When he was close enough I grabbed a bit of freeze-dried liver from a nearby bowl and gave it to him, then put my hands on his sides. I paused to let him acclimate to the sensation. "Up," I said, lifting him, and he settled into my arms.

"You make it look so easy," Paula said, shaking her head.

"You'll get it," I reassured her and handed Ivan over.

After a little more chitchat Paula finally collected her things. She said something as she headed out the door that I couldn't quite hear.

"What's that?" I called to her.

"I said that there are a lot of men out there and I want you to be safe," she said, pausing before walking outside with Ivan clutched in her arms.

Once she was gone I kicked off my heels and slipped on my Birkenstocks, letting out a moan of relief. I wasn't lying when I told Paula I had cleanup down to a science. I'd already run the messy paper towels from the accidental puddles and piles out to the dumpster, and the rest of the trash was bagged up and ready to go. I moved the hay bales and pumpkins to the back door, put the folding chairs in my storage area, and stashed the agility equipment where it belonged.

I was happy I'd hidden two of Roz's frosted ghost sugar cookies at the beginning of the night because the trays of food I'd put out were down to crumbs and I was starving. I shoved one in my mouth, grabbed an overfull trash bag, and headed for the back door.

It was going to be a quick trip to the trash, an in-and-out so fast that I wouldn't need my silly fur coat, which was hanging by the front door because it got too hot by the end of the party. I hip-checked my way outside, pausing to kick my trusty propping rock into place to hold the door open. The cold slammed into me and I instantly regretted my no-coat decision. My black dress was made from thin velvet with spaghetti straps and I might as well have been naked in the freezing night air. I shuffled as fast as I could, considering my black nylons made my Birks slippery, and readied myself to toss the heavy bag into the bin Highland games shot put–style.

Was the twinge in my shoulders as I hoisted the bag a remnant from my workout with Andrew, or just proof that I *wasn't* strong like ox? I was too tired to think about either option. I glanced toward Andrew's side of the building, half expecting to see people overflowing out here too, but it was dark. I could hear Myrtle meowing in the distance as I flip-flopped to my door.

My *closed* back door.

I let out a groan of frustration. It wasn't the first time my not-so-trusty propping rock had failed to do its job. Now I'd have to sneak around the building to slip in the front main door without anyone from Andrew's party seeing me.

I cursed my stupid nineteen-dollar dress as I speed-shuffled with my arms crossed tightly over my chest. I was freezing, overtired, grumpy, and hungry. I pitied the fool who got in between me and the end of my night.

Andrew's DJ was still cranking club hits that drifted out his open front door. The party had thinned, but there was still a group gathered hobo-style around a firepit at the edge of the parking lot. It had to be a building violation, but I was too tired to call him on it. One of the guys was seated in an Iron Throne and I had to give him props for the realism. They seemed drunk and rowdy, chanting something and laughing. It sounded like they were saying "give it to me" over and over until I realized that they were actually saying "Gib it to me." Andrew Gibson had a *catchphrase*. I slunk against the building, staying in the shadows until I finally reached the door, then placed my hand on the handle and pulled.

Nothing.

I wrenched it a few times even though I knew it was locked, my frustration and anger making me want to scream. *That* was what Paula had said to me as she left. She'd locked me in, to protect me from the swole-bros.

I leaned my head against my door as I spooled through

possible solutions, trying not to shiver while the wind sliced through my dress. My phone was locked inside. Roz, the keeper of my spare key, was gone. The only option was to go to Andrew's, beg to use his phone, and get my mom to drive over with her spare key. Maybe Patricia was still there and I could summon her without anyone else seeing me? Because at this point my messy wig, dress, and Birks combo was scarier than any zombie.

"You okay?"

I whirled around and there was Aqua-Andrew in all of his sleeveless fake-tattooed glory, acting like it wasn't thirty degrees. There was something a little dangerous about him standing in the shadows with his arms crossed, making his biceps look bigger than normal. Even in the darkness I could tell he was sizing me up, trying to make sense of what the hell I was doing and if he should intervene.

"No, I'm obviously not okay," I griped before I could temper my frustration. "I'm locked out."

He worked hard to hide a smile but not hard enough. "You seem to have a problem with doors."

"And?"

"And . . . I'm a little afraid to help you, given what happened last time."

The vapor puffs around my face gave away the fact that I was frustrated and breathing hard.

"I said I was sorry."

That got a rumbling round of laughter out of him. "You absolutely did not. In fact, you gave me a list of rules I needed to follow, remember?"

As much as I didn't appreciate Andrew laughing at me while

I slowly froze to death, there was no denying how genuinely pleasing the sound was. But it didn't have the effect he wanted, as I refused to crack a smile.

"May I please use your phone?" I asked more politely than I felt.

"Only if you tell me what you're supposed to be." He gestured up and down my body, pausing on my Birkenstocks.

I bristled and pointed at my lopsided black and white wig. "You're seriously telling me you don't recognize Cruella de Vil?"

"I mean . . . I guess?" He cocked his head and pursed his lips. "But the shoes are throwing me off. You look more like high school art teacher Cruella. Or food co-op Cruella."

I glared at him.

"Bluegrass fan Cruella."

"Oh, *come* on. You saw me in the full costume, with the red lipstick and fur coat and heels. I know you did."

"You're right." Andrew took a step closer, so that he was completely hidden in the shadow from the building. "I did."

I tried to ignore the intensity in his glare as goose bumps skittered along my skin. "And?"

He dragged his eyes down my body again and I was happy that my arms were crossed, so he couldn't see my nipples poking through the thin fabric.

"And I think Roger Radcliffe would've happily handed over those puppies if you'd been the one asking for them."

I made a disgusted noise and reached out to push him away, but he caught my wrist. "I'm kidding, I'm kidding. I do *not* condone puppy coats, I promise."

Andrew didn't let go and his white-hot hand made me forget the chill in the air. My breath came in shallow puffs, the clouds around my face betraying any sense of calm that I was trying to project.

Here it was again. My angry, mortifying, clawing hunger for Andrew Gibson, boiling inside of me, urging me to do something I'd regret, like rising up on my tiptoes to kiss his stupid, beautiful mouth. There was no alcohol to blame for it this time, but if I was honest with myself I'd admit that wanting Andrew didn't require intoxication.

"You don't need my phone," he said.

I struggled out of the quicksand of my desire for him to try to make sense of what he meant. "So you *won't* let me borrow it?"

He shook his head and finally let go of me. "Wait here. Unless you want to come and join my party for a few minutes."

"Absolutely not." I shook my head so vigorously that my wig shifted even more. Zadie could be in there and I was in no mood to see her. "But what are you doing? I don't understand—"

He held his finger up at me, then walked back toward his side of the building without another word.

I paced in circles, rubbing my now freezing bare arms. How long had I been out here? Five minutes? Two hours? I'd lost all sense of time.

The guys clustered around the fire hooted at Andrew as he walked past and I shrank back into the shadows. I heard a noise from the far end of the building and spotted Myrtle in loaf position watching me. She looked relaxed, but I knew how quickly she could spirit away.

"You've *got* to be cold, Myrtle. Why do you insist on being an outside cat?"

The local rescue had tried to trap her tons of times over the years, but she always managed to grab the food without getting caught. Even if they could snag her I wasn't sure she'd be content being relegated to house or barn cat status. She alerted to something beyond me, then took off right as I realized that Andrew was headed back.

"Here," he said, handing me a black hoodie. "You're freezing."

I was too cold to refuse it and slipped it on. Even though it looked new I could swear I caught a whiff of his campfire scent as I pulled my head through. It was one of those perfect oversized sweatshirts, fleecy soft inside. I glanced down at the front and saw his logo on the chest.

"You got merch. Looks great. I'll buy this one from you."

Andrew shook his head. "That's the prototype. It's mine, but you can borrow it for tonight. And here's this."

He reached into his pocket and held out a key on a brass bulldog key chain.

"How did you . . ."

"Roz gave it to me on her last day here and told me to give it back to you. I keep forgetting to, but I guess it worked out."

He dropped it into my open hand.

"Now we're even. You rescued me off the roof and I rescued you from freezing to death."

"Are we keeping score?"

His mouth twitched into a smile. "When it comes to you, yes."

chapter seventeen

It was prime leaf-peeping season on the expansive Gibson homestead, but I only had eyes for Darling, and the feeling was mutual. Thistle and Petunia stood behind their queen bee like they were in between classes waiting to see who was going to make the first move in the schoolyard throwdown.

It wasn't like I was asking for much from the trio. We weren't at the point where I could even think about trying anything impressive. All I was looking for was the tiniest *literal* baby step in my direction, something we'd conquered at the first lesson but had lost in the weeks since.

Backsliding was the worst.

Patricia was on a call with her accountant so she'd left me to work on my own, which was perfect, considering I was floundering. At least we had a perfect fall day to not make any progress. My black knit cap and lined red flannel shirt were warm enough despite the wind that kicked up every so often, sending a confetti of gold and orange leaves to the ground around me.

"Girls, c'mon, I have pears and animal crackers. You'll love them."

They blinked at me, unmoved by the feast in my treat bag.

"Still at sixes and sevens with that lot, eh?"

I turned and saw Gerard passing by carrying a bucket filled with tools.

"Hello." I waved at him. "Yeah, I'm feeling a little defeated at the moment. Goats, one, Chelsea, zero."

He walked to the fence and propped his muddy boot up on it. "Don't blame yourself, they're an odd bunch. Not what we're used to."

"But I really feel like I could get through to them if they'd just give me a chance."

"Well, they're not going anywhere, to my dismay, so you're welcome to keep trying as long as you like. I know Patricia appreciates your efforts."

The more I studied Gerard the more impossible it seemed that he was Andrew's father. At least with Patricia I could see hints of their shared family tree around his eyes and the shape of his face, but there was nothing that linked the two men. Granted, Gerard had thinning white hair to Andrew's mane, but even the way he carried himself was different. He had a professorial vibe, and a quiet, observant way that was the antithesis of his son's life of the party persona.

"I'm not quitting until they're eating from my hand, just you wait. This is exactly the kind of challenge I enjoy."

"Ah, determined. You sound like Andrew," he replied with a wry grin. "No wonder you two get on."

I'm sure my confusion registered on my face. What exactly was he telling his parents about us and why did he feel it was necessary to lie? I didn't know how to respond so I dodged the comment.

"You missed a great launch party at Crush," I offered. "At

least that's what it looked like. I couldn't actually go because I had an event that night as well, but his side of the parking lot was full."

Every feature on Gerard's face pulled downward into a frown, which was an unexpected reaction to his son's success. "So I heard."

His expression didn't invite further conversation so I deflected to my reluctant students. "Do you have a favorite in this group? I don't know their personalities yet."

He reached up to scratch his chin with the back of his gloved hand and squinted at them. "I do. I like Darling, despite her propensity for havoc." He gave me a wink, then picked up his bucket of tools. "But then again, perhaps that's *exactly* what I like about her. Until next time, Chelsea."

"Sounds good." I turned back to my students, expecting them to still be frozen on the other side of the paddock. But no, in the time I'd been chatting with Gerard they'd tiptoed their way closer to me. Not enough to do any real work yet, but close enough to acknowledge their bravery with some animal crackers. I reached into my treat bag slowly and watched them shift their weight at my movement.

"Well, hello," I said in a soft voice. "Look how brave you are. That's good." I tossed a few animal crackers toward them and they startled at the movement then dropped their heads to examine the treats. Darling picked one up first and chewed slowly, rolling the cookie in between her lips and teeth like she was checking for poison, while Thistle and Petunia swallowed them down quickly. They somehow communicated with each other telepathically and took another step toward me as a group.

"So brave!" I knelt then tossed a few more cookies to them, which they ate quickly.

The approach/throw pattern continued until they were about ten feet away from me, which was slightly better than where we'd left off when I was there a few weeks prior. From this point on I couldn't let as much time elapse between sessions if we wanted to keep making progress.

"Look at you!" Patricia's voice rang out from behind me. "They're so close."

I grinned back at her. "Getting there!"

She kicked her leg up on the fence in the exact spot where Gerard had just done the same thing. "What exactly are you hoping they'll do?"

"Well, first I need them to not be petrified of me, then you, then we'll do something called 'targeting.' It's getting them to touch their noses to my fist, which is a low-stress way to start making contact with them. Once we have that foundation of trust I'll start trying other stuff like sending them to stations and maybe a few tricks."

"Maybe they'll end up as sweet as my other babies?" She brightened. "You haven't met them yet, have you? Why don't you come down to the other pen and see what sweethearts they are."

I'd already been there for an hour and a half, but I wasn't in a rush to leave. "Sure, I'd love to."

I heard the bleating before I saw them. Loud, pitchy, demanding shouts that sounded more than a little human. The duo were crowded together, sticking their heads through the fence and screaming at us to hurry up.

"I usually bring them treats. They're going to be disappointed," Patricia said.

"Oh, I still have plenty."

"Wonderful, they're going to love you even more."

The minute we slipped through the gate I felt like I was meeting a different species. Unlike the Mean Girls, who acted like I was a sniper in their pen, Rainbow and Happy greeted me like I was a celebrity, jumping up on me and letting out exuberant bleats.

"Aren't they perfect?" Patricia laughed at their happy hops around us.

I sidestepped away from the goats, since jumping up was an impolite greeting no matter the species. "Who's who?"

"The black one with the racing stripes on her head is Happy, and the white one is Rainbow."

Their behavior was so different from the other goats that I felt myself holding back from touching them despite the fact that they were practically begging me for scratches.

I finally squatted down to pet them and Rainbow's tail started wagging. "They're like dogs!"

"Very similar." Patricia nodded, rubbing Happy's forehead. "Oh, don't let me forget that I still need to settle up with you for today."

Rainbow pushed her head against me in a cross-species request for more petting. "Let's not worry about that now. We can figure it out once I start making progress."

"We'll see about that." She shot me a look, then closed her eyes and took a deep inhale. "Doesn't it smell fantastic? I just love fall."

I filled my lungs with the cool air. "I love it too."

The scent of leaves and the hint of a distant bonfire conjured up a jumble of feelings inside of me. I'd always loved fall for being the gateway to my favorite time of year. It was the season of family yet here mine was, hobbling along without the heart of ours.

"What are you doing for Thanksgiving?" Patricia asked.

"My sister is hosting this year, she lives in Fishtown. She and her husband just remodeled their kitchen and she wants to show it off. What about you?"

"I'm hosting," Patricia replied, leaning down to give Happy a kiss on the top of her head. "Always do. We invite a big group of people, family and friends. You're welcome to drop by if you have time, I'm sure Andrew would enjoy seeing you."

I choke-coughed and became very focused on rubbing Rainbow's neck. "Thank you, that's sweet of you to invite me, but I'm sure we'll be turkey-napping well into the evening."

"Ah yes." Patricia grinned at me. "All those familiar holiday rituals."

The more we talked about traditions the closer we veered to my shutoff valve. I didn't want to get into the specifics of who would and wouldn't be gathered around our Thanksgiving table. "I should probably head out."

"I so appreciate your help today. We'll get there."

"We will. I need to come back more often, though, to keep the momentum going."

"Well, we love having you here, so come as often as you like."

If Patricia had been anyone else I could envision growing a lovely friendship. But no matter how much I enjoyed being with her, every moment felt like I was behind enemy lines. Thanks to Andrew, I couldn't be friends with her, because I knew that the closer we became the more I'd hear about him. And I wasn't about to smile while she told stories about his weekend trips to

Rexford with Zadie, or whoever his girl of the moment happened to be.

I gave Rainbow one last rub and followed Patricia out of the pen. It was only four, but the sun was already dipping low and the nip in the air was becoming a full-on chill. The Gibson home looked postcard-homey in the distance, with a few lights turned on inside casting an inviting glow.

"Would you like to warm up with a cup of coffee with me?" Patricia asked.

"Thanks, but I should go, I have a puppy who keeps time like a train conductor and it's almost dinnertime."

"That's right, Andrew told me about little Edith! Maybe she can come and meet Murray sometime? He loves puppies."

"That would be cute." I smiled broadly to make my answer seem less vague. I shifted back to a more comfortable topic. "I have a few busy days ahead of me, but I'll try to come work with them within the next week."

"Perfect. You can visit whenever you like, our door is always open."

It made me a little sad that I'd never be able to take advantage of her hospitality.

chapter eighteen

I'd accidentally adopted a tyrant in a dog-suit.

Edith was starting to show some shockingly asshole-ish behaviors and it felt like there was nothing I could do about it. Every dog is a product of nature *and* nurture, but it seemed like whatever backwoods gene pool she'd sprung from was over-powering my efforts to help her become a sweet, well-adjusted dog. She was snarky and bossy with Birdie and it broke my heart that my tired old girl let the puppy get away with it.

If Birdie was barking at something out the window Edith would rush over to muscle her out of the way so *she* could bark. When Birdie took a drink of water Edith nosed her face into the bowl until Birdie was pushed out. I thanked my senior for her patience with the annoying behavior but felt sad that her golden years were being interrupted by a dog with no chill.

I did everything I could to gently redirect Edith when pos-sible, but some of the behaviors were so subtle that I couldn't referee in time. I'd brought the puppy into my home envisioning a sisterly, or better yet maternal, bond between them, but what I'd gotten was low-grade psychological warfare.

The worst part? Edith was *brilliant*. She loved training and picked things up so quickly that I had to sprint to keep up with her amazing little brain. I always joked to my clients that smart dogs were a blessing and a curse and here I was experiencing it in real time. Of course, Birdie was a clever dog too, but there was something about Edith that pushed her into evil genius territory.

Birdie was up on my bed as I got ready for my evening, her eyes flicking between me and her tormentor. The puppy was taking her frustrations out on a particularly challenging food puzzle, alternating between barking at it and angrily gnawing the knobs instead of pushing them around like she was supposed to.

"I know, I know." I sighed, giving Birdie a sad smile. "I'm trying. At least she's not bothering you."

I pulled the flat iron through my last section of hair, then craned my neck to make sure I'd gotten all of it. Tonight I was actually getting my butt up off the couch and making good on the rain check I'd promised Carly at my Howl-o-Ween party. She'd conned me into going to the closing night of the fall festival at Abbot Farm with her and Joe, before the farm shifted into prime Christmas tree mode. It was the second week of November and I appreciated that they didn't try to rush the holiday, since there was so much to love about autumn.

"What's the right look for Hallmark holiday movie activities?" I asked the dogs.

I settled on jeans, a thick black knit sweater with a few layers underneath, and my favorite black lug sole lace-up boots. I had a red buffalo check jacket that I never wore that was perfect for the doing-it-for-the-'gram vibes of the evening.

I hustled the dogs out for a quick walk and Carly and Joe pulled up right as I was leading them back inside. "Gimme three minutes."

Carly flashed me a thumbs-up from the passenger seat.

Once Edith was settled in her crate with a stuffed Kong and Birdie was finally relaxed now that her tormentor could no longer reach her, I headed downstairs.

"Hey!" Carly turned around in her seat and welcomed me in an overly excited voice as I climbed in their old Cherokee. "I'm so glad you agreed to come. This is going to be a fun night."

"Yup." I managed to meet her level of enthusiasm as I fastened my seat belt. "Thanks for letting me be a third wheel."

Joe glanced at me in the rearview mirror as he eased away from the curb. "You're actually not a third wheel. We're meeting someone there."

I mentally scrolled through their friend group, trying to figure out who it could be. "Anyone I know?"

"Yeah. My new trainer and your neighbor."

I grabbed for my seat belt, my thumb on the buckle like it was an ejection button. "You invited *Andrew*?"

"I did." Joe eyed me in the rearview mirror again. "He's a really cool guy."

I looked over my shoulder at the retreating sidewalk and wondered if I could jump out of the car and run home.

"Is that okay with you?" Carly asked, still swiveled and studying me through appraising eyes.

I was reminded that I hadn't told her anything about my history with Andrew and kicked myself. It wasn't exactly the moment to get into it now either. I'd gossiped in front of Joe before, and he was always ready to offer the male perspective when necessary, but now that he was training with Andrew it changed things.

Joe wasn't exactly discreet. The truth was, he was more of a gossip than his wife. I loved getting the dirt about his colleagues and friends, but I knew that his willingness to spill the tea on them meant he'd probably also be capable of doing it to me. But not maliciously. Joe just enjoyed being chatty, it was part of his friendly, affable appeal. I could totally picture him letting something I'd said about Andrew slip accidentally.

"Yeah, it's fine," I said in as neutral a voice as I could manage.

I tried not to pout all the way to the farm, keeping up my side of the conversation while my mind spun out of control about the possibility of enduring a hayride next to Andrew. What we were about to do felt suspiciously like a double date. Was it planned? Were they trying to force something between us?

I sighed. This night was going to *suck*.

"Don't worry, it's not a double date," Carly said, as if she'd read my thoughts. She turned to Joe. "Didn't you say there were a bunch of pictures of him with a girl in his Insta?"

I froze as dread fishtailed in my chest. And *here* was where Joe's tendency to gossip was going to work in my favor.

"Not sure," Joe said as he pulled onto the property and followed a teen in a reflective vest to a parking spot in the crowded field. "I accidentally requested his private Instagram account and not the Crush account, but he accepted me, so I snooped around. There were photos of him and a girl, but there's nothing recent. They were from last year."

"What did she look like?" Carly asked, and I wanted to high-five her for getting to the important question.

"Hot. Like, superhot. Kinda Zoë Kravitz–ish but with more

oomph." He made a vague sweeping movement in front of his chest. "I think she's a fitness model in Miami or something?"

Zadie. He was definitely talking about Zadie.

Carly gave him side-eye. "And how would you know *that*?"

"I looked her up," he admitted sheepishly. "I was curious! Anyway, she didn't have any pictures of him on her feed so I don't think they're together."

I'd looked up Zadie Palmer a few times myself but couldn't find her, and I assumed it was because she'd named herself something like "The Real Zadie Palmer" or "Zadie Palmer Official." There was no need for me to tap into my full stalking abilities because I already knew that she was beautiful and perfect and I didn't want to subject myself to photos of her looking incredible in swimsuits.

I tumbled out of the car, suddenly feeling grumpy about all things fall. The happy family throwing leaves at each other? Awful. A cute couple sharing a caramel apple? Revolting. I wanted to grab a spiked cider and get lost in the corn maze until it was time to go.

Joe rushed ahead of us, looking down at his phone, and Carly threw her arm around my shoulder as we followed behind him to the strung-up café lights and crowds. Abbott Farm was the go-to holiday destination for the entire county so the place was crawling with people looking for their fall fix.

"Sorry about surprising you with that," she said in a low voice. "I didn't know until right before we left the house. I think Joe is hoping for a little bromance. Total hero worship. I actually caught him flexing in the mirror!"

"Sure, I get it," I muttered back. "But I'm not Andrew's biggest fan. I haven't told you this yet, but we have some . . . *history*."

Her eyes went wide and she drew back from me. "Do you now? And why did you keep it from me? Spill it."

Joe spun around before I could answer her. "Andrew is at the log-chopping contest! They're getting ready to start. We need to hurry!" He jogged back and grabbed Carly's hand, and she grabbed mine.

I allowed myself to be pulled along, trying to come up with not only an excuse to leave early but also a way to get home. Uber wasn't exactly booming in Wismer. I glanced around the crowd for familiar faces, hoping that I could bum a ride with someone.

We came up to a small raised platform where Andrew and two other people stood behind massive sawed-off tree trunks, with piles of logs behind them.

"All right, folks," the event organizer said over a handheld megaphone. "We've got three hardy contestants for the first round of chopping. Who can split the most logs in a minute? Is it Pamela, Kenny, or Andrew? The winner gets to come back to pick a complimentary Christmas tree on December first and a basket of goodies from our holiday farmstand. You folks ready? Let's wish them good luck!"

The crowd cheered. Joe pulled us into an open area so we could see better and I slunk down behind him. Andrew was shrugging off his black jacket, making him look the part in a yellow-checked flannel shirt and jeans. He rolled up his sleeves as if to prove that he meant business and once again I had to wonder if the man was immune to cold. Here I was in four layers and I still felt the night air creeping under my sweater and nipping my fingertips.

"Oh, Andrew's definitely going to win," Joe said, his gaze

jumping between the contestants. "Kenny could be a contender, but Pamela? No way."

Carly waited until Joe turned back and snorted at me. "Oh my God," she mouthed, rolling her eyes and pointing at her husband.

But he was right. Pamela looked like a mom who'd been put up to the competition by her girlfriends and Kenny was a bean-pole of a man compared to Andrew.

A whistle sounded and the trio started chopping. Pamela managed to get her ax stuck in the log immediately and tried in vain to wrench it free while Kenny split the logs so quickly that the pieces went airborne each time his ax sliced through the wood. Andrew chopped at a respectable pace, but he was no-where near as fast as the dark horse competitor.

"I guess that guy's a ringer," Joe said over his shoulder, look-ing disappointed. He turned back and started clapping with the rest of the crowd. "C'mon, Andrew!"

Andrew clearly didn't have experience with the mechanics of chopping wood. My dad had made me try it and with his tu-toring I'd actually gotten pretty good at it. Strength was im-portant, of course, but there was also physics to consider, and ax handling.

Andrew glanced at Kenny as he picked up his next log and I could almost see the calculations going on in his head. I watched him adjust his grip on the handle and shift his stance so he could get more momentum in his swing and *boom*, he split the log in half the time.

And damn it, he looked sexy as hell doing it. Even though he was learning with each log, there was a confidence to the way he moved. He knew everyone was watching him and he leaned into it, glancing up to smile at the crowd as he grabbed logs, like he was in on the joke.

"There you go!" Joe cheered as Andrew hot-knifed through another stump. "You got this!"

Andrew's strength plus his cribbed understanding of how to chop proved to be a lethal combination. His stack caught up to Kenny's as the clock ticked down and by the time the buzzer sounded there was no question who'd chopped the most.

"Looks like Andrew is the winner of our first round!" the em-cee said, smacking him on the back, getting an embarrassed grin out of him. "Congrats, buddy, we'll see you at the final round later tonight."

Andrew scanned the crowd and when he spotted us gave us a nod of recognition, like a celebrity who was going to grace fans with an autograph.

"Told you he'd win," Joe said to us. "That dude is *strong*!"

"He's something," I muttered, staring at the spiked-apple-cider-tasting tent wistfully.

The crowd parted as Andrew walked over to us, sliding his jacket back on.

"Hey, guys, good to see you," he said, shaking Joe's hand and leaning into Carly for a side hug. I gave him a little wave from a safe distance away. "So that was different, huh? Some functional training that I wasn't expecting tonight. Now I could use a drink."

"Same," I admitted.

"Let's grab cider, then line up for the hayride," Carly said. "I think the next one leaves in fifteen minutes."

Joe started chattering about how his biceps were sore from their last workout as he and Andrew led the way to the tent, leaving me and Carly to bring up the rear.

"So you *clearly* don't like him," she whispered to me. "But what I need to know is why. Because he seems like a good guy and then there's"—she gestured up and down his body from behind—"all that."

"Long story, and now isn't the time."

As if to prove it Andrew turned around quickly, catching us both off guard. "First round is on me. Four, then?"

"Oh, yes, please!" Carly grinned and came close to batting her lashes at him, and I knew then that she was yet another fallen soldier in my war with Andrew Gibson.

chapter nineteen

The spiked cider wasn't nearly spiked enough for me to loosen up and enjoy the bumpy tractor amble through the forest.

The "fall hayride" was the middle place between Abbott's haunted hayride in October and its Christmas lights tour starting the day after Thanksgiving, which meant there were no zombies *or* LED reindeer to enjoy as we rolled through the property in the uncomfortable wood cart. Carly was on my right side and Andrew was giving me a wide berth on my left. I was a little surprised and disappointed that Joe had opted to cozy up under a blanket with his wife instead of his crush from Crush. It meant that Andrew and I were forced to acknowledge that we were side by side in the dark.

"You cold?" Andrew asked me, holding up the woven blanket that had been on his hay bale. "You can have this."

I shook my head. "Nope, I'm fine. Toasty." I lied.

We were coming to the end of the ride and passing under arches of white lights that stayed up no matter the season.

"Ooh, pretty lighting," Carly said, pulling her phone from her pocket. "Selfie, get close!"

She held her phone up as she and Joe pressed their cheeks together. Andrew leaned a centimeter toward me and I managed an unconvincing grin.

The tractor finally lurched to a stop and we filed out behind teenagers holding hands and parents clutching sleepy toddlers.

"Well, that was fun," I began in my let's-wrap-this-up-and-say-goodbye voice.

"And now it's time for the main event—the corn maze," Carly said, pointing in the distance to where the entrance of the massive field was lit up by stadium lights.

"Right." I sighed as I realized that I was stuck. "The corn maze."

I brought up the rear as we headed toward it, and the three of them chattered about their prior experiences outwitting corn mazes. I eyed the thing as we got closer, wondering if I could squeeze between the dried stalks in the middle and cheat my way out of it.

"They say it takes at least thirty minutes to get through the whole thing, and that's if you have a good sense of direction," Joe said. "We should have a competition to see who can make it out fastest."

There was no way I wanted to spend a half hour wandering around the thing. I was about to set a new speed record.

"In teams," Carly said, grasping her husband's hand. "Us against you two."

I shot her a look that could've sent the dried husks up in flames.

"Sure, that works," Andrew said, shocking the hell out of me. "Joe, if we beat you you're going to owe me *so* many pull-ups next time I see you."

"Don't worry, won't happen," he replied, full of bravado. "Honor system. We'll each set our timers as we walk in."

A bored-looking teen handed us flashlights at the entrance and I realized that the interior of the maze was dark, lit only by the stars.

"Is there, like, a cheat code?" I asked the attendant as Joe and Carly headed in. "Can you give me any pointers to get out quickly?"

The kid's expression didn't change. "Nope. Good luck." He slapped a flashlight in my hand, then got out of his chair and fumbled with a yellow plastic chain.

"Wait, are you closing?" I asked him, feeling a little panicked.

He nodded. "You two are the last ones for the night. We had a group get lost in it and call 911 at midnight at the beginning of the season, so we shut it down a little earlier, just in case."

"It's *that* hard?"

"Well, it's not easy, I'll tell ya that."

I glanced over at Andrew as a shiver zipped through me at the thought of being trapped in corn-land with him. "Maybe we should skip it? I mean, you've got the final round of the wood-chopping contest to win, right?"

"I'll get us out in time," Andrew said confidently, fiddling with the on-off switch and beam width on his flashlight.

I felt my jaw tighten. "I thought this was a team effort?"

"Sure, it is." He glanced at the entrance, then down at his phone. "We'll give them a few more minutes before we go in and smoke 'em. Let them get good and lost."

I'd seen this side of him before. The touch football games that morphed into tackle, the trivia nights that led to shouting matches. It seemed to me that Andrew saw life as a series of challenges that needed to be conquered, even if they were as ridiculous as finding the way through a labyrinth made of cornstalks.

"Joe's the only one who has to pay up if he loses," I said. "It's a one-sided bet."

"Because I won't lose."

"*We* won't lose," I corrected.

"Right." He nodded. "Okay, they've been in there for five minutes, let's go."

I followed Andrew in reluctantly. The lights at the entrance were swallowed within a few feet inside, leaving me to fumble to get my flashlight on. At this point in the season it wasn't a fright maze with zombies and witches jumping out to scare us—that part ended after Halloween—but the dead cornstalks in the moonlight and the giant man a few feet away from me still felt like the beginning of a horror movie.

"This way," Andrew said, pointing in the exact opposite direction that I wanted to go.

"But . . ." I pointed to the obviously correct route.

"Nope, I'm sure this is the way. I have a good feeling."

I kept my mouth shut against my better judgment and followed him. The path was clear and gave me more than enough room to drag behind Andrew like a teenager trying not to be spotted with a parent at the mall.

We came to a split in the path and Andrew pressed on without even glancing at me, as confident as a museum tour guide.

"I really think we should go this way." I pointed. "It makes sense that the exit would be at the opposite corner from the entrance."

"Corn mazes don't make sense. I'm following my gut and my gut says this way."

"Well, my *brain* says this way," I huffed at him, taking a few steps in the direction I wanted to go. "But using one's brain is something you don't have much experience with," I muttered.

He whipped around, his scowl obvious even in the darkness. "What did you just say to me?"

Had I meant for him to hear it? Maybe. Yes.

No.

"Nothing, I was kidding," I squeaked out, throwing my hands up at him.

He stormed a few steps closer and as much as I wanted to retreat I held my ground until he was right up in my face, hunched over me with his nostrils flaring. "I knew you always thought I was a meathead when we were in school. Clearly you still do."

There was pain mixed with the fury in his expression, and I wished I could take it back.

"No, I—"

"Just stop," he said, the disgust in his voice clear. "If your big brain wants you to go that way then go."

I expected him to step away, but he stood his ground in front of me, blocking my path, daring me to move past him.

"Andrew, I'm sorry, that wasn't what I meant," I said quietly, staring up at him as his black eyes searched my face. The damage was done and my apology sounded hollow.

He was hovering too close. Angry, hurt, and scrutinizing me the way he used to so long ago. I felt exposed under his gaze, like he could see through me to everything I was desperate to keep buried. That my jabs at him were a defense mechanism against my mortifying one-sided attraction. I wanted him to look away, to finally take a step back so I could breathe again, but he continued to claim the air around me until I felt like I was suffocating.

The wind blew through the stalks, setting off a ghostly clatter. Neither of us seemed to comprehend the insanity of hashing out old hurts under the stars surrounded by acres of dead corn.

"I'm sorry," I repeated, but his face still didn't soften. The crease between his eyebrows etched deeper and it set off something primal in me. I'd really hurt him and I needed to make it right.

Andrew started to say something, then stopped himself, moving slightly away from me and immediately making me wish that he hadn't.

"You . . ." He shook his head like he was angry that it was all he could manage to get out. "I just . . ."

I opened my mouth to apologize for the third time, but before I could, he grabbed my wrist and wrenched me closer to him, pulling me off my feet and sending the air rushing from my lungs in a single startled gulp. His grip was tight, pinning my arm against his chest, where I could feel it rising and falling like he'd just run a race. My heartbeat sped up and my entire body tensed, poised for whatever was going to come next.

His black eyes settled on my mouth and I shifted, uncomfortable as ever under his scrutiny.

"You drive me fucking insane, do you know that?" he finally grunted at me, still gripping my wrist in his hot hand, holding me way too close.

I lifted my chin, ready to say the feeling was mutual, but he kept talking.

"You always have. You're judgmental. You're bossy. And you think you're the smartest person in the room."

He ended up inches from me, breathing hard, but instead of scaring me each insult just made me angrier.

"*I'm* judgmental?" I roared back loudly enough to get a blink of shock out of him. "You used to call me 'noodle arms' and said that you were surprised I could lift my backpack. You said I had flipper feet. You told me I was so pale that I was practically neon." I could've kept going about the many ways he'd made me feel insecure, but I felt like I'd made my point. "You had no right to talk about my body. You made me so self-conscious!"

As I repeated his little digs back to him I was struck by the realization that they were all pretty tame. *Everyone* told me I was pale, but only Andrew saying it had left me feeling bruised.

It was his turn to look remorseful. Each reminder of the way he used to judge me chipped away some of the hard edges from his expression.

"Well, I'm *sorry*." It came out as a roar. "I didn't mean to make you feel bad. But you have no right to talk about my brain. Or lack thereof."

He was still clinging to me like he knew I'd take off running the second he let go. But what Andrew didn't seem to realize was that I wasn't going anywhere.

I couldn't.

Something sticky and complicated was cementing my feet to the ground and keeping me from looking anywhere but at him. A big part of it was because I didn't want him to think that he was intimidating me, but even more, his scalding grip was a sense memory of what had happened between us the last time we'd been this close. And because despite everything that was going wrong between us in this moment, I still had the completely unhinged hope, deep down, that maybe it could happen again.

"And I haven't said a word about your body lately," he grumbled in a low voice. His eyes slipped down to take me in and I let out a shuddering breath.

"I'm sorry, Andrew. I shouldn't have said anything—"

"*Stop.*" It was a command, and I got the feeling that he was over my apologies.

What the hell were we doing? Why was Andrew holding on to me, standing so close that he could drop his frowning, angry mouth just a few inches and do what we both knew we wanted?

A bigger gust of wind blew through the stalks and I shivered despite the heat bouncing between us.

"You're cold. We should go."

There was no way I could disagree without him knowing exactly what I was thinking.

"Okay."

With that he dropped my wrist, and all the tension that had been coursing through my body drained to my feet, leaving me limp.

"We're going your way," Andrew said, moving past me in the hollowest victory I'd ever won.

chapter twenty

I wish you would stop being so formal—it's just lunch, Joan," Aunt Helen called to my mom from her place at the table, where she was trying to pet Edith without getting nibbled. "We could've eaten takeout and I would've been thrilled, as long as I was with all of you."

My mom hustled around the kitchen solo despite our offers to help. She was in her element when she was cooking and serving and didn't want anyone in her way until the last dish had been placed on the table.

"I'm not being formal, this is what family does. It's how I show love, you should know that by now." She placed a steaming tray of lasagna on a woven trivet, kissed Aunt Helen on top of her head, and headed back to the kitchen.

My aunt had arrived the night before to spend the week before Thanksgiving with my mom and she'd insisted on a family meeting to finalize who was bringing what on the big day. We all knew the truth was that she wanted to squeeze in as much togetherness as possible. I loved spending time with her even though her uncensored take on life occasionally led to ruffled feathers and hurt feelings. It wasn't that she was mean-spirited. Much like my dad, Aunt Helen just didn't have a filter.

We were gathered at the long table that flanked the fireplace, with Birdie camped out on her spot on the worn stone in front of it. Aunt Helen was wearing her typical glamorous it's-a-tracksuit-but-it's-also-cashmere getup in spotless cream, paired with thick-soled black Givenchy sneakers and a black scarf that had "Chanel" hidden in the mass of colorful scrawls. Her short white hair was tucked behind her ears. She had the kind of look that got her automatic upgrades to first class.

A typically stunning Taylor was seated at the head of the table in what had always been my father's chair, and even though it hollowed me out seeing her there and not him, it sort of worked. She represented the future of our family, a continuation of the legacy. The promise of the little Higgins Engelman she was growing was the perfect distraction from the void at the table.

"You're up next," my aunt said, turning to me and pulling her red-rimmed glasses off the top of her head and back onto her nose. "Taylor's got me up to date on all things baby, but what about *your* baby, hm? What's next for Frolic?"

My mom placed a bowl of salad on the table then pulled an orange and blue floral apron over Aunt Helen's head.

"What in the county fair is *this*?" she sputtered, plucking at the apron like it was a rag.

"Lasagna and white cashmere are a messy combination. I won't allow you to risk it," she replied as she settled into her chair.

My mom truly thought of everything.

"Well, Chels?" Aunt Helen asked as she filled her plate with salad then passed the bowl to Taylor. "What's the latest from dog-world?"

I opened my mouth, then snapped it shut, because every part of Frolic was now snarled up with thoughts of Andrew. My busy class roster? Worries about where people would park when Andrew was holding his own group classes? My most challenging client? Obviously Dude, who I hadn't seen since before the corn maze incident. Forecasting into the future? Impossible, not only for me but also for him thanks to what Mike was doing.

I hadn't seen Andrew since the night at the farm. It was no shock that Carly and Joe had beaten us out of the corn maze, and we'd allowed them to bask in their victory for the rest of the night. As expected, Andrew had gone on to win the wood-chopping competition. I'd watched from the very back of the crowd, still feeling aftershocks over what had happened between us. Or *almost* happened. Andrew the showman was replaced by Andrew the workhorse as he chopped his way through the stack. Each swing of the ax felt like it was directed at me.

"Dog-world is good," I managed as I reached across the table to grab a garlic knot. "Steady as she goes."

"There's more," my mom insisted. "Tell your aunt about what you want to do with the space next door to you."

My stomach twisted into its own knot at where the conversation was headed. I hadn't told anyone about the building sale, mainly because I knew what my mom would suggest. And now, with Aunt Helen here to back her up, I was doubly sure that I didn't want to get into it.

"Yeah, um, I'm considering expanding into the vacant space next to mine."

"You didn't tell me that," Taylor sniped at me. "That's a big deal."

"What did your landlord say about taking it over?" my mom asked.

"Holding pattern," I mumbled, stuffing the entire knot in my mouth. "So, why don't we finalize who's bringing what next week? I want time to prepare."

It was the exact right bob and weave to derail my perfectionist sister, who I knew wanted her first Thanksgiving dinner in the new kitchen to be a cozy, pumpkin-spice-scented dream.

Taylor flipped her hair over her shoulder. "Ryan's parents are having an artisanal charcuterie platter sent in from Williams-Sonoma and they're bringing lots of wine. Mom is doing the turkey. I'm taking care of the mashed potatoes and sweet potatoes. Aunt Helen, what would you like to make? We still need a vegetable. And dessert."

"Green bean casserole," she said, scrolling through her phone. "It was your father's favorite."

As if we could forget. It was my grandmother's recipe, so ridiculously creamy and fried-onion-covered that it could hardly be considered a vegetable.

"I'm bringing a vegetarian pot pie that's so good you won't even miss the chicken," I volunteered, knowing that no one was going to eat it but me and Ryan. "And since I'm making crust I'll bring an apple pie as well."

"Perfect," Taylor said with a nod.

"Chelsea." Aunt Helen looked up from her phone, then jabbed her finger on the screen. "Why does it say here that your building is for sale?"

I choked on the lasagna noodle in my mouth. "Wait. How did you—"

"I wanted to see what it looks like since I haven't been there since you opened. I searched your business name and it gave me the address, and when I clicked on it I saw the listing. Chelsea, what's going on?"

I'd always appreciated how Aunt Helen had kept up to date with technology for the sake of her business, but now I wished she'd be a little more like my mom and focus her online abilities on just Facebook and solitaire.

The room was silent except for the sound of Edith gnawing on her treat toy and every eye was on me.

"It's for sale, honey?" my mom asked quietly.

I set my fork down and nodded. "Yeah, it's no big deal. Mike said the new tenants have to honor my lease, so it's fine. Just a change of ownership, nothing to worry about."

"When is your lease up?" Aunt Helen asked, and once again I cursed her for her business acumen. She'd had a brick-and-mortar shop for years so she knew all about the ins and outs of being a tenant.

"A year and a half. It's fine. I'm fine. I'll figure it out." I grabbed my second garlic knot.

"I wouldn't agree with that," Aunt Helen mused, focusing her laser eyes on me. "Where would you go if the new owner decides to kick you out?"

"They're not going to kick me out. I'm a good tenant who pays on time. I pay *early* some months. What's not to love?"

Andrew's fledgling business flashed through my mind. He didn't have any history with Mike. He'd be easy to get rid of. As much as he pissed me off, I didn't want to see him lose everything he'd worked so hard to build.

"What if someone wants to take the whole building over and turn it into a shipping warehouse?" Taylor asked. "If they have a business plan your good tenant record won't matter."

"Your sister is right," my mom said softly.

"You really need to think about this," Aunt Helen chimed in, completing the pushiest Greek chorus ever.

"You're ganging up on me."

"Chelsea," Aunt Helen scolded, sounding way too much like my dad. "We are *not* ganging up on you. We're trying to help you. Now, have you considered buying the building yourself? Because I saw the asking price and I know for a fact that your father left you—"

"Helen." My mom shook her head.

Aunt Helen didn't know the unspoken rule in our household. That we didn't talk about the money that was sitting in an account, waiting for me to claim it. I glanced at Edith and wished she'd start chewing the tassels on the rug, or peeing on it, so I could jump up and focus on her instead of the mess spilling across the table.

"What?" Aunt Helen pressed on despite the warning, glancing around the table at us. "Why can't we discuss it? Avoiding it isn't going to make this problem go away, and not talking about your father's gift won't bring him back."

"Yikes." Taylor sucked in a breath and threw down her fork. "Here we go."

To hear it spoken so plainly sent a shock wave through me. My mom and Taylor knew that I didn't want to talk about it, yet here was Aunt Helen refusing to read the room.

"I don't want the money," I offered, hoping it would be enough to end the conversation. "Mom knows."

"And why not?" Aunt Helen asked, propping her elbows up on the table and leaning toward me. "I know that the money your father left the two of you helped Taylor get that beautiful baby in her belly. Why wouldn't you use it for your own baby?

He would want that. He believed in you." Her voice went softer, but it didn't help blunt her words.

Taylor had shared every step of her IVF journey with us, from the initial hopes of the first set of shots to the eventual crushing blow. That they'd been able to go for another round thanks to the money my father had left her felt poetic, but it wasn't something we talked about. Tears filled my eyes as I stared down at my full plate.

"Say something, Chels," Aunt Helen urged. "Let's talk through this together."

I sniffled and cleared my throat a few times until I felt composed. I knew that she'd just keep bulldogging me until I broke, so it was better to get it over with now, so it wouldn't ruin the rest of her visit.

"That money shouldn't exist. The only reason it does is because Dad gave up," I managed, finally looking at Aunt Helen. She was frowning, but I could tell it was over concern for me, not disapproval. "You know that I found *so* many treatment options for him. Like, cutting-edge clinical trial stuff that he qualified for. And the success rates were good too."

"They were decent, not good." Taylor corrected me. Her arms were crossed and resting on top of her bump.

"They were better options than what *he* chose," I fired back at her.

"Chels, honey," Aunt Helen said in a soft voice, "your mom forwarded those trials to me and I sent them to my friend who's an oncology nurse practitioner. They were promising, yes, but they weren't a fit for your father's diagnosis."

"Okay, but there were other treatment protocols. Instead of fighting he just . . . gave up." My voice faltered.

"Chelsea, *stop*," my mom scolded. "I've told you not to say that. It's not true."

"Which is exactly why it's impossible for us to talk about it," I shouted at her, feeling the usual desperate anger clawing at my insides. "I see the facts and you're lost in the fiction."

We all went quiet, thinking about the man we'd lost. In moments like this my dad was always the first one to break the tension, to try to get us to laugh. I could picture him leaning back in his chair, a little smile on his face and his finger in the air, saying, "Check, please."

"I'm sorry, but I don't see what that has to do with the money," Aunt Helen said, glancing around the table at all of us. "You have a problem and the inheritance will solve it, it's as simple as that."

"I don't want the money."

"Well, I think you're making a mistake," Aunt Helen said, putting out there what I'm sure my mom and sister were thinking. "A building like that is an investment. And you'd be a wonderful landlord."

I barked out a laugh at the thought of collecting rent checks from Andrew and felt three sets of eyes swing my way at the outburst.

"Nothing," I said at their questioning looks. "I, uh, I need to get Edith outside for a potty break. Keep eating."

None of them recognized the fact that I was rousing a perfectly content Edith in an effort to stop the conversation. I picked her up and snuggled her against my neck, waiting for her to give me a typical nip on the ear. But even Edith seemed to be able to feel the vibe, offering me a nuzzle of support instead.

chapter twenty-one

I t took everything in my power to keep from whooping.

I'd walked into the Mean Girl pen expecting more of the same long-distance glaring I'd been enduring from Darling, Petunia, and Thistle, but here they were, eating animal crackers directly from my hand.

They were tentative at first, taking a treat then backing away to eat it, but once they realized that I was essentially a frozen human treat machine they decided that crowding me was perfectly fine. I was shocked by how gentle their mouths were, and the way they studied me as they took the goodies. At one point Thistle tried to sample my fingerless glove along with the treat. And Petunia bleated, which I took as a good sign.

"Oh my *gosh*," Patricia stage-whispered from the fence line. "You did it!"

"And now it's your turn," I whispered back. "I'm going to toss a bunch of cookies across the pen to distract them. Come in quietly when they go to eat them."

I dug into my treat bag and crunched up a handful of crackers, then underhanded the crumbles just beyond where the

goats were standing. They turned to start cleaning up the goodies and Patricia slid into the pen and walked over to me in slow
motion. Thistle raised her head to glance at her but went back
to eating without a complaint.

"I'm nervous," Patricia admitted with a soft laugh. "I just
want them to like me."

"What's not to like?" I laughed, bumping my shoulder against
hers. "I'm no goat expert, but what's true with dogs seems to
also be true with goats: don't push. Let them set the pace. Here,
I brought the big guns for you." I reached into the second com-
partment in my treat bag and gave her a handful of nickel-sized
balls. "I made these; they're oatmeal, molasses, and pumpkin
seeds from my Howl-o-Ween pumpkins."

Patricia looked at the goodies then up at me with wide eyes.
"You *made* them? Chelsea, you didn't have to do that."

"I wanted you to give them something they've never had
before, to make sure they associate you with extra-special
stuff."

Petunia and Thistle were back at my feet, snuffling at my
boots and looking up at me expectantly. Darling hovered behind them.

"Go ahead and give them one," I said.

Patricia held out her hand and both goats sniffed at it, suspicious but still governed by their bellies. Thistle gulped first and
wagged her tail.

"Wagging is good, right?" I asked.

"Very good!" Patricia grinned. "My compliments to the chef."

Petunia bumped her way closer and took the treat in her lips,
rolling it around a few times before actually eating it. Darling
seemed to realize that something exciting was going down in

flavor town and she high-stepped in front of her friends to consider what Patricia was offering.

"Here we go," I said in a low voice. "Does the Queen approve?"

If a goat could look judgy, Darling was excelling at it, extending her long neck to sniff at the treat, wearing a frown. She twisted her head, then finally deemed it worthy.

"And so it begins," I said with a grin. "The real work of training. I want you to give them yummy stuff a couple of times a day until they sprint to you when you walk in. Then the next time I come we'll work on targeting."

Patricia was beaming at the trio, offering them oatmeal nuggets one by one as they clamored closer to her. "This probably doesn't seem like a big deal to you, but it means the world to me."

"Oh no, I think it's a huge deal. But we're not done, because I have a feeling if we start walking or moving they're going to scatter."

"Should we test that theory?"

I shook my head. "Nope. No reason to stress them out. We'll keep things calm until we're sure they can handle little tests. That means when you want to walk around the pen you need to toss food and get them to move away from you before you do. Make sense?"

"Got it," she replied with a nod. "Now that we're done, can you come in and warm up with a quick cup of coffee? Your cheeks are all red, you must be chilly."

I'd worn my black wool cap with the rainbow pom-pom and a bunch of layers, but standing still in the cold morning air had sent a chill straight through the down of my parka. I considered the scenario before answering her. It was Saturday, a few hours before my first class of the day and an unlikely time for an Andrew drop-in.

"Sure, I'll have a cup. That would be great, thanks."

Patricia raised an eyebrow at me. "Toss and go?" She gestured with a handful of treats.

"You got it, toss and go."

We made it out of the pen with minimal goat scatter and headed for the house.

"I can't believe next week is Thanksgiving," Patricia said as she climbed the porch steps. "Are you ready for it?"

"Yeah, I am." It was an honest answer. We'd all get caught up in the traditions of the day, both new and old, and wind up too busy to think.

She held the door open for me and welcomed me into the cozy yellow kitchen, which was warmed by the woodstove in the corner. The table had a stack of newspapers still spread out in front of what I assumed was Gerard's chair, and a novel with glasses on top of it at the spot across from it. I envisioned quiet mornings of the two of them reading and tried to figure out how Andrew fit into the picture.

"Leave your coat and hat on the chair by the stove, they'll be nice and toasty when you have to go. Now sit," Patricia ordered, pointing at the table. "Cream and sugar?"

I nodded. "Please."

Murray met us in the kitchen with a few hops and wags, followed by Gerard in a barn jacket and an orange knit cap. He clasped his hands at his waist and raised an eyebrow at me. "Well? Success, I presume? You're both smiling."

"Oh, I always smile when Chelsea's around. Hard not to,"

Patricia answered, placing a white faux bois creamer and sugar bowl on the table. "Will you join us, dear?"

Gerard leaned down to pet Murray and shook his head. "No, I'm heading out to trim the branches along the driveway."

Patricia tutted as she poured the coffee. "The man can't sit still."

"What?" He spread his hands in frustration. "It needs to be done. And Andrew is coming to help."

I froze as air-raid sirens went off in my brain. We'd managed to avoid each other for weeks and I wasn't about to get caught on his home turf looking chummy with his parents.

"Good, I'm glad," Patricia said as she walked the mugs to the table. "He'll keep you from doing anything dangerous."

"If he ever gets here. I told him to arrive an hour ago." Gerard shook his head, eyebrows furrowed. "So typical. But I'm off to get started without him. Lovely seeing you, Chelsea."

"You too. Stay warm," I said.

Patricia let out a long sigh that interrupted my brain-storming ways to make a graceful exit before Andrew arrived.

"Those two . . ." She frowned.

As much as I needed to leave, the gossip in me was desperate to get some intel on the bad blood between father and son. "What's going on?"

"I can only imagine the bickering to come. They're just too similar but they refuse to acknowledge it."

I took a sip of coffee to hide my dubious expression. How could the mountain and the reed be similar?

"Strongheaded," she continued.

Okay, that part was true.

"Each convinced that their way is the right way."

Yup.

"And too smart for their own good."

Record scratch.

"Hm," I managed.

"They recently stopped speaking for two weeks because they had an argument about the relationship between nihilism and existential dread."

I nearly choked on my coffee. I could barely remember the *definition* of nihilism yet Andrew was having scholarly arguments about it?

It didn't compute. The sole reason why I'd been able to look past my annoying physical attraction to Andrew was because anytime I tried to envision having a serious conversation with him I came up blank. We had nothing in common. I didn't want to talk about fantasy football, or protein smoothies, or theories of strength training, and they seemed to be the only things he cared about. But based on what his mother was telling me I was way off target.

"That's the heart of the issue between them," Patricia continued, fiddling with the handle on her mug. "Andrew is an optimist, like me, and his father has a glass-half-empty outlook on life. Gerard and I balance one another out, but the similarities between them with that one glaring difference make things . . . bumpy."

Andrew was an optimist, all right. I'd never met anyone else who could spin a rained-out charity football game into a giant coed mudslide.

"Is it always tense between them?" I asked, not sure if the question could be considered prying.

A smile flickered across her face. "No, thankfully. Deep down those two adore one another. They just tend to forget it in the heat of the moment and then they make stupid decisions. Like Gerard not showing up to Andrew's grand opening."

I felt a stab of sympathy for Andrew. I'm sure it hurt not seeing his dad in the crowd, especially because it sounded like it was a decision he'd made, not because he was under the weather that night.

"Well, you were there," I said carefully, not sure how deep I wanted to wade into the family drama. "I'm sure that made him happy."

"And he was so busy that night, I'm sure he barely noticed." Patricia seemed grateful for the redirect. "He told me what happened with your key. You two are lucky to have one another so close."

I gave a noncommittal nod and drained my mug. "Speaking of, I should get going. I have classes today."

Patricia hopped up to grab my jacket. "Thank you so much for your help this morning. It's going to be too cold to work outside soon, but hopefully we can get a few more lessons in."

"We'll make it happen, I'm sure of it."

She held my jacket open like a tailor and I slipped my arms in. Patricia patted my shoulders. "You're one too."

I swiveled to face her. "One what?"

"An optimist. What a wonderful club to be a part of."

I pulled my hat over my ears and considered it as I walked back out into the cold. Maybe I used to be in the club, but it sure hadn't been true lately.

Murray ran over to walk me to my car, but right as I reached out to pet him he alerted then dashed away, barking his head off.

No, no, no, no. It was Andrew, blazing up the driveway.

I quickly weighed my options. The driveway was too narrow for two cars so I couldn't make a clean getaway, plus Gerard was at the midpoint of it with a chain saw. And it would be weird to ignore Andrew, especially if Patricia happened to glance out the window at us. I pretended to fiddle with my phone as he pulled up next to my car.

Andrew climbed out looking like he was settling into his role as "hot lumberjack" after his win at the fall festival. The brown and orange flannel matched the leaves as if he'd planned it, and the black beanie and thicker beard gave him a longshoreman vibe.

"No jacket?" I asked as my greeting.

He frowned at me as he patted Murray. "I'll be sweating in about five minutes."

His eyes swept up me and I realized that I looked like a kindergartner in the oversized coat and ridiculous hat. But I was dressed for warmth, not to impress him.

"How were the goats?" Andrew asked.

"Good. Really good. We're making progress." I figured animals were the only safe topic for us. "How's Dude?"

He shifted and looked down at Murray. "We, uh, we had an incident. The other day he took off after Myrtle again on the way into Crush and was missing for an hour."

I opened my mouth to lecture him about being off leash, but something in his face stopped me. He looked . . . embarrassed. And he could've kept the incident to himself, but he'd *chosen* to tell me.

"That must've been scary. I'm sorry to hear it."

It struck me that Andrew needed my help but didn't know how to ask for it. The last thing I wanted was for something to happen to Dude, so I bottled my feelings for the human end of the nonexistent leash and made the offer.

"We should probably get back to training him. I have a few slots open on my calendar."

The tension in his forehead relaxed and relief spread across his face. "Seriously? I'd really appreciate that. I can pay you instead of doing the trade. I mean, I'm guessing that you don't want to come to Crush anymore—"

"Oh no, I'm definitely coming back," I replied quickly, surprising even myself. "We made a deal, three for three. I'm getting my swole on whether you like it or not."

He grimaced. "Never say that word again. I'm begging you."

"What? You don't think I can be part of the swole patrol?" I puffed up my chest. "I might surprise you with my massive trapezoids."

His eyes crinkled as laughter tumbled out of him. "Please stop. It's called the *trapezius*."

"Whatever." I shrugged. "Just know that I'm going to get shredded."

"In three sessions? Doubtful."

We both seemed to realize at the same moment that we were veering into uncomfortable territory, and any more discussion of my body could lead us back to our fight. Murray trotted off, leaving us without a distraction between us.

"So, you can text me when you have a chance to look at your schedule," I offered. "And good luck with the branch trimming."

"Thanks."

I opened my car door and slid in as Andrew turned to head down to where his dad was firing up the chain saw.

"Hey, Chels?"

He was standing in the middle of the driveway with the bright sun backlighting him. It was incomprehensible to me that I could see swirls of steam coming off his shoulders despite the fact that I was shivering from the cold. But then again, I knew firsthand that Andrew ran warm.

"Yeah?"

"I just want to say sorry for the stuff I've said to you in the past. I never meant to hurt you."

This apology felt different from the one he'd given me in the maze. There was a weight to his words, like he'd had time to think through the way he'd made me feel all those years ago. I paused, half in my car. "Thanks. I think we've both said and done things we regret. I'm sorry too. It's probably best if we move past everything."

The words were out of my mouth before I realized the double meaning. That we also needed to move past the night in the storage closet. I was too far away to try to read his expression.

"Agreed. Let's just be good neighbors from here on out, okay?"

"Deal," I answered as I tried to imagine what he considered good-neighborness. I swallowed my speech about garbage and parking spots and leashes and slammed my car door shut.

Good neighbors.

At least for a little while.

chapter twenty-two

Edith whipped around and snarled at Ivan.

"Immediately no," I said, stomping over to where she was cornering him and swooping her up into my arms. "I've seen what I needed to see."

"Oh, they're okay," Paula protested. "It's fine, Ivan needs to be taught a lesson."

It was nearing the end of my weekly seven p.m. puppy play and socialization class and a few of my students were getting punchy.

"Some dog-to-dog corrections are okay, but all Ivan did was sniff her," I explained, raising my voice a little and looking around at my half dozen human students to bring their attention to what was going on. Edith was panting in my arms and still staring at her victim. "Ivan wasn't being pushy or inappropriate with Edith, he was just curious. The way Edith snapped at him means that she's overstimulated. Remember, there *can* be too much of a good thing when it comes to socialization, and that's when we need to intervene. Or better yet, before they snap."

Carly pointed at Geneva, who was gnawing on her class bestie, Sassy the Pomeranian mix. "I think these two could go all night."

"It might seem that way, but even if the puppies are having fun it's a good idea to take breaks," I answered, walking Edith toward my office. "They're like toddlers; they don't realize when they're overtired. That's when things get ugly. It's time to wrap up for the night anyway."

I ignored the fact that my puppy had become the biggest a-hole in class and deposited her in the room so I could answer any questions before people headed out. As usual, the group was slow to pack up, but I loved that my classes turned strangers into community. Paula and Sassy's person, Donna, walked out chattering together.

"Do you have a sec? I wanted to tell you something in person," Carly said, watching the door shut behind them. "I have news."

I immediately glanced at her midsection and she laughed and punched me. "No, not that. The *other* millennial milestone."

"Well, you've already got the puppy." I ticked it off on my finger. "And if it's not a baby . . . is it a house?"

She nodded and bounced up and down. "Yes! We put in an offer on a place on Broad Street. It happened super fast. If all goes according to plan we'll be moved in before Christmas."

"Carly, congrats!" I pulled her into a hug. "Tell me there's a yard."

"The *yard*." She sighed, her face glowing. "It's an absolute nightmare of dirt and weeds and I love it! It's almost two acres."

"Are you kidding? Pictures, please."

She pulled out her phone and scrolled through photo after photo of an adorable white Cape Cod with green shutters.

"It's perfect," I said.

"Oh, come on." She frowned at me. "Did you miss the pink and black bathroom tiles and dark wood cabinets in the kitchen? It's awful, but it's got potential."

"And that's all that matters."

My phone went off in my pocket and I was shocked when I pulled it out and saw the international number on the screen. Why was Sam calling me? I held my phone up. "This is my friend in Tokyo, I need to grab this. She usually doesn't call."

"Ooh, yikes," Carly said. "I'll grab G and head out."

"Congrats again," I shouted to her as I answered the call.

"Congrats for what?" Sam's voice echoed through the phone.

"Oh, hey, sorry, I was talking to someone else. Are you guys okay?" There was a delay and my heart sped up as I waited for her to respond. "Sam?"

Her voice came through muffled and I couldn't make out what she was saying.

"Sam? What was that?"

It was a clumsy beginning to our conversation after not talking for so long. I felt a hollowed-out ache in my chest at what we'd become. Strangers, when we'd once been so close that our periods were synced to the day.

What I still couldn't wrap my head around was how it happened. There was no big blowup to blame for the awkwardness. The distance between us had grown slowly, a leaky faucet, until the drip-drip-drip of our different life phases became an ocean we couldn't cross without a major effort. Samantha had been caught up in new motherhood, and I'd been trying to navigate life without my dad. We'd tried to be there for each other but we were each depleted in our own ways.

"I said I'm fine, nothing's wrong." The echo on the line made it sound like she was calling from the moon. "I thought we could catch up a little before I came back. Is this an okay time to talk?"

I breathed a sigh of relief. It was nothing more than a temperature-check call to get a read on where we stood before she came home. It was still going to be weird, but at least we could deal with it before we were face-to-face. I headed back to my office and climbed over the fence to find Edith dozing on my futon. I settled next to her and she snuggled closer to me, placing her head on my lap and smacking her lips a few times. "Yup, I just finished a class. What time is it there?"

"Eight fifteen on Tuesday morning. I'm calling you from the future."

I chuckled at the joke she used to use when they'd first arrived in Japan. "And how is it?"

"Noisy," she answered, and I heard Mia squealing in the background.

I cleared my throat. "Are you excited to come home?" I sounded a little stilted, like I was talking to a receptionist at the dentist's office.

"Beyond," she said. "You're going to be around, right?"

"Of course, you know my life. Nonstop nothingness."

She made a noise I couldn't translate.

"What's new with you?" I pressed on. "How's Mia?"

"Oh, she's great. She's a super-busy baby."

"Yeah, the pictures on Instagram are adorable," I said quickly, and realized that I'd seen them but not actually *Liked* them and had basically outed myself as her stalker.

"Thanks. I can't wait for you to see how much she's changed."

She paused and I held my breath. "I mean . . . if you have time to hang out."

I leaned my head back and closed my eyes to keep them from welling up with relief. "Of course I do. I'll always have time for you, Sam."

It struck me that everything between us had basically frozen when she left. The funeral and the mess afterward, when she tried to be there for me and I'd pushed her away. Then the over-whelming feeling of her packing up, and the speedy, awkward goodbye. And the lonely feelings that followed after she and No-lan left, like I was losing another part of my heart, but for a com-pletely different reason.

"Okay, good. I'm glad." Mia's squeals filled in the silence while we both grappled with what to say next. "I miss you, Chels. Like, a lot."

No matter how much time had passed since talking there was no mistaking the subtext in her voice. Something was up, but it wasn't the time to talk about it.

"I miss you too." I answered back quickly.

Admitting that our stupid exile from one another was over was enough to shift the temperature between us and it felt like we both exhaled the lingering stress at the same time.

"How's your neighbor?"

"Yeah, that." I snorted. "We've found a way to cope, I guess. It was pretty bumpy at first."

"So we heard."

I felt a pang envisioning the three of them gossiping about me. "Why, what did he say?"

"Honestly, nothing bad. He said you had a bunch of rules, which, duh. Has he met you?"

"Did he say anything about the building being for sale?"

"Yeah, he's pretty freaked out about it. He's looking into other rental spots as a backup."

Andrew hadn't even hinted at it to me, but then again, when had we had the opportunity to talk? I frowned at the thought of him moving on without a fight. "Really? Where?"

"Not sure, we didn't get into it. Anyway, is it weird seeing him all the time?"

I could hear an edge in her voice, the tone that suggested that she was ready to excavate the past if I was. "Honestly, I don't see him much."

"Hm. Not to start something, but he said you look incredible."

I sat up, startling Edith. "Wait . . . *what?* In what context?"

"Don't know. Nolan told me he said it, so I don't have the details, but I thought you might want to know." I could hear the smile in her voice. "Do you want me to find out more?"

It was a trap. If I said yes she'd think that something was percolating between us, which it definitely wasn't.

"No, not necessary. He probably meant my Howl-o-Ween costume. I went all out, heels, smoky eye. Very not me." That had to be it, because it was impossible to believe that Andrew would find everyday me incredible. I didn't want to overthink it. "How are you guys celebrating Thanksgiving over there?" I asked.

I settled in as Samantha described the take-out turkey and sides that she was going to get for a group of fellow expats as well as a few of Nolan's colleagues who'd never experienced the tradition before. It was just like her to open her home to celebrate. She was the extrovert to my introvert, the reason I got off the couch for concerts and beer tastings and late-night clubs through school and beyond. In the beginning we'd been forced together because of my history with Nolan, but in time we realized that our friendship was fated.

"I can't wait to see you," I said after she described how lost she was in her language immersion class.

"Same. We're splitting the time between Long Island and Wismer. I'll let you know the exact dates soon."

"I'm around," I said, stating the obvious. "I might have to get any nights out cleared with Birdie and Edith, but other than them and work my calendar is wide-open."

"Yeah . . . I know. We definitely need to talk about that. Hold on, *who's* Edith?"

It sort of broke my heart that she didn't know about her. "I have a puppy now. I was sort of pushed into an adoption by a former client. I'll tell you the whole story when I see you."

"'When I see you,'" Samantha repeated back to me. "I like the sound of that."

"Same."

By the time we hung up it felt like no time had passed.

chapter twenty-three

"Happy Thanksgiving," my mom croaked into the phone. "But, Chels, honey, I've got bad news. I have it now too."

"Mom, *no!*" I switched my phone to my other hand so I could redirect Edith away from nipping Birdie's tail, then settled back on the couch. "How bad?"

"Let's just say I've cleared a path to the toilet," she answered in a weak voice.

"Okay, that's TMI, but I'm really sorry to hear it. So it's the same thing Aunt Helen has?" Her intestinal bug had come out of nowhere and sent her dashing between bed and the bathroom for the past two days.

"It is. She's a little better so we've swapped caregiver and patient roles."

"Wait, does that mean you're *both* not coming to Thanksgiving?" I frowned at the thought of the holiday at Taylor's just consisting of Engelmans. They were fine but they weren't family.

I had more than half the day to relax before heading to Taylor's and I'd been reading a book since I'd forced myself to leave my laptop at Frolic. I was actually excited for the holiday, to spend time eating and drinking and trying not to think about how different the day felt. My mom's call was changing everything I'd convinced myself to accept about our new holiday.

"No, honey, we don't want to put Taylor and the baby at risk. Or anyone for that matter. It's not worth it. We can get together and do a Thanksgiving part two as soon as we're better."

I frowned into the phone. "Do you want me to come over and help? Do you need food?"

She made a gagging noise. "The *last* thing we want is food, trust me. The most I can handle is toast and water. Aunt Helen has graduated to oatmeal and bananas. And I don't want you anywhere near us. We're doing fine, okay? You go to Taylor's and enjoy the day. Oh, and on your way please pick up the food I ordered from MacMurray's since we can't bring what we were supposed to. It's already paid for."

"I'm so bummed."

"We are too, honey. But what can you do? We'll FaceTime with you all at some point."

"Remember, I have an Android so you have to call Taylor's phone, not mine."

"Right, right," she said as if the technology made sense to her.

"Call me if you need anything, okay?"

"We will, thank you. Please try to have fun."

I sighed. "It's not going to be easy."

We hung up and suddenly reading a biography about the life and times of the British artist Rowan Barnes was the last thing I wanted to do. I shut my eyes and was starting to twitch my way to a nap when my phone rang again. Taylor, probably calling with last-minute instructions now that our guest list was down two people.

"I talked to Mom," I said as I picked up. "It sucks."

"Chelsea, *everything* is canceled," she wailed.

Her voice had that out-of-control pitch that always made my heart freeze, but then again, my drama queen sister deployed it for everything from Emmy nom announcements to snowfall predictions.

"The pipes burst," she sobbed. "Our whole first floor is under water!"

"No! What happened?"

"Ryan's mom did laundry yesterday and we didn't realize that something was wrong at first," she hiccuped. "The pipes drained in the ceiling all night and then this morning the whole ceiling collapsed into the kitchen. It was a *waterfall*!"

I felt a little sick. Her dream kitchen was barely three months post-renovation. The project had been a hellish experience of delays, missing components, and cooking on the grill and washing dishes with the hose in their tiny backyard.

"I'll be there in an hour," I said, easing off the couch. "I've got buckets. We'll get it cleaned up, don't worry."

"No, Ryan said not to come." Her voice was shaky and it broke my heart. "We . . . we need to get everything figured out with insurance first. And we've got an emergency plumber on the way."

"Tay, are you sure you don't want me there?"

She sniffled. "Yeah, don't come. I'm sorry I ruined your Thanksgiving."

It was typical Taylor, taking the blame for something that was out of her control.

"Stop, don't worry about me. I feel awful for *you* guys."

"You don't even know. We don't need this stress right now." Her voice rose. "The baby will be here soon and we don't have a kitchen!" I heard Ryan saying something to her in the background and her voice went muffled to snipe back at him. "He told me that I need to stop stressing out."

"I mean, he's sort of right?" I said gently. "It's probably not good for the baby."

More rustling from her. "Okay, the plumber is here, I gotta go, I gotta go."

She hung up before I could respond.

And just like that, within the span of an hour, my Thanksgiving celebration had gone down the drain, literally. I threw myself back on the couch and reached for Birdie, who was camped out in her usual spot behind my knees.

"I guess it's just us."

I glanced around my sunny apartment and tried not to feel sorry for myself. It was just a day, after all. And I had plenty to be thankful for. A veggie pot pie I could pop in the oven when I was ready. My four-legged besties I could take on a hike later. A new hardcover book about a quirky recluse that had cracked the *New York Times* bestseller list and was close to four hundred pages long. I sighed.

"Maybe some pre–Black Friday online shopping will help?" Edith wandered over to me and stood on her back legs with her paws resting on the edge of the couch, surveying me. "You really are adorable." I rolled over to rub her shoulders and she met my hand with her teeth.

"Why are you such a little jerk?"

The difference between my two dogs was striking. Bird was the quintessential good girl, a sweet and loving companion who after a lifetime of big ball-fetching energy had mellowed into the perfect couch potato. Edith was clever to a fault, catlike with her affections, and way too big for her black and white britches. Things were stable between the two opposites, but I was still bummed that they weren't besties yet.

I picked up my phone again. I liked a full-screen scroll when shopping and I kicked myself for leaving my laptop at work. It had seemed like a great idea at the time, a forced separation from the demands of self-employment, but that was before, when I had a full day of socializing and eating ahead of me. Now I needed to stay busy, to keep my brain from fixating on how different everything was.

To prevent the bleak feelings from taking over.

Exactly ten minutes later I pulled into the parking lot at Frolic expecting it to be empty but no, of course Andrew's Jeep was there. I wasn't in the mood to talk about my newly craptastic holiday so I ran in and threw my laptop in my backpack. I was about to dash through the front door when I saw him through the glass, talking animatedly to someone out of my view. I shrank back so it wouldn't seem like I was spying, which I totally was. Who was with him on Thanksgiving morning, and where was the person's car?

I envisioned the possibilities and wasn't at all prepared to see a young man in a wheelchair roll into view. Andrew paused and seemed to demonstrate some kind of arm exercise for him, pointing to his triceps and then encouraging the guy to try it himself. I watched them and realized that the guy in the wheelchair had been in the *Games of Thrones* costume at the Halloween party, with his chair decked out as the Iron Throne.

A Subaru pulled in and parked near them. I felt bad for watching, but I couldn't look away as the woman who was clearly the guy's mom got out and gave Andrew a hug. The guy wheeled himself over to the passenger side and Andrew opened the door for him and stood by as he maneuvered himself into position by the car. I could see Andrew coaching him, but gently and without the rah-rah cheerleading he'd done the day I had to lift the ladder. Andrew nodded and did a single satisfied clap as the guy made the transition from wheelchair to car, then broke the chair down so quickly that it was clear that he'd done it many times before. The mom popped open the hatchback and Andrew slipped the thing in like it was made of paper. They laughed about something and Andrew waved as they drove away.

I waited for him to head back into Crush and dashed out when he'd disappeared from view, speed-walking toward my car with my Nantucket hoodie pulled up and my head down like I'd just shoplifted something.

"Hey."

I whipped around and there he was, arms crossed and leaning back against the building.

"Hey. Happy Thanksgiving."

"Same to you. What are you doing here?" He headed toward me, scanning me for clues.

I did a half spin so he could see my backpack. "Forgot my laptop." I figured it was better to not go into detail.

"You're working today?" His eyebrow arched.

"Look who's talking." I gestured to where the car had just been parked.

"Yeah." His expression shifted as he nodded. "That was Aiden. High school sophomore who was in a car accident. Fell asleep at the wheel. He's transitioning from rehab to strength training with me. Incredible kid."

"Oh, wow." I wasn't sure what else to say.

The corners of Andrew's mouth turned down. "He was a sprinter on the track team."

I hugged myself against the cold and thought about all the ways life could turn upside down in an instant. "Is it going . . . okay? I mean, training with him."

"Better than okay. He's strong as hell mentally and he's got more grit than anyone I've ever met."

"Is it a stretch for you to do that type of work?"

He shot me a confused look.

"Post-rehab stuff. Like, focusing on health and wellness instead of physique."

I saw the hurt flash over his face before he managed to right his expression. "You really think all I do is powerlift with the bros, huh?"

"No, that's not what I meant at all." I backpedaled even though it was exactly what I'd assumed about him.

"Let me enlighten you about what I do at Crush." He deployed the Gibson Glare at me. "Yeah, I work with a lot of people who are in it to look good, but I've got half a dozen clients over seventy who know that motion is the lotion for long-term health. I've got a yogi who lifts to complement her practice. I've got a guy who's a caretaker for his father with Alzheimer's who needs to be strong enough to lift him if he falls. I've got a guy who almost destroyed his shoulder doing CrossFit with a trainer who got his certification online. Crush isn't just about vanity, Chelsea. And people who are interested in fitness aren't all muscleheads. What I do is *science*."

I felt my cheeks go hot as he called me on my assumption. "You're right, you're right. I'm sorry."

We stared at each other as our cold breath made little storm clouds around our faces.

"Speaking of training, you and I both need to get back to it. Back to our agreement." Andrew said it gently and I understood that it was his olive branch, a way to move past what could've been another argument.

"Next week," I offered quickly. "I'm wide-open Monday night."

"And I can swing Wednesday morning before nine or Friday before eight."

"Okay, I'll text you to confirm," I said.

We both fell silent again.

"I need to run, my mom's got a full house on the way," he said as he started back toward Crush.

"Lucky you." It slipped out before I could stop myself.

Andrew paused, like he could sniff out the sadness in me. "How are you celebrating today, other than working?"

I didn't want to get into it, but the way he was looking at me made it feel like I *had* to tell him the truth. It all tumbled out of me before I could stop myself. "I was supposed to go to my sister's for the day, but her kitchen flooded. And my mom and aunt were supposed to go too, but they both have the flu, so I'm on my own." I shrugged and tried to play it off, even though the more I thought about it the worse I felt.

"Oh, no way. That sucks."

"Don't worry about me, I'll keep busy." I pointed at my backpack again. "Anyway, happy Thanksgiving." I headed for my car.

"Higs."

Andrew's shout stopped me cold.

"You're coming to Thanksgiving with me."

chapter twenty-four

The fact that I was seated beside Andrew at a long, crowded dining room table was proof of his powers of persuasion.

Patricia had folded me into a hug when I arrived and welcomed me like I belonged, when the truth was I was an extra plate to fill at an already overflowing celebration. She'd introduced me as the "goat whisperer" to the sixteen or so family members and friends gathered in their living room and within a few minutes I was absorbed into the group, eating appetizers and laughing along with them as she told the story about getting headbutted into the mud.

I'd expected to feel out of place, a charity case, but by mealtime I was right at home sitting down at the table with Gerard at one end, Patricia opposite him, and the rest of us jammed elbow-to-elbow between them.

The tight quarters meant that the chairs were nearly locked in place at the table. Andrew had given his chair from the dining room set to one of his mom's friends, leaving him in a wobbly little folding thing that made him look like a giant in a dollhouse. I watched him load his plate up with mashed potatoes before passing by his cousin on the other side of him.

"I see I'm not the only one who's hungry." I nodded toward his overfull plate.

"Yup. Good food and good people. I'm going to enjoy every bite."

His eyes lingered on me a second too long, causing me to add an extra spoonful of unfortunate-looking corn pudding on my plate.

He leaned closer to me and pointed at the yellow pile taking up too much real estate on my plate. "You're going to regret that. Aunt Barb always overcooks it."

I poked at it. "It's a corn *brick*," I whispered.

"And now you've got to eat it or face the wrath of Barb. She watches everyone's plate. Trust me, you don't want to get on her bad side."

I sampled a tiny bite and followed up with a gulp of wine. "Looks like I'm taking one for the team today."

Andrew gave me a satisfied nod. "Your mom raised you right."

"Hey, what's going on with the Redskins, Andrew?" His uncle Teddy, a ruddy-faced guy who seemed to want to be the center of attention, shouted down the table. "You keep in touch with those guys?"

Andrew winced. "They're the Commanders now, remember?" He lowered his voice so only I could hear him. "Of all days to use the old team name."

"Whatever you call 'em." Teddy waved off the correction. "Do you miss it? I bet old Millville can't compete with those perks."

"It's not a competition," Andrew responded. He looked around the table as he spoke and I realized that we shared the "it's time to listen to me" instructor voice required for anyone who taught people. "I loved my time with the Commanders, but my new direction with Crush is exactly what I want to do. And it's going great, thanks."

"He's always been entrepreneurial," Patricia said, beaming at Andrew. "He set up a lemonade stand at the end of our driveway all by himself when he was seven!"

Gerard chuckled and leaned forward on his elbows so that everyone focused on him. "Yes, but unfortunately he was too young to understand that Cedarhurst Lane gets an average of three cars per day. The poor boy didn't have a single customer. Let's hope his business acumen has improved since then."

I started to laugh along with the rest of the group but stopped when I noticed the scowl on Andrew's face.

"If you'd ever come by the place and see what I've done maybe you'd be able to figure that out for yourself."

The side conversations halted until the only sound in the room was the clanking of silverware on china.

"I suppose I should," Gerard said, nodding thoughtfully, his eyes on Andrew. "I'd love to see what prompted you to leave an excellent job that had benefits and a path for advancement. Because it must be *extraordinary*."

I heard Andrew let out a long, slow breath. When I glanced over at him his head was bowed and his hands were balled into fists on his lap. For the first time ever the mighty Andrew Gibson looked . . . *defeated*. Small. Seeing him that way made my heart ache. I was tempted to reach out and give him a squeeze of support, but all eyes were bouncing between the two men, waiting for the next parry.

"How's the corn pudding?" Aunt Barb finally asked in an overloud voice.

The room came alive with compliments for the monstrosity and even I added that it was the best I'd tasted. Conversations cranked back up all around me, but Andrew remained quiet. I made half-hearted small talk with an intense gray-haired woman on the other side of me whose name I'd forgotten but I knew was a neighbor, shooting looks at Andrew as he shoveled the contents of his plate into his mouth.

Once the table was cleared and coffee was brewing for dessert I walked from room to room trying to track him down. I finally found him leaning over the baby gate in the laundry room near the back door, petting Murray.

"He gets overwhelmed." Andrew nodded to the dog. "The crowds are too much for him."

"I get it," I said, leaning against the wall. "Hey, you okay?"

"Yeah, why?" His tone went sharp and I realized that I was venturing into territory where I didn't belong.

"Your dad . . ." I offered then trailed off with a shrug.

"Par for the course. It's always like that. He thinks I'm a fuckup." Andrew looked at Murray and massaged his shoulders.

"Seriously?" I quickly tallied the wins in the Andrew Gibson Hall of Fame and couldn't imagine how anyone, particularly a *parent*, wouldn't see them too.

"He thinks Crush is a huge mistake and he's not shy about letting me know it. Walking away from job security doesn't make sense to him. The man has worked for the same company for his entire career; obviously he can't relate."

I glanced down the hallway to make sure no one was nearby. "So he hasn't been to see Crush at all?"

Andrew shook his head and let out a gruff laugh. "Not yet, and at the rate I'm going it won't matter. If the building sells he'll think he was right."

I didn't want to let him know that Samantha and I had talked about him. "Yeah, have you thought about what you're going to do?"

Andrew stood up. "I've been looking around, but there's nothing that comes close to our building. And even if I do find something comparable there's the financial hit to rebuild everything in a new space." Murray jumped so that his front paws were on the gate and Andrew gently pushed him off.

"I'm really sorry, Andrew."

It was such a foreign concept to me, a father who didn't support his child's dream. My dad was my biggest cheerleader. I'd always leaned on him and he'd seemed to relish being my adviser. He was the one who'd told me it was okay to start over after I'd packed up my life and moved to California to help launch a dog boarding franchise, only to discover that it wasn't a fit for me.

The nagging feeling came back, the knowledge that the solution was there, right in front of me. All I had to do was accept my dad's gift and we'd *both* be able to carry on. The problem was I couldn't think about the money without feeling like I had to vomit. It was tainted, no matter how my family tried to spin it. The inheritance only existed because someone I loved dearly had given up.

I glanced out the window on the door and saw that the blue skies had darkened to a stormy gray. "I'm going to go say hi to the goats before the rain. Want to come with me?"

"Yeah, I do. I need to get out of here." He gave Murray a quick kiss on the top of the head and followed me.

The wind nearly ripped the door from my hand and I wrapped my arms around my body as I stepped out onto the porch.

"You need a coat, hold on," Andrew said, and jogged back into the house. He returned a few seconds later holding out a black corduroy jacket with a shearling collar. "It doesn't go with your dress, but at least you'll be warm."

I slipped the giant thing on and glanced down. "Thanks. Obviously you're not cold." I gestured to his thin navy sweater.

He shook his head. "Never." He paused to scan me from head to toe. "Hm. You actually make my work jacket look good."

I hid a blush that lasted all the way down the driveway to the Mean Girls pen. The moment the trio spotted us standing at the fence they rushed over, eliciting a laugh out of Andrew.

"You *are* a miracle worker. Never thought I'd see the day."

"Well, we're on the other side of the fence. I have a feeling they'd have a problem if you went inside with me." I handed a piece of bread to him. "Here." He gave me a questioning look and I showed him the pockets in my green dress that I'd filled with two leftover dinner rolls. "I refuse to wear clothing without pockets."

We fed the goats in silence, laughing about the way they butted in front of one another to grab the bread from us. The wind and sky felt ominous, like the weather wasn't quite sure what to do.

"Uh-oh," Andrew said, pointing up. "We better get inside."

And then, as if he'd poked a hole in the clouds with his finger, the rain began. First a few cold drops, then a downpour, sending the goats running for cover under their lean-to.

I started for the house, but Andrew grabbed my wrist and

pulled me to the little tin-roofed storage shed by the pen. "We can wait it out here."

We ducked inside and he pulled the door shut behind him. The only light seeped through the cracks in the wood.

"Cozy," I laughed as I took a half step backward to try to put some space between us. It was pointless, because we were basically toe-to-toe. The rain pounded above us on the tin roof.

He didn't laugh. In fact, his expression looked dark, his eyes stormier than I'd ever seen them. I pressed back against the plywood wall to stabilize myself because I suddenly felt light-headed by his nearness and smoked cedar scent. My breathing went shallow as he continued to stare at me. I felt like a fraud because no matter how much I tried to talk myself out of it, *this* was what I fantasized about. Us, alone together, with nothing else registering but the sound of our heartbeats.

"Say something," I said, trying to break the tension, because everything about where we were felt familiar. The confined space forcing us to be close. The dim light. The realization that no one knew where we were.

And the unmistakable pull to kiss the very person we hated.

"No."

Andrew reached out and gently clasped the nape of my neck, drawing me to him so quickly that I let out a gasp. The idea that he wanted it too felt like a revelation even though I knew deep down that he did. This wasn't drunken horniness like the last time; his warm hand on my skin was intentional. My breathing went shallow and I tried not to tremble as he slowly dropped his head until his lips were just inches from mine. Time seemed to stop as the faint pulse of his breath tickled against my mouth.

"Can I?" he whispered as he leaned closer.

I didn't trust my voice and a tiny part of me worried that I might accidentally correct his English so I nodded. I was absolutely desperate for him. He waited a few painful seconds longer, letting his eyes travel around my face one last time, before finally placing his lips on mine.

chapter twenty-five

It was a million times better than I remembered.

There was no frenzy between us, no prelude to a potential hate-fuck like the last time. This kiss was achingly slow. I had to fight to keep from letting the little moans in the back of my throat from escaping as Andrew slanted his mouth against mine and leaned into me. I was embarrassed at just how badly I wanted this. I was so focused on the pressure of his lips and the delicious flick of his tongue that I didn't even feel him easing me against the wall until my back was flat against it. It was as if my entire body had gone numb and the only thing I could feel was the brush of his mouth against mine and the fire he was igniting inside me.

This kiss was the promise of so much more, whether we wanted to admit it or not.

The last time we'd kissed, his body was all smooth planes and lean muscle. Current Andrew had new mysteries to uncover. I was desperate to touch everything I'd only been able to fantasize about since that night, to catalog the changes that had turned the man into a mountain. My hands slid up his chest to his shoulders and rested there with the slightest pressure, and Andrew jerked away from me abruptly like I'd scorched him.

"Do you want me to stop?" he rasped, his expression injured, like not kissing me was causing him physical pain.

"Oh my God, no," I whispered, feeling woozy. "I want you to *never* stop."

His dark eyes turned predatory and he claimed my mouth again. The sweetness between us was slipping away, replaced by a hunger I could feel in every cell of my body. Andrew reached down to collect both of my wrists in his giant hand then pinned them against the wall above my head, trapping me as he kissed his way down my neck. Each press of his lips was a brand on my skin. I shuddered against him and I felt his lips curl into a triumphant smile. He used his thigh to part my legs and I let out a whimper as he pressed closer. I felt like I was holding my breath every time he shifted, worried that he was going to come to his senses and stop touching me.

He finally let my hands drop and I dragged them over his back, caressing him like I needed to make up for lost time.

"I hate what you do to me," Andrew whispered in my ear as his hand found its way beneath the hem of my dress and started climbing my leg.

"Why?" I asked, my lips flush against his ear. I pressed a kiss to it and he groaned.

"Because you wedge yourself in my head and you're all I can think about. *This* is all I can think about."

Hearing him admit it sent a tiny thrill of victory through me.

Andrew's palm felt like it was searing my thigh. I arched into him, hoping the thumb that was smoothing the skin on my inner thigh would travel a little higher.

"Fuck!" Andrew jumped away from me like he'd been electrocuted, staring at the wall next to where I was standing.

"What's wrong?" I looked around frantically.

He pointed to Thistle's muzzle coming through a hole in the wall. "She bit me!" He reached down to rub his leg.

I suddenly grasped the absurdity of the moment. We were making out like horny teenagers in a *goat barn*. Andrew almost put his hand in my panties in a *goat barn*. I started giggling helplessly.

"Goat-us interruptus," I managed as my cackling grew more unhinged.

Andrew laughed with me, still rubbing his shin. Thistle bleated a warning and we knew the moment was over.

"We, uh, we should probably get back," he said in a thick voice.

I tilted my head and went quiet for a few seconds. "Yeah, sounds like the rain stopped."

We stared at each other as the music of Thistle chewing plywood ruined any chance of us ending on a romantic note. Andrew took a reluctant step backward and pushed the door open, still watching me.

"Look!" I said, pointing beyond him.

The rain had been transformed into a swirling snowstorm. Three of the neighbor kids that had been at lunch came tearing down the driveway as Andrew and I stepped out of the shed, squinting in the brightness. Luckily there were no adults to witness our guilty exit.

"Thanksgiving is dead. Long live Christmas," he said.

And long live whatever we'd just kicked off in the goat barn.

Karen Foster wasn't getting the hint.

I'd wrapped up the third session of my adult beginners class fifteen minutes prior and was trying to prep for Andrew and Dude, but she hadn't budged from her chair. Her chubby beagle Bella was rightfully exhausted, dozing at her feet.

"I really think she's got dominant tendencies," she said, flicking her hands toward Bella. "How else would you explain her still pulling on her leash after all of these classes?"

Karen was one of those students who tested my diplomacy skills each week. She drove a giant black Cadillac and was quick to mention the fact that her husband, Dr. Glen Foster, had run the most successful ear, nose, and throat practice in the tri-county region for the past twenty years. She liked to complain about the fact that Bella wasn't making progress, but I could tell by her confused expression and endless questions during class that she hardly ever worked with her dog.

"It's all about consistency," I replied in an even tone. The trick was to frame her lack of effort in a way that didn't directly call her out. "Three lessons might seem like a lot of time to *us*, but the reality is it's just three hours in a week consisting of one hundred and sixty-eight. And if Bella doesn't get a chance to practice her homework"—again, I kept the blame out of the equation even though I totally wanted to throw her under the bus—"her progress will be slow."

"Hm," she sniffed. "Well, I still think it's her dominance."

I'd already spent a good part of our first class debunking

canine dominance theory with her and I didn't have the time to debate it again. Andrew and Dude were about to show up and I needed a few minutes to hide in the bathroom and do deep breathing exercises since it was going to be our first time seeing each other since the goat barn. The rest of Thanksgiving had been a blur, and he'd told me that his entire weekend was full of family commitments. Our texts firming up our training schedule had ended with him saying that we could talk when we were together, which could mean anything.

"We can get into it more at our next class, okay? I have a private lesson in a few minutes," I said, hoping that she'd take the hint and leave. "It's a deaf dog so I really have to focus."

She perked up. "My nephew in Tulsa just adopted a deaf dog! Perfect, I'm going to stay and observe what you do so I can give him pointers."

I had to fight to keep smiling at her. "I'm so sorry, Karen, private lessons are just that: private. My clients pay a premium to have one-on-one sessions with me." I neglected to tell her that Andrew was an exception to the rule.

She made a pouty face. "Please? Maybe I can ask your client if I can stay and watch?"

There was absolutely no way I wanted Karen hovering around while Andrew and I tried to figure out what the hell we were doing with each other. Not that I wanted to hash out the details of the kiss with him while we worked with Dude, but still. It was going to be hard enough to focus on the work without her interrupting the whole time.

"I'm sorry, Karen, I can't agree to that." I backpedaled at the last second. "It's up to my client."

"What's up to your client?"

Andrew had taken advantage of my prop-rock to let himself in the back door, striding into the room with Dude on a leash beside him. I glanced at Karen and saw her posture shift into coquette mode when she spotted him, breaking into a smile and crossing her legs prettily. Bella barely glanced at Dude and for the first time ever I actually wished for a canine confrontation so I'd have a reason to kick them out.

"Well, *hello* there!" she cooed in a syrupy voice I'd never heard before. "Chelsea said you have a deaf dog and I was hoping I could stay and observe your lesson. My nephew just adopted one too."

Andrew took her fawning in stride. But then again, he probably didn't even notice it.

"Sure, that's fine." He glanced at me a second too late and seemed to realize his mistake. "That is . . . if it's okay with Chelsea."

"Oh, she already said I could if you agreed to it," Karen answered quickly. "Just pretend like I'm not here."

And for the next hour that proved to be impossible. My agenda for the session was packed and included starting the critical "watch me" cue, fine-tuning Dude's "sit," teaching "down," introducing recall training, and helping *both* ends of the leash learn that wearing one was a good thing. Instead we barely got through "sit" and "watch me" thanks to Karen's incessant questions and commentary. By the end of class I was ready to murder her.

But a tiny part of me appreciated the fact that she absorbed any of the potential awkwardness between me and Andrew. With Karen why-ing the entire time I couldn't obsess about how incredible he looked even though he was just in his usual black sweats/pants hybrid and a slim-fit gray Crush hoodie. I was too busy dealing with her to wonder if he meant to brush my hand that way when he gave me Dude's leash. I was forced to pretend Andrew was any old client even though it felt like we kept exchanging secret glances while Karen chattered on.

"That was wonderful!" Karen sang as she finally collected her things. After hanging out in Frolic for two hours Bella only had eyes for the door. "I picked up quite a few tips."

"It was nice to meet you," Andrew said with a friendly wave. If he was frustrated he sure wasn't showing it.

I managed a nod in her direction as she and Bella headed out and let out a long exhale when the door finally closed behind her.

"Well, that was the worst," Andrew laughed. "Not the lesson, *her.*"

"She eats up more time and attention than anyone else."

He smirked. "It's always like that. One person who sucks the life out of you. I have a few clients I'd like to fire, but every time I even hint at it they book another package of twelve sessions."

I pointed at Dude, who was circling around Andrew looking worried. "He needs to go out for a potty break." As much as I wanted to finally talk to Andrew one-on-one I wasn't about to make Dude suffer.

"Yeah, and I have a client coming in thirty minutes and I need to run him home." Dude pulled toward the door and Andrew followed behind him.

"Hey, be careful. The pulling." I grimaced and pointed at Dude. "If that strategy works for him he'll keep doing it."

"Right, right," he said, reorienting himself so Dude wasn't sled-dogging. "You're teaching me as much as him."

I watched them walk politely toward the door and felt my

heart sink despite the progress I was witnessing. We weren't going to talk about it after all. The kiss and all that it meant, or could mean. But I wasn't about to bring it up. I'd been burned once before thanks to the text never answered.

Andrew was nearly out the door when he stopped. "Did you hear that Sam and Nolan are back?"

My heart warmed at the thought of my friends so near. "I did. Can't wait to catch up with them."

"I'm having them over to my place Thursday night for pizza. You want to come too?"

It was perfect. The four of us together again, ignoring whatever weirdness remained. We all hadn't been in the same room since their wedding. Hope surged through me at the thought of smoothing over our rough edges.

"Yeah, that would be really great."

"Perfect, I'll throw you on the group text." Dude scratched at the door and Andrew got the hint. "Bring Edith too," he yelled as the door shut behind him.

chapter twenty-six

As I placed the vintage pink bulb on the Christmas tree I realized that I'd never been happier for catastrophic flood damage.

While Taylor and Ryan had been able to deal with their massive kitchen renovation during the summer, there was no way she was going to suffer through it during the holidays, especially with her pregnancy further along. My mom had opened her home to them until the renovation was completed, which meant that she would be totally focused on fussing over them as Christmas got closer. Imagining the three-point-five of them together was a weight off my mind. My mom would be too busy caring for them to overthink everything, which in my opinion was the best way of coping with those heart-fracturing memories that popped up as the holidays got closer.

"Mom likes to put that one toward the top of the tree because it's so old. It's safer up there," Taylor said, pointing to the bulb that I'd just hung in the perfect spot.

"Yes, ma'am," I muttered and moved it higher.

"Thank you, honey," my mom said, beaming at me.

Ryan and Taylor had brought home a tree for Mom and invited me to help decorate it, so we were gathered together in our great room with a fire crackling in the fireplace and hot chocolate at the ready. Despite the stupid old jokes about in-laws not getting along, it was obvious that my mom and Ryan adored each other. We all loved him, it was hard not to. Taylor had picked a good one. He had shaggy brown hair, a quiet, dry wit, and a devotion to my sister that verged on sickening. But I could see him treating my mom with the same care, as well as assuming bottle- and jar-opening responsibilities and other assorted dude chores.

The tree was already filling the room with that familiar piney scent, bringing back memories of so many happy moments. The rest of the room had been decked out for weeks, with holiday rugs on the floor and garlands strung up on the wood ceiling beams. Everything felt familiar and comfortable despite the vacant recliner yawning in the corner.

"Tay told me about your building being for sale," Ryan said as he hung up a Santa ornament. "Any movement on it?"

"I've seen people checking it out, but with the holidays coming it's tapered off," I said, reaching into the plastic tub for the next ornament.

"Aunt Helen had a really good idea—"

"Mom, let's focus on the tree, okay?" I interrupted quickly, shocked that she was going there. "I don't feel like talking about work stuff."

"Okay, fine," she sniffed and pulled a knotted red and green beaded garland from the box.

Taylor wobbled over to grab another ornament. "Tell us about your Thanksgiving with a house full of strangers. I'm sure it was a million times better than ours."

I felt my face go hot at the mention of being with Andrew, and Taylor shot me an odd look.

"What? What happened?" she demanded, studying me.

"Nothing," I said, suddenly very focused on finding the perfect spot on the tree for the long-legged elf ornament in my hand. "It was great. Better than I expected."

"Where were you again?" Ryan asked. "Taylor said something about a guy you went to school with?"

I nodded. "Yeah, Andrew was my friend Nolan's roommate. He opened a gym at the other end of my building so we sort of reconnected."

I wondered if they could see me blushing at the mention of "reconnecting."

"He's hot, right?" Taylor asked. "I met him once and I remember that he was really good-looking."

Taylor's type was exactly who she'd married, so the fact that she considered Andrew attractive came as a shock to me. Of course, it was impossible to ignore his sheer animal magnetism, but still.

"He's very handsome," my mom agreed before I could answer.

I shrugged. "If you go for that sort of thing."

"What sort of thing?" Ryan asked as he turned to give me his full attention. "What kind of competition am I up against?"

I laughed at him. "He's, like, a . . . a gym guy. It's obvious he works out. He's big. Muscular."

"'Roided up?" Ryan asked, holding two sparkly ballerinas in his hands.

"No." I shook my head and frowned at the thought. "Not like that. He takes up space in the world, but not just because of his body. He's got this super-friendly, outgoing personality.

Everyone loves him. He's one of those people who has, like, an *aura* around him. He draws people to him." I shrugged and hung the elf haphazardly. "It's hard to describe."

"Are you two hearing this?" Taylor glanced between Mom and Ryan. "She's totally into him!"

"Oh, God, no! Absolutely not." I laughed unconvincingly. "We are *so* different."

"Well, your father and I were different," my mom said as she brushed past me with the now untangled garland. "Opposites, even."

I frowned at the thought and watched her rise up on her tiptoes to start threading the garland through the branches. "That's not true. You guys were perfectly matched."

"You don't have to be exactly the same to have a wonderful match, Chels," she chided.

I had a flash of my dad telling a story during a dinner party with every eye on him while my mom watched him with a small smile, probably because she'd already heard the story a dozen times before. He was always the one speeding toward glory on the track while she was his faithful pit crew.

"Well, it doesn't matter because I'm not looking," I said. "And he probably isn't either."

"Yeah, why would you *le rush* into anything?" Taylor shot me an evil look. "I'm sure your calendar is simply buzzing with activity."

I grabbed a plastic bulb from the box and chucked it at her head. She ducked and it bounced off the window.

"Girls, *stop*! You're going to break something."

We all laughed and got back to the job at hand: staying focused on anything but the missing bright star in our lives.

. . .

"I'm sorry to say this, but Edith is acting like a jerk."

Carly gave up trying to pet the puppy after getting nipped every time she reached for her. We'd spent thirty minutes outside in the dusting of snow, letting Edith and Geneva run wild in Carly's new fenced-in yard and now we were settled at the kitchen table, ready for coffee and gossip. Geneva was curled up in her bed in the corner of the room and every time Edith even looked at her she raised her lip in warning.

"Yeah, she's a lot. But I think she might be the smartest dog I've ever met."

In the weeks since I'd brought her home we'd sped through basic training, which meant she was the equivalent of one of those preteens that graduated from college. And she *never* got tired. She came to Frolic with me most days and despite the nonstop stimulation she was still raring to go when we got home. Poor Birdie spent most of her time up on my bed, the one spot where she was safe from Edith's harassment.

I dug through my backpack then handed over one of the busy toys I'd packed for her. She settled down to work on it and I breathed a sigh of relief.

"Can we talk about tile for a second?" Carly asked. "I have a bunch of samples for the floor in here and I'm stumped."

"*Anything* will be an improvement," I laughed.

The kitchen looked like it hadn't been touched since the house was built in the 1940s. The linoleum floor was a worn coppery block pattern and the cabinetry was flat-faced dark wood. But it didn't take much to see past the cosmetic flaws to the beauty waiting to be uncovered.

Carly dumped a dozen different tile samples on the table in front of me. "I have Pinterest boards for every room. Look." She handed me her tablet.

As I scrolled through her ideas I was reminded of my own Pinterest boards that I'd put together for a Frolic expansion. I felt a little sick at the thought that maybe I'd spent all of the time creating them for nothing. Mike was being typically cagey about what was going on with the building. Anytime I asked him about it he told me that there was "lots of interest," but then he let it slip that he'd dropped the price. It made sense, though. Not everyone saw the bland industrial building for the gem that it was.

I looked up from the tile options. "Don't kill me, but would you ever consider hardwood in here?"

Carly's mouth dropped open. "You read my mind! I've been so set on tile, but I keep seeing all of these amazing wood options and I was too afraid to switch gears." She glanced down at the tiles spread on the table. "Crap. Now I have to start over."

"You've got time," I reassured her.

"Time for what?" Joe strolled into the kitchen and dropped his gym bag on the counter, causing both dogs to run to him. He stooped to greet them both.

"Kitchen stuff, don't worry about it," she replied, gathering up the samples. She widened her eyes at me and I realized that her indecision was probably frustrating Joe.

"Just saw your neighbor, Chels," Joe said as he refilled his water bottle. "He *killed* me today."

"Is that good or bad?" I asked, watching as he searched through the cabinets, finally settling on a handful of almonds.

"Very good." He popped one in his mouth. "That guy is a

genius. He knows *everything* about the human body. Like, I asked him a simple question about squats and he goes off about Newton's second law of motion and the new thinking about knees over toes. I don't understand half the shit he says, but obviously he knows what he's doing."

Carly settled in the chair across from me. "Someone's happy he lost four pounds."

Joe wagged his finger at his wife. "It's not about weight loss. It's a journey."

"Right, of course." Carly laughed at her husband's intensity. "You might want to leave now, we're talking about kitchen design options."

"Yikes, I'm out." He grabbed his bag. "One parting word: *budget.*"

After he'd left the room Carly pulled her legs up on her chair and gave me a Cheshire cat smile. "Speaking of Andrew, you never told me the whole story of what happened with him."

I rubbed my eyes. So much had changed between us since the night in the corn maze, yet it still felt like there was even more that I didn't understand. I decided to focus on our history rather than our confusing present.

"Please keep this between us, okay? I don't want Joe accidentally saying anything to him."

"Promise. I can tell the man has split allegiances already so I'll keep it to myself."

I felt a little woozy at the thought of revisiting the night with her. Despite how things were evolving with Andrew the primary emotion I still felt when I thought about it was embarrassment. But Carly needed to know, especially as Joe and Andrew became closer.

"Andrew is best friends with one of my friends from high school, Nolan. Nolan and my roommate Samantha started dating so we were kind of forced into a foursome. But Andrew *despised* me. It was so obvious. He thought I was a dork who did nothing but study."

"Were you?" Carly asked.

"I mean . . . yes, but he was the only one who judged me for it."

She laughed. "We were all such assholes back then, right?"

"Yeah, but he was the biggest." I cringed internally at the fact that I'd been just as judgy about him. "Anyway, we barely tolerated each other, made it through graduation, and didn't connect again until Sam and Nolan's coed bachelor party on a boat in New York Harbor."

Carly's eyes lit up. "Okay, I like where this is headed."

I swallowed hard. "I got really drunk. Obscenely, make-bad-choices, *blackout* drunk."

"Yes, I love bad choices!" Carly clapped her hands gleefully. "Keep going."

"I don't remember how, but Andrew and I both ended up in a storage closet and . . . we hooked up."

"Seriously? This is way juicier than I thought."

"We didn't have sex, I'm sure of that," I added quickly. "But everything else? Yeah."

Carly glanced toward the doorway Joe had just walked out, then leaned forward. "Was it good?" she whispered. "Please tell me it was good."

The memories of his hands and mouth exploring me as my body responded to his every move were seared in my memory, and even thinking of them in the light of day at my friend's kitchen table set off a shiver inside of me.

"Amazing," I squeaked out as my face went hot.

She let out a breath. "Thank God. I'd be so disappointed if he looked like that and couldn't deliver. So what happened next?"

This was the part in the story I wished I could erase. I pressed on. "We were both half-dressed and I . . . I felt sick and I . . ." I cringed at the thought of it. "I had to run to the edge of the boat so I could vomit."

Carly threw back her head and let out a room-shaking cackle. "No!"

"Yeah." I didn't blame her for laughing. If I hadn't been the one puking I'd think it was hilarious too. "I was sick for the rest of the night, and then I passed out."

"And what did he do?"

And here was the other part of the story, where my cringe shifted to sadness; the part that showed Andrew's true colors. "Nothing. I texted him right before I passed out and I woke up when we docked. I lost my phone that night but I never heard back from him. And I sent him an incoherent . . ." I made a face then forced myself to keep going. "Incoherent *love* letter. I said things that I didn't even know I was feeling. I bared my soul."

"Oh *no*. He ignored it?" Carly said softly. "I'm so sorry, Chels."

I shrugged the sad feelings away. "I was a drunken mistake for him. It happens. The good news is neither one of us feels the need to talk about it. It's history."

"Is it awkward now?"

I took a deep breath and tried to come up with a way to explain what happens when you mix a rainstorm, goats, and someone you can't get out of your head.

chapter twenty-seven

My worry list was longer than ever, and to stress myself out even more I dissected each item in detail during the drive to Andrew's.

Seeing Samantha for the first time in forever.

Being back in a foursome with dicey history.

Trying to act normal with Andrew nearby.

Not letting on to Samantha that Andrew and I had hooked up.

And on a completely different level, bringing Edith even though she hadn't met Dude yet.

Then there was all the usual stuff to obsess about, like if my outfit was cute, and would I be able to eat despite a simmering belly. I glanced at Edith in the rearview mirror.

"Be good tonight, okay?" She tilted her head to the side and gave me her most innocent look. "Exactly. Keep it up."

It didn't surprise me that Andrew was renting a place I'd always been curious about. The restored 1800s schoolhouse was fifteen minutes from Crush, a cute little brick building with a peak over the arched door and big windows everywhere. It didn't have much of a yard, but it backed against preserved fields, which meant that Dude had hundreds of acres to get lost on if Andrew let him off leash without practicing his recall homework. I made a mental note to remind him to keep at it.

I fought off the jangly, queasy feelings at the sight of Nolan's old Honda already parked in the driveway. I didn't allow myself to think about how much I'd missed both of them until I was seconds away from hugging them again. I'd been stupid to not be better about staying in touch. Sure, it was a two-way street, but I felt like I'd been the one idling at the stop sign.

I opened the back door of my car, grabbing Edith's leash and the six-pack of craft beers I'd picked up. It was going to be a great night. Old friends, cute dogs, and lots of laughs. I had to keep telling myself that as I walked up the steps and the front door opened.

"Chels!"

Samantha's scream cut right through me. In that single syllable I could hear the crack of emotion in her voice. A little pain mixed in with her happiness.

"Sammie!"

I dropped the six-pack, crashed into her, and burst into unexpected tears.

Hugging Samantha stripped away any of my worries about things being awkward between us. I could feel her cry-laughing too as we embraced. I'd been bottling up how much I missed her, pretending that it didn't matter that we'd drifted apart.

Edith pogoed next to us until we finally broke apart, smiling as we wiped away our tears.

"I'm so happy to see you that I can't stop crying." She had her hand over her mouth, laughing as the tears trailed down her cheeks.

Edith seemed to realize that I was getting more attention than she was and jumped up on Samantha.

"Oh, Chels, she's *perfect*!" Sam dropped to her knees to pet Edith.

"Well, Birdie would beg to differ," I laughed.

Samantha looked up at me as she tried not to get nibbled, then jerked her head back dramatically. "Oh my God, you look good. Like, really good. What's different about you?"

Even after our time apart she was still in tune with me enough to pick up on the fact that there was something wild rumbling around inside me. We'd always had an almost psychic connection, where a glance or raised eyebrow could hold an entire conversation's worth of context. Now, though, I wasn't sure I was ready for her to know my innermost thoughts. I didn't want Andrew crowding out all of the other catching up we needed to do. Plus, I didn't want her to resume her pro-Andrew campaign until I had a better understanding of what the hell was going on with him.

"Oh, stop." I ducked my head to avoid her curious stare. "I got a good night's sleep maybe? Anyway, look at *you*. Love the haircut."

I was shocked that Samantha had chopped off her mahogany-streaked crowning glory, but the new shorter bob suited her too. Then again, she was naturally gorgeous enough to get second looks in sweats and a ponytail at breakfast. When we used to go to bars together, before she and Nolan got serious, Sam's dark eyes and showstopping smile were the siren songs that lured men to their doom. I was fine with her castoffs.

"You really like it?" she asked, wrinkling her nose. "Mia kept pulling my hair and honestly, this is just easier."

"Did you bring her?" I peeked past her to where the blue door was flung open and letting all the warm air out.

She shook her head. "Nolan's parents wanted to take her for the evening and I was more than happy to let them. Mommy needs a break!"

Nolan's voice echoed out to us. "Would you two stop gossiping and get in here?"

It was typical of us to get so caught up in the moment that we forgot about the rest of the world. Sam swooped Edith up and I followed her in. I had a few seconds of sensory overload after I crossed the threshold, trying to absorb Andrew's shockingly cozy space, giving him an appropriate smile and nod while simultaneously heading to Nolan for a bear hug.

"Hey, gorgeous, missed you," he laughed as he wrapped his arms around me. Edith came over to jump up on us and I realized that she was becoming one of those dogs that hated hugging.

Nolan was the brother that I'd always wished for. We'd been in the same friend group since middle school, but going to college together had strengthened our pretend siblinghood. And the marrying-my-best-friend part had sealed it for life.

"You're so skinny," I said, pulling out of our hug to take him in. His sandy hair was cropped shorter than I'd ever seen, and he had dark rings beneath his bright blue eyes.

"Just what every man wants to hear, thanks." He pretended to take a blow to the chest. "I prefer 'lean.'"

"I think he looks great," Andrew said from the kitchen, where he was flipping caps off beer bottles. I tried not to notice how snug his white Henley was. "Wiry and strong."

"He's running again," Samantha said. "At least one of us has time to exercise."

A loud bark interrupted us.

"There's Dude," Andrew said, glancing down the hall. "I guess he can sense that his favorite teacher is here." He fixed a shockingly friendly Gibson Glare on me. "Is it okay if I bring him out so he can meet Edith?"

I felt a ridiculous thrill at being called "favorite" even though he was talking about his dog's opinion of me. If I was going to twist everything he said I was in for a long night.

"Yup, just keep him on leash until we figure out how this is going to go."

"Oh, trust me, I know how you feel about leashes," he said as he walked out of the kitchen.

I looked around the house for an appropriate spot for the introduction since it was too cold and dark to try it outside. The brick-walled space was mostly open, but there were enough places for Dude to hide if Edith went into piranha mode. I had a feeling that he was going to act like Birdie: kowtowing to the bossy baby. I leashed her up as well.

The sound of too-long nails on hard wood echoed down the hallway.

"This is gonna be good," Nolan said under his breath. "Dude is a maniac."

I felt a little injured by the comment, considering he was in training with me, but then again, if Andrew wasn't practicing with him then I couldn't be blamed.

Dude spotted me and went into a full-body wag, but Edith let out a bark and his attention shifted as if he could hear it too. It took a few seconds of leash juggling, sniffing, and circling before I felt confident that they were okay to be off leash together.

They were both interested in each other, and Dude seemed appropriate with Edith. The puppy, however, was anything but.

Edith launched herself at Dude's face with her mouth wide-open. She seemed to pause, then twisted in midair when he let out a low growl and raised his lip.

"Is that okay?" Andrew asked, sounding like a nervous parent at the playground.

"It's perfect," I reassured him. "This is exactly what she needs. She's kind of a jerk and my dog Birdie is too sweet to tell her off."

Edith kept up with the same ridiculousness that she always pulled with her sister, nipping at Dude's ears and bumping against him with her nose repeatedly. I crossed my fingers that Dude wasn't going to take it.

It only took a few more nose punches and nips before Dude had clearly had enough. He let out a string of fierce barks and leapt at Edith, startling her so badly that she fell over backward. She stood up slowly, seemingly dazed by the first real correction she'd ever gotten. Dude shook off, then walked away with his tail wagging.

"That was *amazing*," I said even though I knew he couldn't hear me, leaning down to pet him. "Thank you for teaching her a lesson, sir."

Now that the dogs had sorted themselves out we grabbed beers and headed for the couches in the open family room. Edith stuck close to me and pretended she couldn't see Dude.

"So what's it like being neighbors?" Nolan asked as he settled in.

Andrew and I glanced at each other. Such a loaded question.

"Once she laid out all the ordinances, several times, we were fine. Parking, garbage, and mandatory leashes were the biggies," he said. "It was dicey at first. We all know Higs and her rules."

I felt a flicker of anxiety as Nolan and Sam laughed with him. This was how it used to go, back in the day. Andrew would start off with a little joke about me, some "good-natured" teasing, and the next thing I knew my neck felt tense and I was searching for light insults to lob back in his face. But everything was different now. Make-out-session-in-the-goat-barn different.

At least I hoped so.

"Yeah, but we also know how you don't aways listen, so I don't blame her for repeating the rules," Sam said, making me want to high-five her.

Andrew was directly across from me on a leather lounger and it felt like we were both trying to avoid looking at each other, as if Nolan and Sam would be able to figure out that something had happened and would then subject us to relationship Q&A for the rest of the night. Everything felt weird, like the lights in the room were too bright and the thermostat was set a little too high. But it wasn't like I'd expected a totally casual hang, considering how many things were evolving, both with Andrew *and* with Sam.

"Are you going to decorate this place for Christmas?" Nolan asked, gesturing around the room with his beer. "It's looking pretty sad."

"I'm going to, yeah. Get a tree, throw up a wreath on the door. I actually won a tree—" Andrew stopped abruptly and glanced at me, probably thinking about the corn maze incident. "I, uh, won a Christmas tree at a fall festival. I need to go back to the farm and cut one down."

I sneaked a look at Sam, hoping that she wasn't picking up on any weird vibes, but she'd pulled out her phone and was texting with a frown on her face.

"Your mom says Mia got out of her bath and won't put her pajamas on. She's running around naked."

"Takes after her daddy," Andrew laughed and pointed his beer bottle at Nolan. "You used to get drunk and sleep naked." He shuddered at the memory.

"Let's not get started on the topic of nakedness, okay? Because I could tell the story . . ."

"Oh God, not the ass-in-the-air story." Andrew rolled his eyes. "How many times have we heard this one?"

"I've actually never heard it," I said, perking up. Nolan was a great storyteller and I wanted to laugh at Andrew as a payback for his rules comments. "Tell me."

Andrew's face shifted into a distressed scowl. "Nolan, don't. That's ancient history."

Suddenly I wasn't so sure I wanted the details, but Nolan was already warming to the idea of trying to embarrass Andrew. "So, it's sophomore year and I get back to our room after a party. We'd agreed to leave a shoe outside the door if we had someone in the room, which happened a lot more for one of us than the other. But I did okay."

Sam made a disgusted noise as she typed on her phone.

"There was no shoe that night, so I was all clear." He paused dramatically. "I unlocked the door and all I saw, lit by a tiny desk light, was Andrew's gigantic, white, naked ass jiggling in the air on the bed. I don't know *what* he was doing, but the dude was contorted." Nolan cackled. "The girl he was with screamed and they both dove under the blanket, but not before a vision of

Andrew's brown eye was seared in my brain. I can still picture it now. I'm scarred for life."

"Nolan . . ." Sam looked up from her phone with a disgusted look on her face. "Come on."

"What? I can't complain about the fact that he forgot the signal a *lot*? Which means I saw that naked volleyball butt way more than I wanted to. I mean, we all know the guy had a revolving door, right?"

Andrew's expression was somewhere between embarrassed and pissed off. "Long time ago." His eyes flicked to me before I could look away.

Everything had changed, yet nothing had, really. Here we were, falling back into familiar patterns like no time had passed.

Conversation moved on to Andrew's business, and as I watched the three of them I started to relax. Andrew and I still hadn't had a chance to talk about the goat barn incident, but something had shifted between us and we both seemed to know it.

Because every time I caught his eye the Gibson Glare softened into something that made my heart fumble.

chapter twenty-eight

Abbott Farm had Christmas music piping through speakers on tall poles, so even if the act of cutting your tree didn't put you in the spirit, Mariah shrieking in the distance forced you to feel it. And for the first time in ages, I sort of did. The pervasive holiday cheeriness that I'd sidestepped for the past few years was finally rubbing off on me.

I was actually getting excited for Christmas.

Part of it had to be the balm of time passing, of us getting used to our new family unit. Taylor and Ryan staying with my mom combined with the excitement of the baby shifted us closer to a "normal" holiday season, pukey and flooded Thanksgiving notwithstanding. And as much as I didn't want to admit it, the promise of whatever was unfolding with Andrew helped too. Everything felt a little more sparkly. Hopeful. Magical.

Exactly what the season was supposed to feel like.

The texted invitation to go back to the farm with him to cut a tree had come as a shock, along with the line at the end of it that said, We can talk about everything. I'd reread the text a few times to make sure I wasn't misinterpreting it, because it felt like . . . *something*. Something Hallmarkian and sweet and incredibly date-like. I'd tried to look as cute as possible, considering we were going to be trudging around outside, opting for my pom-pom-free cashmere hat and a slim black parka that didn't make me look like a chocolate-covered marshmallow.

"How about this one?" I asked Andrew, pointing to a squat, dense pine tree that was at the edge of a row and accessible on all sides for easy cutting.

"Hm." He took a step back to scan the tree then shook his head. "That's a Scotch pine. They smell great, but I think the branches are too crowded. Let's keep looking. We'll find the right one." He walked on ahead of me, gripping the hacksaw in his gloveless hand.

I liked that he said "we" as if my opinion mattered.

I'd half expected him to charge in and cut any old tree, preempting our adventure before it had even begun. At the rate we were going, with Andrew stopping to pluck a branch or step back to calculate the height of a tree, it was going to take him hours to choose. But if anyone could appreciate mulling over a decision it was me.

Andrew came to a stop and pointed at a perfectly shaped tree. "That's a blue spruce. Great needle retention, unique color, long-lived, but not for me."

"*How* do you know so much about Christmas trees?" I asked.

"Dunno, I just do. Shocker, there's more to me than just lifting weights." He tried to make it sound like a joke.

"I know that," I shot back.

"Do you?"

He smiled as he said it, but something in his eyes told me that the question was half-serious. I would forever regret what

I'd said to him in the corn maze. But then again, he'd felt it even without me saying it out loud.

Andrew turned to me. "Is there a certain kind that you like?"

We'd always gotten the same type growing up since my dad was staunchly Team Fraser Fir, but for the past two years I'd wound up buying whatever sad Charlie Brown tree was left in the precut lot four days before Christmas. And this year, with Hurricane Edith in the house, I wasn't even sure if I should get a tree at all.

"I like symmetry. Tall and skinny, with nice long branches so I can load up the ornaments. But it can't be too big since my apartment is tiny."

He paused in front of another picture-perfect contender. "That's right, you're in that old building with the big round window."

"Yup, that's my apartment." I frowned as the realization struck me. "Wait, how do you know where I live?"

He shrugged and started walking again. "Nolan must've told me."

We dodged a little boy whose hat was falling off his head, trudging behind his parents and sister, crying that he was cold and wanted to go home.

Andrew chuckled then glanced at me. "Are you getting close to toddler meltdown status yet? I know I'm dragging you all over this place."

I shook my head vigorously. "Not at all. I like being out here."
With you.

The little boy's cries faded away and we were alone on the path, surrounded by pine trees of all shapes and sizes.

He tipped his head as he studied me. "But your cheeks are all pink. Your nose too. You sure you're not freezing?"

I barely felt the cold, especially with Andrew looking at me that way. "I wore layers."

"Of *course* you did." He chuckled and pulled a few needles off a nearby branch.

"I'm surprised you're even wearing a jacket."

"Oh, it'll come off once I start sawing, trust me."

"That's assuming you're going to find a tree. Because so far you're striking out." I gestured at the trees. "Trash, every last one of 'em. Absolute garbage. Disgusting."

His laughter echoed around us. "Okay, okay, I get it. I'm being too picky. You know what? *You* pick my tree."

My eyes went wide and I waved my hands in front of me. "Oh, no way. Too much responsibility. If I choose wrong I'll have to hear about it for weeks."

"Weeks?" He shook his head. "If you choose wrong I'll never let you forget it. Ten years from now I'll be reminding you of the time you made me get a Leyland cypress." He shuddered.

I felt a tiny surge of joy even though Andrew probably didn't catch the implication of what he'd said. Ten years. A lifetime. And we'd still be talking?

"I'm serious, Higs. You're picking." He pointed the end of his hacksaw at me. "You've got five minutes."

I narrowed my eyes at him. "Challenge accepted. Try to keep up."

I took off at a jog, scanning the trees as I passed them. I could hear him laughing behind me.

"I was kidding, you don't have to run."

"Nope," I shouted over my shoulder at him. "I figured you out. I know exactly what you want."

I skipped the rows of squat pine trees with fat branches, and the ones that were so tall that they could only fit in McMansions. I backed up cartoon-style when I came to the part of the field that had what I was looking for and headed down the narrow path to make my choice. Andrew caught up, but hung behind me as I scanned my options.

I stopped in front of *the* tree. "This one," I said confidently.

"Interesting." He adopted a thoughtful expression, like we were in a museum looking at a sculpture. "And why do you think so?"

"You said you don't like crowded branches, and this tree has some space in between them. You didn't like the blue spruce so I'm guessing you prefer a deeper green, which . . ." I gestured up and down the tree like a spokesmodel. "Plus, it's uniform, pleasingly plump, and still tall enough to look impressive in your house." I leaned closer and shoved my nose into the branches. "And it smells amazing."

Andrew stalked around the tree, taking it in from every angle. "There's a little bare spot back here."

"Are you putting it in the center of the room?"

"Of course not."

"Then put that part against the wall and no one will know. Come on, that's like Christmas Tree 101."

Andrew walked on down the row checking out the trees near the one I'd selected.

"Well?" I demanded, trying to shove down the feeling that he was judging me yet again, and of all things for a damn Christmas tree. "I picked a good one, right?"

He walked back and came to a stop right beside me, so close that our shoulders touched as we stared at the tree in question. "Yup. It's perfect. Thank you."

It was stupid to feel proud about the victory, but I did. It was the new and improved version of our old dynamic, where Andrew judged *and* complimented me.

"Let me get under there and start cutting." He pulled a pair of leather gloves out of his jacket pocket, then shrugged it off. "Just hold the trunk in the middle, okay?"

He made his way beneath the low branches and started sawing, slicing through the trunk so quickly that I barely had time to reach in to grab it before it started swaying. His chopping abilities had won him the tree in the first place; it shouldn't have been a surprise that he could slice through a live one too.

"Got it?"

"Yup!" I had a face full of pine branches, but I wasn't about to let go until he told me to. A second later the weight of the entire tree was falling through my clenched hand. I used all my strength to keep the awkward thing from toppling all the way over.

"Nice!" Andrew said as he stood up. "You *are* strong like ox."

His compliments weren't even really compliments, but they still made me feel warm inside. I could pick out a good Christmas tree and manage to keep it from falling over, be still my heart. But after feeling like I was never quite good enough I lapped up every morsel of his praise.

"Yeah, but . . ." I managed as I continued awkwardly hugging the tree.

"You can let go now."

I realized that he was going to drag it to the car and dropped it to the ground.

When we finally got back to the shed where the workers were wrapping the trees in mesh and saw the line ahead of us I realized that we'd be waiting for a while.

"Rush hour at the tree farm," Andrew said, nodding at the hustling workers.

"Yeah, probably not a great idea to come on a beautiful Saturday."

A teenager in overalls, a Nordic-looking hat, and braids walked over to us. "Would you like a ticket for your tree? That way you can get some hot chocolate instead of waiting in line."

She pointed down the lane to another shed, where people were sitting around a small bonfire in Adirondack chairs.

"Do you have time?" Andrew raised his eyebrows at me.

"I never say no to chocolate in any form."

She handed us what looked like a poker chip with a number and hung a corresponding chip on the tree. We headed down the lane toward the hut, serenaded by Bing Crosby and the occasional deli counter voice calling out tree numbers. All we needed were a few flurries and the whole scene would've been worthy of a movie.

"Look, they're leaving, grab their chairs," Andrew said, pointing to where a couple was vacating two prime spots close to the fire. "I'll go in and get drinks."

I hustled over and staked our claim. Sitting close to the fire made me realize that I'd been freezing the whole time but too busy enjoying myself for the cold to register. I wasn't nervous being around Andrew, at least not in the way I used to be, where I was always second-guessing myself. What I was feeling was something I'd forgotten I was even capable of: that buzzy, disorienting sensation of wanting to grin at the person I was with nonstop, because I just liked being near him.

Andrew came out of the hut carrying two steaming cups and a little brown bag. "These people really know how to open wallets. Between the tree concierge and all the snacks in there I might go broke." He sat down next to me and handed me a cup.

"At least the tree was free," I offered.

"Now hold on, I *earned* that thing. I paid for it in sweat."

I took a sip and considered it. "I guess you did."

"Here." He held out one of the little bags.

I peeked inside. "Christmas tree sugar cookies? And I thought this day couldn't get any better."

"Wow, you're easy to please." He bit his cookie in half.

A voice came over the loudspeaker. "Twenty-two is ready. Merry Christmas!"

The family next to us hopped up to claim their newly wrapped tree, leaving us alone at the edge of the bonfire. Andrew glanced around furtively.

"So . . . should we talk now?" he asked once he was satisfied that no one was in eavesdropping distance. "About Thanksgiving?"

The nervous anticipation that flared up inside of me felt a little like heartburn, a hot knife to the chest. "We probably should." I looked down and fiddled with my cup.

This wasn't going to be like the last time, where we left everything unspoken. We were going to hash it out and have some sort of resolution before we claimed the shrink-wrapped tree. I mentally scrolled through the possible outcomes and decided that there was no way he'd bring me to cheery Christmas-tree-land to tell me the kiss had been a mistake. That was a conversation for our parking lot, so we both could make a quick getaway. Then we could go back to scurrying into our respective businesses and pretending that we didn't see each other.

Based on the way he was looking at me, scurrying wasn't going to be an issue.

"I guess you could tell that I wanted it to happen." His serious expression finally cracked. "I was pretty obvious, huh?"

"In a good way," I reassured him quickly as my nerves settled a little.

"Yeah, but I probably should've found a better spot. I mean, the *goat* barn?"

"You saved me from the rain. I'd call that chivalrous."

Andrew cocked an eyebrow. "I like how you spin things." He downed the cup of hot chocolate like he was taking a shot of liquid courage. "So, I'm going to cut to the chase and put it all out there." He cleared his throat. "I'm not sure where *your* head is, but I had fun. And I'd like to continue having fun with you during the holidays. So if there's a way to make that happen, I'm all in."

Obviously I knew a declaration of love was off the table, but I wasn't quite sure what he meant by "fun." I craved something more descriptive than the "f" word he'd opted for. I wanted terms and conditions. Boundaries.

And maybe a few promises.

But then again, if I was honest with myself, after what had happened in the goat barn I was willing to accept any scrap Andrew was offering me. I wasn't proud of it, but I also wasn't going to deny myself what I'd wanted for longer than I was willing to admit. Plus, there was something to be said for the chance to head into the holidays with him by my side. And if there was anything I needed more of in my life, it was fun. Hanging out with Andrew basically guaranteed it.

He seemed very invested in turning his paper cup into origami as he waited for me to say something. When he finally looked up from the smashed cardboard I met his anxious expression with a smile.

"I'm in. Let's have fun."

chapter twenty-nine

I wasn't a fan of holiday shopping, but I loved the fact that I was doing it with Sam and Mia.

We were stealing as much time together as we could before they headed to Long Island to spend Christmas with her parents. We'd opted to visit the quaint river town across the bridge in New Jersey, hoping to finish up our Christmas lists under a blustery sky that promised snow. Mia was toddlering it up in our latest stop, a twee, breakable-filled housewares shop.

"Do you think Nolan's mom would like this?" Sam held up a navy polka-dot teapot, keeping one hand on Mia's stroller. "I brought her a bunch of stuff from Japan, but I feel like I need more."

I paused. "Does she drink tea?"

"Not sure, but maybe if she doesn't she'll start?" I stared at her for a beat and she let her shoulders sag. "You're right, you're right. Terrible idea."

"I'm sure whatever you brought is plenty. And you guys being here is gift enough."

"Aww." She jutted out her bottom lip in a pout. "I've missed you so much, Chels."

"Same. Plus, I love getting to spend time with *this* little one!" I squatted in front of the stroller so Mia and I could smile at each other. "She's amazing. But I still can't tell who she takes after. Her hair is so light."

"*Hmph.* Let's just hope she doesn't inherit her daddy's bad attitude." I glanced up at Sam, but she was busy flipping dessert plates over to check the prices. "What do you still need to get?"

"I'm basically done after everything I bought today." I gave Mia a final nose-wrinkling grin and stood up. "I need a little something for Taylor's husband, Ryan, that's it."

I was still grappling over whether I should buy a gift for Andrew as well, but I wasn't quite ready to commit either way. After all, I had no idea how the next few weeks before Christmas would unfold with him. Given our history, "fun" could blow up in our faces. Our next scheduled hang was helping him decorate his tree, which seemed safe enough. I knew better than to overthink the possibilities of what could happen between us during yet another rom-com setup.

I knew better, but that didn't mean I was completely successful at it.

Because we were going to be alone and I knew I wouldn't be able to resist him any longer.

I was jerked from my daydreams by the sound of Sam shrieking. "Mia, let go!"

Sam must not have realized that she'd parked the stroller right next to a Christmas tree decked out with hundreds of tiny porcelain forks, spoons, and knives. Mia had managed to grab a handful of them and was trying to yank them free, causing a symphony of clinking as the tree swayed back and forth. Sam wrenched them out of Mia's hand, closed her eyes, and huffed out a sigh.

"Can we please be done? I want food."

The desperation in her face triggered my protective instinct. Samantha was going through something and it wasn't just a busy toddler.

"Sure, let's go eat."

"And can we make sure they have alcohol? I'm not going to say I *need* a drink, but a drink would be really, really, really amazing."

Fifteen minutes later we were in a surprisingly good take on a British pub, ensconced in the world's coziest booth next to a crackling fire. Sam had begrudgingly let Mia put on headphones for some screen time so we could chat.

I watched her take a long drink from her pint. "Are you okay?"

She shrugged as she placed it on the table. "We'll get to me. You're up first. How is the holiday season going for you?"

"Fine?" Sam's furrowed brow suggested there was more to the question, but I wasn't sure what she was getting at. "Busy, the usual."

"No, I mean . . . everything." Her expression softened. "Your dad, Chels. I've been thinking about him. And you."

I fought against the surprising jolt of grief. Sam had only met him a few times, but she was well aware of what our relationship had been like. "I'm doing okay. I mean, I'll never stop missing him. The holidays are tough."

It was as much as I was willing to give, even with Sam.

She reached across the table to squeeze my hand. "Is it better or worse to talk about it? I don't want to upset you, but I want you to know that I'm here. Always have been."

A flash of pain shot through me at her admission. I knew it was true, but I'd pushed her away.

"Honestly? Right now I'd rather focus on you, because I can tell something is going on."

Plus, I didn't want to bring down the mood any more than it already was.

"Shit." Sam fell back against the booth looking drained. "It's that obvious?"

I reached for her this time as her eyes welled. "You're a pretty good actress, but I can see right through you. What's going on?"

Nat King Cole crooning "Merry Christmas to you" felt at odds with the cloud hanging over our table.

Sam glanced at Mia then back at me. "I'm just . . ." She bit her lip. "Overwhelmed. And lonely." The dam broke free and she gave in to silent tears. "Japan is *hard*. Nolan works so much and when he's home he's exhausted. We've been fighting." She let out one of those shuddery, heartbreaking sighs that signified more was being left unsaid. "And I don't know many people, so it's basically just me and Mia. I feel like an asshole because it's a great opportunity for Nolan. And obviously I adore her." She nodded toward her daughter. "But being back here is making me realize how lonely I am."

I knew that if we'd been alone Sam would have entered ugly-cry territory by this point. I reached across the table to grab her hand. "I'm so sorry. Why didn't you call me?"

She made a sweeping gesture to convey the chasm that had grown between us, which made me well up too. "At least I know when I go back I can. That helps."

The server showed up with our appetizer, forcing Sam to fake it so Mia wouldn't notice she was upset. True to form, she managed a gorgeous smile for the waiter despite her damp eyes.

"Anyway." She grabbed a pita chip and dug it into the guac. "It's a lot, you know? But I'll figure it out."

Mia stood up on the booth and reached for a chip, nearly toppling her water glass over. Sam caught it just in time.

"What can I do to help?" I asked, mopping up the water that splashed out. "I'm a great babysitter. Want me to hang with her for a few hours next week?"

"That's sweet of you to offer." Sam gave me a grateful smile. "I think Nolan's mom would kill me if I left her with anyone else. She's practically mainlining this child so she gets her fill before we go back."

"I don't blame her. She's amazing."

We both stared at Mia while she munched on a chip. I still couldn't believe that the woman I'd watched do body shots on top of a dirty bar was a mom.

"Okay, would you distract me, please," Sam begged as she tried to keep Mia from throwing ripped-up bits of napkin on the floor. "How's your love life?"

I took a suspiciously heaping bite of chip and guacamole to buy myself a few seconds while Sam studied me.

"Something's going on. I can tell by your face."

"What? I'm chewing." I pointed to my overfull mouth. I managed to smile at her and she crowed victoriously.

"I *knew* it! You have that freshly fucked glow!" She slapped her hand over her mouth and looked down at Mia, who was mashing pita chips with the wrong end of a fork.

"Oh, hold on, I absolutely do not." I paused to prepare myself for the epic play-by-play to come once I told her. "So have you heard anything about the goats?"

"I was right! The second I heard you were training his mom's goats I knew something was up." Sam rocked back and forth like she was putting the final pieces of a mystery together. Mia stared up at her with a worried expression. "He's been all cagey with Nolan, and you two were acting so formal the other night. Like you were strangers in line at the grocery store. I *told* Nolan I thought something was going on, but he didn't think so. He said Andrew would've told him. When did it happen?"

It took me a second to process the fact that Andrew hadn't said anything to Nolan. I knew the guys didn't gossip like me and Sam, but they were tight enough that he could've mentioned it.

I laughed at Sam's serious expression. "Are you okay? I mean, do you need a minute to process?"

"Well, yeah. This is how many years in the making?"

I shrugged. "You need to know that 'this'"—I made air quotes—"is nothing official, okay? We agreed to have fun, that's it. No promises."

She scanned me. "And you're okay with that?"

"I don't think he's capable of much more, so, yeah."

She frowned at me. "Are you forgetting his two-year relationship with Zadie? He's not afraid of long-term, Chels."

As much as I didn't like thinking about Zadie, she *was* proof of his ability to commit to someone. Not that that was what I needed from him, but still.

"Well, that's not where we are, so whatever." I fiddled with a chip. "And I'm fine with it."

Sam pulled the goat barn details out of me and wound up

fanning herself by the end, despite my euphemisms to keep the story acceptable for young ears. Confiding in Sam felt like old times. I didn't realize how much I'd missed it, and her.

The sensation crept up on me. That warm, buzzy feeling of the magic in mundanity. We were just two old friends catching up, so why did it feel special? Maybe it was the midday beer, or the crackling warmth of the fireplace, or the pine tree with white lights glittering in the corner. I'm sure the holiday sound-track helped too. It was still early enough in the season that I wasn't sick of "Last Christmas" yet. It all added up to a moment I wished I could bottle up and then drink down the next time I was feeling sorry for myself.

Sam moved the guacamole farther away from Mia and of-fered her the tablet again. She waited until Mia had the head-phones back on before she started talking. "I know you probably thought I was going to freak out when you told me, and I totally am on the inside, but I'm not going to meddle." I laughed at her and her face fell. "What? I'm serious. Nolan and I would love to couple hang with the two of you before we leave for Long Island, but if you guys are opting to keep it strictly horizontal I respect that. *You* tell *me* how you want things to go."

I drained the rest of my beer as I considered how to answer her, because the truth was even I didn't know what I expected from the little "fun" pact with Andrew. I mean, if I was honest with myself I knew what I hoped for, deep down. But it wasn't on the table. "Fun" was, and I had to be fine with it.

"I'm going to his place tonight to help decorate his tree, so I'll let you know if I foresee any ice skating double dates in our future."

"His place? Just the two of you? Boom-*chicka*—" Sam stopped herself and slapped her hand over her mouth for the second time. "Sorry, old habits." She sat up straighter and folded her hands on the table primly. "I hope you two enjoy the pleasure of one another's company as you bedeck his tree."

"Thank you."

"And make sure to take special care of his Christmas balls, Miss Higgins. I do hope Santa won't be the only one coming."

"Sam!"

Mia's eyes jumped between us as we collapsed into giggles.

chapter thirty

"What's all of this?"

Andrew grabbed two overfilled bags from my hands and stepped back to welcome me into his place.

"You said you don't have many decorations so I figured I'd help so your tree doesn't look pathetic. I mean, unless you're going for a minimalistic vibe."

I stomped the dusting of snow from my boots before going in. I'd expected to feel nervous when I walked through his door because even though I was there to decorate, the real goal for getting together on a cold winter night was clear to both of us. We were going to see *exactly* how much fun we could have together in as many different ways as possible. I mean, I'd worn my cutest bra and panty set so they could be enjoyed. As I crossed the threshold all I felt was . . . right.

Within a few seconds I heard the sound of paws racing toward me and I braced for impact. Instead, Dude came to a screeching stop and folded himself into a quivering sit in front of me.

"Wow!" I flashed the "yes" hand signal at him and dug a treat out of my pocket.

"We've been practicing, Teach," Andrew said. "Wait till you see his recall."

I kicked off my boots, then dug through my bag and handed Dude a giant bone that I hoped would keep him occupied for the whole night.

The tree I'd picked for Andrew was in a place of honor in front of the picture window that faced out to the fields in back, already decked out in tiny white lights. There was a fire burning because of course there was. He had music playing low and I gave him points for opting for something chill and loungy instead of Christmas music. There was no way to feel sexy listening to "Mele Kalikimaka."

"You didn't have to buy stuff for me," he sputtered as he walked the bags over to the tree.

"Oh, I didn't. I used to do a different Christmas color scheme every year at Frolic and these are leftovers from the past few years."

"You don't have any decorations up at Frolic yet." He frowned as he took a box from my arms. "Are you going to decorate soon?"

I was the one who'd kept it minimalistic for the past few Christmases, sticking with a dog bone wreath on the door and a few sad garlands inside. But this year I could feel the old creative holiday magic taking hold of me again. Granted, it was later in the season than normal, but not too late to help my students feel merry while they learned "sit," "down," and "come."

"Yup, I'll get it all done this week. But we're not here to worry about me. *You're* the one with the naked tree." I felt heat rush to my face at my word choice.

"Not for long," he said, gesturing to the bags and boxes at his feet. "Thank you, I really appreciate all of this."

When he looked at me I realized that the Gibson Glare was long gone, replaced by something that sent a wave of warmth through my chest. *This* was his weapon, the look that made me feel like I was the most beautiful woman he'd ever seen and he couldn't bear to glance away from me. No wonder his body count was so high. Who could resist a man capable of making you feel cherished with just a glance?

I wanted him so badly that I was having trouble focusing on anything else. After the way things had ended all those years ago I'd never imagined that we'd be here, but the truth was, deep down I'd always hoped we'd find a way. After hating him for so long I considered it my dirty secret, something I could barely admit to myself. And here we were, talking about Christmas decorations like we both didn't know that the night would end with both of us naked.

I cleared my throat and tried to be present instead of thinking about ripping his hoodie off. "Happy to help. After all, I picked that tree. Gotta make sure it looks amazing, to make up for that unsightly bald patch."

He laughed. "Yeah, the deer and rabbits outside have been complaining about it." Andrew headed for the kitchen. "Let's eat first. I made soup."

Yet another shocking discovery in the man I thought I had all figured out. "Wait, you *cook*?"

He moved to the stovetop on the kitchen island and lifted the lid off a large pot, looking at me through the steam. "Of course. Doesn't everybody?"

"Smells really good," I said, breathing in a slightly nutty aroma. "What is it?"

"Mushroom soup." He pivoted to look in the oven. "And bread that I almost forgot about."

If I could've melted into a pile of lovesick goo at that moment I would've. Bread? Bread took planning. It meant he'd put forethought into our meal. He'd bought *yeast*.

"Don't be too impressed," he said as if he could feel the swoon rolling off me like mist on a morning lake. "It's four ingredients and you don't have to knead it."

"Too late. My jaw is on the floor."

He put on the world's unlikeliest oven mitt, a bright red thing with a gnome on it, and pulled out a loaf pan that had a mound of golden crust peeking over the top. "Perfect. Would you like honey butter or regular?"

I slapped the counter. "Stop it. Butter choices? What are you trying to do to me?"

He laughed and the rumbly timbre filled the room. "If it's that easy to make you happy then I've got nothing to worry about."

Once again he didn't seem to realize what he was saying. He wanted to make me happy? After years of sniping, it was something I needed to train myself to believe. But it *wasn't* hard to believe that he'd be good at it. Because Andrew Gibson was good at everything.

"I feel bad I didn't bring anything to contribute," I said, the dinner party training my mom had instilled nagging at me.

"Excuse me?" He pointed at the plastic bags and boxes at the foot of his Christmas tree. "Anyway, this was easy."

I watched him fill two mismatched bowls and realized that the meal was vegetarian. Had I told him that I was veg?

"Let's eat on the couch, these chairs are awful." He nodded toward the two hard stools in front of the island.

I grabbed my bowl along with two slices of warm bread and then followed him to the couch. Despite the fact that Andrew and I were about to eat dinner he'd *cooked for me*, with his own hands, it all felt shockingly normal. Like it was something we'd done before even though the closest we'd come to sharing a solo meal was the time Nolan left the dining hall early and we were stuck glaring at each other across the table for four minutes until I couldn't take it and walked away.

Dude eyed us from his bed as he gnawed on his bone. Andrew settled in on the couch, kicked his feet up on the coffee table, and let out a contented groan. "Perfect."

I tucked myself in the opposite corner and drew my legs up beneath me. "What is?"

"This." He made a vague gesture around the room. "A fire. Good food. Excellent company. There's no better feeling."

"I never took you for a homebody," I laughed. "The Andrew I knew considered every night a Friday night."

He pulled the spoon from his mouth slowly, his eyes locked on mine. "Then maybe you didn't know the real me."

The intensity in his expression sent a shudder up my spine. Of *course* I knew the real Andrew. He was the life of the party, always the first one on the dance floor, who tormented everyone else into joining him. He knew which songs to program on the jukebox to get the crowd singing. Open mic night? The guy could do a ten-minute riff on his professors that left people rolling. Whoever this cozy-vibes person was sitting on the couch across from me was an imposter for the real Andrew Gibson.

"Okay, help me understand, then. What's a typical night for you like these days?" I took a mouthful of soup and let out my own groan of satisfaction. "Hold on, do I taste truffle oil?"

He grinned at me and nodded. "Yeah, you do. But you know it's all fake, right?"

I frowned but didn't stop shoveling the soup into my mouth.

"You can't buy real truffle oil at the grocery store. It's all olive oil that's flavored with an organosulfur compound, not real truffles."

"Look at you with the ten-dollar word!" I laughed.

His mouth went tight for a millisecond. "Yeah, I'm full of surprises."

I realized my mistake too late and tried to recover. "Anyway, you were going to tell me what you do for fun these days."

He was already scraping the bottom of his bowl. "Work, obviously. You get it. Entrepreneur life is twenty-four/seven. I don't go out much. Most of my high school friends left Millville, and I don't know many people in Wismer yet. I mean, I know my clients, but there's a tricky balance. Can't cross any professional boundaries, you know? So I work, I hang out with Dude"—he gestured to his dog, who was nose-deep in bone rapture—"I cook a little. I read." He shrugged. "Lame."

"Are you me? That's pretty much my life." I ripped off a hunk of bread and dipped it in the soup. "What are you reading? Grisham? Clancy?"

He furrowed briefly, another microexpression that let me know exactly what he thought about them without saying anything. "I finished the entire George R. R. Martin series and now I'm on a nonfiction kick. I'm reading about the science of the placebo effect. It's so cool."

"Tell me the most interesting factoid about it." I licked a dollop of melted honey butter off my fingertip.

"I've been fascinated by the placebo effect forever. It plays a *huge* role in what I do. It's not exactly the same thing, but if I tell you to 'drag' a weight down it'll get a different response than if I say 'pull.' You'll fatigue faster if I say 'drag.' We have no clue how much power we have up here"—he tapped the side of his head—"and what we could do if we really put it to work."

"Speaking of dragging and pulling, I'm ready to get back to Crush. We never scheduled my second session." I never imagined that I'd willingly subject myself to weightlifting, but I suddenly wanted to be anywhere Andrew was.

"Seriously? I thought you were lying about wanting to come back. I was sure that you were one and done. Honestly, I was a little insulted that you practically ran out of our first session."

I shrank down into the corner of the couch. "I was, um, having a hard time following everything."

"Well, shit. Was I going too fast? Or was it confusing? I need your feedback because if you were having a hard time as a beginner then I guarantee some of my other new clients are too."

He almost looked nervous as he waited for me to respond. I needed Andrew to understand that it had nothing to do with his teaching skills and everything to do with *me*. I pushed myself to say it out loud as butterflies crowded my heart.

Andrew had moved his empty bowl to the coffee table and was facing me with his arms crossed tightly over his chest, waiting for my critique. His anxious expression sent a hairline fracture through my heart, so I took a breath and forced myself to speak. "Your instruction was perfect. You made me feel like I could bench-press a billion pounds. You're phenomenal at your job, but when you touched me, all I could think of was doing this."

I stood up and then eased myself onto his lap, silencing my nerves as my body came to rest straddling his. Andrew's expression shifted from concern to amazement as he unfurled his arms and placed welcoming hands on my hips. I trembled when his thumbs brushed against my skin where my shirt had come untucked.

He looked like he couldn't believe what was happening, and that he wasn't quite sure what I was going to do next. He'd always been the aggressor and I was the rabbit trapped in his snare, but this time I was the one calling the shots. My breathing went shallow as I enjoyed the power of sitting on top of him, even though it felt like I was sitting on a steel beam and all it would take was a bump of his hip to bounce me off. I'd lived this scenario in my head a million times, where I followed through with what I'd missed out on all those years ago on the boat.

That's why it felt both natural and terrifying as I leaned closer to him and finally placed my lips against his.

chapter thirty-one

He let me lead, at least for a little while.

I sat on top of Andrew and kissed him like it was a welcome-home after a tour at sea. It felt effortless, the way we fit together. With some kisses there was the awkward dance of which way to angle your head, or that sinking feeling of mismatched pressure and speed, but Andrew and I always seemed to find a perfect rhythm immediately whether we were drunk in a closet or fighting off goats.

My fingers danced over the contours of his face and found their way into that hair. I pulled the little rubber band out and coaxed it free, running my fingertips along his scalp. He made a satisfied noise against my mouth that sounded like victory to me. I wanted to see what he looked like all tousled and undone, but I was afraid to stop kissing him, worried that the spell would be broken yet again. But this time we were alone, in his perfect little house with a fire crackling a few feet away, speeding toward the inevitable. I'd always thought that when it finally happened Andrew and I would crash into each other with all of the angry, pent-up emotions that had kept us in a decade-long sniper war. But what we were doing felt . . . *tender*.

I arched my back so that I could press my chest against his and claim more of him as we kissed. His hands moved from my waist to my back, leaving a trail of hot embers behind. I squeezed my thighs against his and felt his hardness through the jeans he'd mercifully worn that night. If he'd been in those damn sweatpants I'd probably already be pregnant.

Andrew's mouth was gentle, tasting me, teasing me back, leaving me feeling like I couldn't quite catch my breath. I wasn't sure I could last just making out, because I'd been imagining the rest of it for too long, and I didn't want to wait any longer.

His kisses strayed from my lips to trail along my cheek, up to my ear, where he nibbled my lobe, giving it a gentle, tugging suck that set off sparklers in my spine. I remembered what that tongue was capable of and I was more than ready to let it wander anywhere it wanted on my body. I ground against him to let him know.

He pulled back, ever so slightly but still too much for my liking, and his eyes swept around my face, trying to read my expression.

"What?" I breathed, worried that he'd changed his mind and I was about to be banished to the purgatory of wanting him.

He reached up to cup my cheek and my heart swelled from the tenderness of it. There was that look in his eyes again, the one that made me feel precious. "I'm just really, really happy you're here," he said, his voice husky.

"Me too," I whispered back.

His palms scorched the tops of my thighs as we drank each other in. It was like we needed a moment before we let our bodies take the lead again, to make sure that both of our defini-tions of "fun" included what was about to happen. Andrew's hand trailed up my back to the nape of my neck and he gently moved me closer until our eyes were locked and our mouths were hovering just inches apart. It still felt a little reckless, like we were breaking some unwritten rule about keeping a safe dis-tance from one another. My breathing went shallow as I waited for his next move.

"Are you ready?" he asked, his voice a raspy whisper.

I wasn't sure what he meant, but I nodded wordlessly as a wave of goose bumps rippled along my skin.

Andrew quickly slid one hand behind my shoulders and the other under my ass, then stood up abruptly, as if I was nothing more than a throw pillow. He muffled my laugh with a hungry kiss, and didn't stop as he walked us past the kitchen and down a hallway. I locked my legs behind his lower back and tightened my arms around his neck as our mouths crashed together. My entire body hummed with the knowledge of what we were about to do, that the torture of secretly wanting him was about to end once and for all.

The hallway was dark and the next thing I knew he'd kicked open a door and was heading for the bed in a dimly lit room. He lowered me onto it slowly, never taking his lips from mine. I clung to him for as long as possible because I didn't want to let go of him for even a few seconds. Once I was flat on the bed he stood over me, his eyes raking down my body.

For the first time ever, I *loved* the way it felt to have him star-ing at me.

He reached down to pull open the button on the top of my jeans, unzipped the zipper, then tried tugging them off of me, nearly wrenching me from the bed, as if he didn't know his own strength. I rolled onto my side as the giggles overtook me.

"I'm usually way more suave than this," he said, laughing at himself. "You make me feel . . . I don't know . . ."

I sat up when I saw the tension in his face. "What?"

"You make me feel *nervous*. That's not normal for me."

It was impossible for me to believe or respond to. How could anything about me make the mighty Andrew Gibson nervous? He sat down on the bed next to me and it sagged beneath his weight. His thigh brushed against mine and suddenly my mind was off and running with visions of stripping him naked.

"C'mere," I said, grabbing a fistful of his shirt and wrenching him closer to me. "Let's see what we can do about those nerves." I laughed as I said it because the thought of it was so unbelievable to me.

And with that we were back in the moment, getting lost in each other as our tongues explored. Andrew pulled me to my feet, pulling my jeans down as we kissed. He broke away to strip them off me and was already reaching for my ass as I stepped out of them.

"Have I ever told you how much I appreciate this thing?" His voice was muffled against the side of my neck. He cupped my ass with both hands and gave it a light squeeze.

Another bombshell as I tried to remain upright. "I don't believe you."

"That's because you were always walking the other way when I was staring at it." He pulled away from me to lean down and bite a cheek. The feeling of his teeth grazing my skin sent shock waves through me. "It's even better than I remembered."

I took advantage of the fact that we weren't kissing to pull my sweater over my head, leaving me standing in front of him in just my pale pink silk bra, panties, and ridiculous white socks.

"*Shit.*"

It came out in a whisper. Between the way he said it and the awestruck look on his face I knew that there was no higher praise. I swallowed hard as warmth spread in my chest. I straightened my back and thrust out my breasts to encourage more of his admiration.

"This body." His low voice rumbled through me. "I remember this body." He took a step closer and placed two fingertips at the hollow of my throat then traced a serpentine line down my chest. He circled around each breast, slowing down as he ran his thumb over the hard peaks of my nipples beneath the silk. His touch was so light that it almost tickled as he moved down my body to my stomach, before coming to a stop between my legs, cupping me gently. It took everything in my power not to grind against his hand.

I leaned closer and felt his chest go slightly concave as I bit his lobe then planted kisses down the side of his neck. It was like a competition to see who could make the other unhinge faster, and I was losing. His mouth found mine and I was drowning in him again.

"Why are you still wearing clothes?" I whispered with my mouth pressed to his ear.

A beat. Two, as one of his hands resumed mapping my body and the other traced me through the thin fabric of my underwear. Even that faint touch was enough to send pulses of pleasure through me.

"Hm?" he asked, not hearing me as his fingertips moved

closer to the edge of my panties. My breath hitched as he started making a circular pattern against me.

If I didn't move now I knew I'd be powerless from his touch, and I needed him to be naked. I didn't bother repeating myself, cursing the fact that I had to move a few inches away from him in order to grab the hem of his shirt and pull it over his head.

I stepped away to study him before he could put his hands back on my body. The first thing I realized when I saw his bare torso was how unfair it was that he looked like that. Not a freckle or blemish on his skin, just endless, muscled perfection, with a sprinkling of hair along his pecs. My next thought was how badly I wanted to feel him on top of me.

It must have struck both of us at the same moment because as I raced to unfasten my bra, roll down my panties, and kick off my socks, Andrew ripped off his pants and shoes. I reached for him, to help him get out of his briefs, but he leaned away from me to his discarded pants then fished through his pockets. He tossed a condom on the nightstand then froze once he saw that I was naked.

"Oh, Chelsea," he said softly. "You are *so* amazing." He shook his head, the awe right there on his face.

Tears sprang to my eyes at the emotion in his voice, but there was no time for me to get overcome by it all because Andrew swept me up in his arms and deposited me in the middle of his bed.

"Naked," I gasped. It was the only word I could manage as I pointed to the briefs he was still wearing.

He gave me a wicked grin and bent over to pull them off. I'd *thought* I had a good memory of his entire body, but when he stood up I realized that I'd been underappreciating him.

He grabbed the condom and slid it on while I watched him.

"Hurry."

I didn't care that I sounded a little desperate, I was tired of waiting for him.

He eased himself onto the bed then took my hand to pull me on top of him so I was straddling him. I raised myself up on my knees, poised to take him in, but he held me in place while his other hand slipped down between my legs. Every nerve ending jolted to life as he found my heat. I leaned forward to rest my hands on his chest as he teased me with soft circles then slipped a finger inside of me. I wanted to move closer to him, to kiss his beautiful mouth, but I was too paralyzed by pleasure to do anything but pray he wouldn't stop.

Even with my eyes closed I could sense him watching me as he caressed me, but I welcomed it. I *wanted* Andrew to see what he did to me.

"So perfect . . ." he whispered.

He brought me so close to the brink with just his fingertips that my whole body quivered. It was as if he already knew my little noises and trembles well enough to understand when I was about to let go. He pulled his hand away and paused for a few agonizing seconds, making me cry out in frustration, then rocked into me with a single swift push. Andrew inhaled sharply as he buried himself in my warmth.

Everything around us seemed to shift into slow motion as a moment of tender acknowledgment passed between us. After so long we were finally here. Together. Connected.

And it felt even more perfect than I'd imagined.

Our eyes met as Andrew started moving beneath me, slow and rhythmic while his thumb worked its magic. I was close, so close, and he knew it, teasing me with his pace and pressure. It wasn't long before my head fell back and otherworldly sounds came roaring out of me. When I opened my eyes he was smiling at me, devilish, and hungry for more. Andrew shifted me gently as the aftershocks rolled through my body, and the next thing I realized I was beneath him with one leg hooked behind his back. He pushed into me again with a groan, then rocked against me, and it was my turn to watch him. His eyes were squeezed shut like he was concentrating, until he seemed to sense the weight of my gaze.

"I can't wait ... I'm sorry ..." he rasped in a frustrated voice, staring into my eyes.

"Let go," I whispered, reaching up to cup his cheek.

He undulated against me, rolling and graceful, until I felt his body go tense.

"Chelsea ..." he gasped then collapsed on top of me, shuddering.

For a long time, our heavy breathing was the only sound in the room. His hand strayed to rest on my hip, and mine fell against his warm shoulder. It was as if we each needed a physical reminder that we were both still there.

Andrew finally pulled away, then raised himself up on his elbows and looked down at me. "Worth the wait," he said softly, then frowned at me. "No, actually we should've been doing that for ages."

"I agree," I managed as he rolled away and took care of the condom. I still wasn't in full control of my body and my limbs felt numb. "That's *exactly* the kind of fun we should be having."

He moved closer to me and pulled the blanket over us, then wrapped his arms around me. "Gimme fifteen minutes and I promise you, there's more fun on the way."

chapter thirty-two

We never got around to decorating Andrew's tree that night.

By the time we'd finally untangled from each other it was late. Dude needed to go out, and I had to get home to Birdie and Edith. We'd kept it casual as I gathered my things to go, but it felt like there was a blinking neon sign between us advertising "live nude fun."

I'd felt nervous as Andrew walked me to the door. Was he going to give me a high five? A hug? What were we to each other? I'd forced myself to repeat a mantra: *we're having fun, we're having fun, we're having fun.* Maybe if I said it enough I'd figure out what we meant by it?

The goodbye issue was settled when I paused at the door to pet Dude. The moment I'd straightened up Andrew had gently grasped my shoulders, pulled me to him, and planted a kiss on my lips that almost had me dragging him back to the bedroom.

Focusing on my classes the following day was all but impossible. My three privates had gone well enough, but by the afternoon I kept glancing out the door for glimpses of Andrew. I'd seen him walk by with Dude and I was tempted to go out and say hi, but I wasn't sure if we were at the I-wanted-to-see-your-face-so-I-ran-out-into-the-cold-without-a-jacket-and-oh-God-I-really-want-to-kiss-you-now stage. We'd texted, but we were both busy and more importantly, we didn't owe each other anything anyway.

Just fun.

I'd finished my day with my intermediate class, which was a cakewalk filled with overachievers on both ends of the leash. I was on autopilot the entire time, but not a single student was aware of the fact that I couldn't stop thinking about what had happened the night before, and my intense need for it to happen again.

Although I'd have to wait at least until tomorrow.

"Dinner's here!"

My mom's voice echoed around Frolic, and Edith took off for her.

"Please don't let her jump on you!" I warned. "We're working on polite greetings."

I jogged over to them and Edith was spinning in happy circles but not jumping, which was good enough for me. There was something about my mom that all dogs loved. Even ones passing her on the street turned to watch her walk by like the cheating boyfriend in the meme. When I got to them she was greeting Edith with one hand while holding a pizza box up with the other.

"Thanks for bringing it, I'm starving."

"I'm so excited to decorate with you," she said, stepping over Edith, who managed to place her body exactly where my mom was trying to walk. "Thank you for inviting me."

We leaned into a hug and kiss and did the usual compliment inventory on each other's clothing and hair before moving on to her visions for Frolic. No one loved decorating for the holidays more than my mom. She switched out the wreath on the front door for the nondominant ones like July 4th and Valentine's Day, but every other holiday was Manhattan Macy's-window-level decorating. I'd told her that I had everything I needed yet I could guarantee that there was a box sitting in the back of her car ready to be called into service.

I gave Edith a new bully stick and we spread out the pizza box on the table just outside my office. "What would you like to drink? I've got water or beer."

My mom shimmied her shoulders and grinned at me. "I'd love to have a beer with my daughter."

I laughed. Her favorite thing in the world was hanging with me and Taylor. As we ate I explained the logistics of my decorating scheme, which was basically "multicolored explosion" since I hadn't picked a real theme this year.

"That's going to be lovely," she said. "And I have some ideas as well. I brought a box—"

"Of course you did," I laughed and she gave me a guilty shrug.

She caught me up on the latest home renovation gossip from Taylor's kitchen and the state of the union between the parents-to-be, as well as the latest from her book club. We were so focused on deciding if her friend Louise, who never read any of the books, should still be invited to come when there was a knock at my door, then a voice.

"Hello? You still here?"

My heart seized. Andrew.

"Yup, in back, with my *mom*." I put emphasis on the word so he wouldn't yell anything inappropriate about what he wanted to do to me, even though I was curious about the possibilities.

Edith careened toward him with the bone hanging out of her mouth like a cigar and I heard his voice go up as he greeted her.

"Neighbor Andrew?" my mom whispered.

I nodded, trying to remain nonchalant.

Her mouth went into an O of recognition and my heart dropped to my feet. The timing was all wrong. We'd just had sex *last night* and I hadn't talked to him in person since.

He came around the corner looking absolutely devastating and immediately focused on my mom. "Hi, Mrs. Higgins, I'm Andrew. We met years ago, but you probably don't remember."

"Of course I do," she fussed as she reached out to shake his hand. "You and Nolan are friends. It's so nice to see you again. And please, call me Joan."

"Joan," he said with a nod. He turned to me and gave me a smile that sent a zing of happiness through me. "Hi."

Everything about the moment felt important and I was totally unprepared. I mean, did people who were just having fun introduce their fun-partner to their parents? But I already knew Pat and Gerard so I guess it leveled the playing field for him to meet my mom.

I realized that they were both staring at me. "Um, we're decorating!"

"After we eat," my mom added so my non sequitur made sense. "Please join us, there's still plenty."

Andrew watched me for a beat and I felt my face getting hot remembering the night before. "Would you mind?"

I shook my head and did an embarrassingly flourishy gesture to the extra chair at the end of the table. "Please."

I felt awkward and obvious, like I was back in high school again and trying to hide hickeys from my mom. But they didn't seem to notice my nerves as they chattered about the best places to get pizza.

"I totally forgot my whole reason for stopping by," Andrew said, finally looking away from my mom. "Mike texted me about bringing someone to look at the property after hours tonight, around nine. This is the second time the person is coming, so it sounds like they're serious."

"Oh, is this about someone buying the building?" my mom asked as she took a demure sip of beer.

"Yeah, unfortunately," Andrew said. He tossed his crust on the paper plate in front of him. "Can anyone think of a way to sabotage the place so they won't want it?"

My mom pressed on even though I was sure she could feel me shooting laser eyes at her. "Did they say what they want to do with the building?"

He shook his head. "No. It feels like things are starting to move faster now, though. I'm getting worried."

"Andrew signed a month-to-month lease because Mike is the literal worst," I explained, giving the situation more air than I was comfortable with. "That way the building looks more attractive to potential buyers. They have Roz's space open in the middle so they could keep it or jack up the rent and try to find a tenant, then there's me anchoring this spot for the next year and a half, and if they want to they can keep Andrew or kick him out immediately."

"That's awful," she said as she looked back and forth between us. "And you just opened. What are you going to do?"

"Mom," I said sharply. "That's a big question, let's keep it light, okay?"

"No, it's fine," Andrew said. "I've been looking around and

there's nothing comparable. I'll definitely have to downsize. And I'm trying not to think about relocation expenses. It's basically a nightmare."

A shadow passed over his face, but I knew better than to ask if something else was going on with him.

"What a predicament," my mom said. "I'm so sorry to hear it, Andrew."

"Thanks." He reached down to pet Edith, who'd materialized beneath the table.

She shot me a questioning look and I shook my head at her, widening my eyes menacingly. There was no *way* we were going to get into the possibility of me buying the building in front of Andrew. She sighed and took another sip of beer.

"Anyway, would you like to come see it, before I have to shut it all down?"

"Stop," I said to Andrew, more forcefully than I'd meant to. "That's not going to happen."

"She's right," my mom added. "Maybe you'll get lucky and someone wonderful will buy the building."

I glared at my mom, but she pretended not to notice.

"Let's hope. I could use a Christmas miracle." He stood up. "Shall we?"

As expected, Andrew made my mom fall in love with him. Her newfound gym enthusiasm combined with his understanding of the senior brain meant that he had her hoisting free weights six minutes after she walked into the place. Edith and I stood by and watched as he showed her how to use a foam roller to treat her lower back pain.

"I love it here," my mom exclaimed as the tour and mini

workout came to an end. "Do you have people my age training with you?"

"I do. My clients range from eighteen to eighty-five."

My mom glanced around the place again. "If I didn't have my exercise ladies over at Wismer Fit I'd come work out here. You are *so* knowledgeable, Andrew!"

The man had the audacity to blush and bob his head at my mom. "I appreciate that, thank you."

He walked us to the door as my mom kept talking about how wonderful Crush was. She reached for Edith's leash. "I'll give her a quick potty break."

She speed-walked into the cold night, leaving us alone.

"I think she suspects something," Andrew said as he watched her disappear into the darkness.

"That we had sex?" I screeched in horror.

He laughed at me like I'd said something adorable. "No. That we've been hanging out."

How did hanging out relate to fun?

Andrew grabbed my belt loop and pulled me closer. "Hopefully she had no clue that I ravished her daughter just last night," he whispered, his breath hot against my ear. "And I can't wait to do it again."

My knees just about gave out when he placed his finger under my chin and lifted it, quickly grazing his lips across mine. He stepped away from me and his posture shifted back to friendly neighbor.

"Hey, have fun decorating tonight!" he said in an exuberant voice, making me realize that he could see my mom heading back from the grassy patch with Edith.

"Th-thanks," I stuttered and flapped my hand in an approximation of a wave as I tripped back to my side of the building.

I met up with her and we walked back to my door.

"I like him," she said, glancing up at me. "He has such a nice way about him. And *handsome*."

For the first time I could commiserate with a victim of his charms.

"Yup, he's great," I answered simply as I held the door open for her. "Anyway, let's get to work."

An hour and a half later the School of Frolic had been transformed into a dog-friendly, Seussian wonderland. We'd strung up faux evergreen garlands wrapped with multicolored lights, decorated my tabletop tree with so many bulbs that the branches sagged, and even hung up a ball of mistletoe near the door.

"Beautiful," my mom said with an approving nod.

It felt strange seeing the place all decked out after keeping it bare-bones. I realized how much I'd missed getting into the holiday spirit.

"Well, we didn't need my box after all, but let me bring it in for you, just in case."

"Mom, no, don't worry about it . . ."

But she was already heading for the door. When she returned I was shocked to see her carrying a much smaller box than I'd been expecting.

"Since you're all done here maybe you can use these in your apartment?"

I placated her as she gathered her things to go. I still wasn't sure if I was going to do any decorating at home. We hugged our goodbye as Edith did her barky commentary about affection that didn't directly involve her. When we pulled apart my mom stared at me for a beat.

"You seem really happy. And that makes me happy too."

I blushed. Of *course* she could pick up on the butterflies Andrew kept releasing in my chest. Her ability to read people, me and Taylor in particular, was one of her many gifts.

She was halfway out the door when she paused. "I put a little something for you in the box, right on top. I hope you'll appreciate it."

Once she'd left I hurried around the building to close up so I wouldn't be there when the potential buyer arrived. The box she'd brought was sitting half-open on the back table so I peeked in to make sure she hadn't left something edible for me, like a peppermint cupcake. I pulled out a small black box that was nestled on top of a Christmas tree skirt and opened it.

I felt a stone form in my chest when I saw what was inside. It was the ornament, our family joke. I'd made it when I was in grade school, a clay monstrosity of a star covered in red glitter with a photo decoupaged on it. We'd stopped hanging it on the tree at least ten years ago because the piece of yarn on the top had disintegrated, but it had a place of honor on the bookcase every season.

I moved to the light to study it even though I remembered every detail of the image plastered to it. It was a photo of me and my dad, hugging cheek to cheek. His eyes were closed and I was smiling the biggest, cheesiest grin that showed off a missing front tooth. I looked absolutely deranged because the photo had been taken at a neighborhood party and I was high on too many brownies. My dad looked overjoyed with his arms wrapped around me. I could almost feel the weight of them as the tears started.

The me of six months ago would've stashed the box in a storage closet until I forgot about it.

I took it home.

chapter thirty-three

Andrew and I were going on a real date.

And it wasn't *just* a date, it was the datiest date to ever date. I thought the twee factor couldn't get any higher than the fall festival and Christmas tree cutting, but I'd forgotten about the two-day Old German Christmas Market in town. I mean, I hadn't actually forgotten about it, since it happened every year right outside my front door, but recently I'd been more bah humbug toward it thanks to the crowds, noise, and cars. This year? This year Andrew had asked me if I wanted to go with him and suddenly I couldn't wait to stand in line in subzero temps for a ten-dollar soft pretzel the size of my head.

I sat on the window ledge watching everyone on the street below feeling ready to soak up some of the happiness. My phone buzzed in my hand. Hi, I'm outside.

I opted to call Andrew back. "Hey, do you want to come up?" He'd never been to my place and I wanted him to meet Birdie.

"Yeah, that would be great. I wasn't sure if it was easier for you just to come down . . ." I could hear the buzz of the crowd in the background.

"It's totally easier that way, but there's a certain old lady up here who really wants to meet you. Edith's been telling her all about you. I'm on the third floor, the front door is open. Use the stairs, the elevator takes forever."

"I never take elevators," he said.

"Shocker. Anyway, come up."

I paced around my apartment as I waited for him and checked my makeup in the mirror for the millionth time. Birdie and Edith watched me with curious expressions until the knock on the door sent both dogs into a barking frenzy. I hadn't had anyone up in ages. Birdie looked at me like she couldn't believe that she'd been called back into guard dog service at her age and Edith went into parkour mode off every vertical surface.

"Ladies, *please*." It was an important lesson I'd forgotten to work on, so I resorted to an emergency management technique and grabbed a handful of treats to throw down the hallway so I could let Andrew in.

I still felt a little seasick about the whole greetings and farewells aspect of our fun-hood since it was all new terrain for us. I flung open the door and felt the air woosh out of my lungs at the sight of him filling the doorway. This man, this perfect specimen, was someone I could kiss if I wanted to. My brain still had trouble computing it after being on the defensive about him for so long. My heart? Well, that was another story entirely.

"Hi." I had to hold myself back from flinging my arms around his neck and covering his face with kisses.

"Hi."

Before I could step back to welcome him in, Andrew circled his arms around me and lifted me off the ground, pressing his lips to mine in a kiss that told me exactly how he felt about greetings. I'd never considered myself petite, but the way Andrew hoisted me through the door and up against the wall made me feel downright pocket-sized.

I was dressed for the cold outside in layers, but my skin still shivered as he kissed me. Desire unfurled in my belly and suddenly all I could think about was directing him to my bedroom. There'd be another Old German Christmas Market next year, it would be fine to miss this one.

Edith had other ideas. Andrew's mouth curved into a smile as she barked her frustration at us. He gave me one last teasing kiss, then set me back down on the ground.

"She's anti-kissing?" he asked, kneeling to pet her.

"She's anti any affection if it doesn't involve her."

"Sorry, Bug, I'm not into three-ways."

Hearing him use the name he'd called her the first time they met brought me back to when we were still pretending to hate each other. I liked this way much better.

"Come meet Birdie. She's going to hang back as long as Edith is in your face."

I pulled him to my little front room and put the gate up so he could interact with my old girl without having to deal with Edith at the same time.

"Cute place," he said as he looked around. "But where are your decorations? It's a little depressing in here, Higs."

"I'm skipping them this year thanks to Edith. It's just too much to worry about with her around. She's nonstop."

Birdie ambled out from the kitchen and headed right for Andrew.

"Oh, she's a beautiful old lady," he cooed as he sat down

on the ground in front of her. Birdie walked right up to him and pressed her head against his chest. "What a sweetheart. How old?"

"Ten." Birdie started climbing into his lap. "She's never going to let you leave if she gets settled. We better head out."

Five minutes later I was bundled up and strolling among the happy holiday crowds with a much less bundled Andrew. The Christmas market was mainly the usual street-fair merch like candles, art, and jewelry, but the stalls were dressed up in little white tents with Moravian stars on top. What qualified it as the *German* market was the oompah band that played a few times during the event and one massive stand that took up a half block filled with all sorts of German goodies.

"Do you mind if we stop really quick?" Andrew asked, eyeing the most popular stall at the event. "I want to get something for my mom. My grandparents were from Germany."

"Well, no wonder you were such a fan of Oktoberfest at school. And here I thought it was because of thirty-four-ounce beer steins."

He laughed. "Yeah, her maiden name was Biegelmacher, can't get much more German than that."

While he looked around the stall I gravitated to the display of little wooden figurines and couldn't resist the tiny ladybug holding a lily of the valley for Taylor.

"All set," Andrew said, holding up a bag. "Mission accomplished, *Schwein haben*."

"Wait, what? You speak German?" It wasn't known for being a sexy language, but I sure liked the way it sounded coming out of his mouth.

"Ein bisschen," he said with a shrug. "A little. Enough to be

dangerous. I took it in high school, and my mom still speaks it now and then."

It still came as a shock that Andrew Gibson contained multitudes. And that I liked all of them.

"Show me what you bought." I pointed to his bag.

He reached in and pulled out a little pink pig with a gold coin in its mouth wrapped in cellophane. "It's marzipan, it brings good luck in the new year. And this guy, for the Christmas tree." He showed me an adorable wooden gnome ornament, then peered back into the bag. "Oh, and this too. It's for you."

Andrew handed me a dessert-plate-sized heart-shaped gingerbread cookie on a pink string decorated with German words in frosting.

I didn't know how to respond. After all it was just a cookie, but it was a *heart* and it was from Andrew. A gift.

I finally managed to snap my mouth closed. "Thank you!" I read it phonetically. "'Fur mane skats.' What does it mean?"

He laughed at me. "Your pronunciation is a little off. I'm not going to tell you, and you're not allowed to use a translation app. You need to find someone to translate it."

"Challenge accepted." I held my hand over my eyes and looked around the crowd. "Scanning for lederhosen." I pulled the ribbon over my head so the cookie sat on my chest like an Olympic medal.

Andrew wrapped his arm around my shoulder and pulled me closer to him. "You're such a dork."

I loved the feeling of being pressed up against him, but his word choice struck a teeny-tiny nerve inside of me. We threaded through the crowd in step together and I pushed the uneasy feeling down.

"Did you get anything for your dad?" I asked.

I felt his body stiffen for an instant. "Not yet."

"Maybe we'll find something here tonight. Does he like art with dolphins swimming in outer space?" I pointed to a stall.

"Honestly, I have no clue what my dad likes."

I looked up at him and it was as if thinking about his father had drained the happiness from his expression.

"Hey," I said, stepping in front of him. "Can we talk about that for a second?"

His answer was a frown, but I ignored it.

"C'mere." I took his hand and led him to a grouping of tables and chairs beneath a string of café lights. "Let's sit."

Andrew dropped into a tiny red chair that looked like it might break beneath his bulk. I sat down across from him and ignored the way the cold seat cut through my two layers of clothing.

"Full disclosure: your mom told me that things have always been rough between you and your dad. And then what happened at Thanksgiving . . ."

He made a frustrated noise and shook his head. "Yeah, *that* was fun."

"It was awkward for everyone, and I'm sorry it happened." I took a deep breath. "Now, what I'm going to say next is probably none of my business, but . . . maybe you guys should talk? Like, really talk."

A pack of teenagers tumbled past us, laughing and shrieking.

He watched them go by, then threw his hands up. "Why? I know exactly what he's going to say before he says it. 'You made a mistake. Being an entrepreneur is a constant struggle. You have no financial security.' The man has never been shy about telling me the many ways I've fucked up. Even my *major* was an issue. He wanted me to study business."

For a moment I envisioned young Andrew fighting with his father about college. The feel-good sunshine guy had kept some secrets.

"But if you bring him to see what you've created, just the two of you . . ." Andrew was shaking his head before I even finished.

"Don't you realize that with the building up for sale he's going to think he was *right*? I made a risky move and it's going to bite me in the ass, and he'll get to say 'I told you so.'"

I hung my head. It didn't have to be like this for Andrew. I had the power to right the collision course he was on. It was in front of me, but somehow it still felt out of reach.

"And why does it even matter? What's the point in trying?" he asked, the pain of our conversation clear in his voice.

The German band kicked up in the distance to give us the world's most inappropriate soundtrack for our conversation. I steeled myself for what I had to say because it wasn't a conversation I had lightly. I couldn't go there with my family, or Sam, but I felt like I had to with Andrew. Maybe dropping into that raw place with him would help him understand how important it was to try to find common ground with his father, before it was too late.

"Why does it matter? Because the day will come when your father won't be here, and you'll regret all the times you never told him you loved him." Tears pooled in my eyes, but I blinked them back. "The hugs you never gave him. It'll be too late,

Andrew, and all you'll have are the memories of missed opportunities. And I guarantee it'll absolutely gut you."

He moved his chair closer to mine so he could rest his hand on my knee, his face tender with concern. "Is that . . . is that how it was with your dad?"

I wiped my nose with the back of my glove then shook my head. "No. We were lucky. We took every chance we could to hug or say we loved each other. But I can't even imagine how much worse the pain of losing him would be if we hadn't been able to." I paused to see how he was taking everything and he was locked on to me. I pushed on. "Andrew, I know your dad isn't perfect. Obviously no one is, but he's your dad, and I think you should at least try. If it doesn't go well, then at least you'll know that you did your best. You'll have that peace of mind."

He took his hand off my knee and leaned back against the chair, staring off into the distance. There was a weight in him that was probably always there but buried so deep that it didn't even register, which was why none of us ever had a clue. Like an old injury that the surrounding muscles worked to compensate for. Andrew's positivity and the darkness I was seeing now couldn't coexist in him.

"Are you upset with me for talking about it?" I asked in a small voice.

"*Never,*" he shot back immediately.

I wasn't about to overstep any more than I had. I gnawed on the inside of my cheek, worrying that I'd ruined the night.

"Thanks for saying it," he said softly.

I nodded and felt some of the tension drain from my body, making room for the chill in the air. I shivered and crossed my arms, only to feel a crack against my chest. I pulled the cookie into the light. "I broke it!"

Andrew chuckled. "Honestly, they taste like shit, so it's no big deal."

"Will you tell me what it means?"

He shook his head.

I craned my neck to scan the crowd. "Not a dirndl in sight."

"The night is young." He stood up and held out his hand to me. "C'mon, let's get some food."

I grabbed it, wishing there was no glove between us. "Yes, we have the very German food choices of subs, Philly cheesesteaks, or gyros."

He pulled me closer and I leaned into his warmth. "None of which you eat. There's gotta be some veg options somewhere."

"I'm not actually hungry, but I *am* cold." I dodged a double-wide stroller that was headed straight for us.

"I'm not hungry either," Andrew said, raising an eyebrow at me. "If I told you I was cold too would it convince you that we should go back to your place immediately?"

The implication of what he was suggesting suddenly became clear. "Oh yes. These temperatures are downright unhealthy. And you're always cold, am I right?"

"Brr," he said unconvincingly. "Whatever could we do to warm up?" He sounded like a kid in a high school play.

I struggled to maintain a straight face. "I've heard that body heat is the best way to help someone suffering from hypo-thermia."

He nodded sagely. "Ah, so that's my diagnosis? Hypothermia? Sounds really bad."

"Indeed." I frowned up at him. "Severe. We should probably begin treatment immediately."

"Oof. I *like* how that sounds. Race ya." He cocked an eyebrow at me and I took off before he could lower it.

We chased each other through the crowd, laughing like idiots as the holiday magic finally, finally grew my grinchy heart three sizes.

chapter thirty-four

I was having more "fun" than I ever thought possible.

We had fun at my place the night of the Christmas market. Twice. And after we finally decorated Andrew's tree, beneath the lights and borrowed ornaments. In the supply room at Frolic, officially christening it. And now Andrew was doing everything in his power to keep my personal training session at Crush on track while I tried to seduce him.

"Stop," he said in mock exasperation as I repositioned myself so he had a front-row seat for my butt while I bent over to do a row. "Are you serious about this or not?"

I gave him a coy look over my shoulder as I leaned down to grasp the bar. "I'm definitely serious about one thing." I glanced at his crotch.

"Higgins." He sighed. "C'mon, would you want me to act all sexy while you were trying to train Dude?"

"Yes. I absolutely would."

It was like my body had been possessed and all I could think about was getting naked with him. I'd had good sex before, but sex with Andrew wasn't just good. It was indescribable. I found myself drifting off throughout the day with fantasies so vivid that they left me trembling. It took all my willpower to keep from running to Crush for quickies, but he was so busy with clients it would've been impossible anyway.

Andrew let out a groan that echoed around the room. "C'mon, *focus!*"

"I'm starting to get a little insulted." I pouted and put my hands on my hips. "How are you even resisting me at this point?"

He stared at me for a beat.

"I'm not."

Andrew steamrolled over to me and swept me off my feet, carrying me from the center of the room to the corner where his extra mats were stacked three feet high. Our naked bodies were reflected in the mirrors all around us, but I kept my focus on him until we both collapsed in a sweaty heap.

We rested on our sides on the mat, staring at each other.

"You're the worst." He was still out of breath as he reached over to smooth my hair off my forehead.

"Hm, and here I thought that was an excellent idea. I'd even consider it a workout. My quads are still shaky from riding you."

His eyes flicked up and down my body then paused at my chest. "Hey, why do you always hide yourself like that? I literally just saw you naked."

I looked at myself and realized that he meant my arm draped across my breasts. I'd never been self-conscious about them, they were fine, but he was right, I always found myself quick to put something on after we were done. The fact that he'd picked up on it unnerved me. It meant that he was studying me, like before.

"Not sure. Maybe I'm worried I don't measure up to what you're used to." I said it as a joke, but the moment it was out of my mouth I realized that there was a grain of truth to it. Zadie's breasts were perfect enough to make a career out of showing them off.

"Stop." Andrew said it softly but his expression darkened. "That stuff doesn't matter to me."

Okay, *ouch*.

It was a verbal paper cut, minuscule in the scheme of injuries yet painful enough to ruin a day. He could've countered with saying that I was beautiful, or that he loved my body, but no, he claimed looks weren't even a consideration for him. So why had he screwed his way through the most beautiful girls at school? I couldn't recall a single ginger-haired, strong-jawed, modest-breasted woman in his body count. It made me feel small to admit that part of me wished that Andrew was with me because he thought I was hot too. I rolled onto my stomach, feeling even more exposed by the way he was looking at me.

"Well, it clearly *does* matter to you, otherwise you wouldn't have dated a swimsuit model for two years."

"Oh shit," he mumbled in an annoyed voice that sounded way too familiar. "Here we go."

I frowned at him as worry kicked up inside of me. "What's that supposed to mean?"

"I had a feeling Zadie was going to come up eventually. And she's a *fitness* model, not a swimsuit model."

"Well, that's even worse," I snorted, reaching over the side of the mats for my discarded T-shirt. I slipped it over my head and crossed my arms over my chest. "She gets paid to look good *and* work out."

"Hold on, hold on, what's happening here?" Andrew sounded a little panicked.

I searched for my discarded leggings so I didn't have to look at him. "Nothing's happening. We're talking." It came out snippy.

"Are we? Because it feels more like you accusing me of being shallow."

"Not at all. I never said that." I tried to sound casual. "You like what you like, you can't help it."

I spotted my leggings in a heap and snatched them up. Andrew reached for my wrist before I could put them on, leaving me standing there in a shirt and no pants, like a porno Winnie the Pooh.

"I like *you*. For fuck's sake, Chels, isn't that obvious by now? Modeling was Zadie's life. Looking perfect was her job, and that was fine for her. But I know that superficial stuff doesn't matter to you."

The comment burned a white-hot hole through me. There it was, flayed open and bleeding out between us. When it came to the way I looked I'd never measure up to her.

I got dressed quickly without saying a word.

"Something's wrong. Tell me why you're upset." He hopped off the mats and pulled on his workout pants. "Chelsea, stop."

Andrew grasped me by both arms and turned me so that I had to face him. My stupid bottom lip quivered and he pulled me against his bare chest, hugging me tightly. I could hear his heartbeat pounding away as he stroked my hair. As much as I wanted to push back I clung to him, like I was afraid that everything was at risk of evaporating. He kissed the top of my head then leaned back to look into my eyes.

"I think you're absolutely beautiful, okay? Is that what you want to hear?"

I did, of course I did, but not like that. It felt like he was offering me a consolation prize, like he'd figured out why I was upset and backpedaled so the teary woman he'd just had sex with would feel okay about herself.

"Thanks," I sniffled, trying to play it off like my nose was stuffed and not that I was feeling wounded.

"I mean it. You're amazing."

"If you say so," I said, and managed a smile.

He gave me another kiss on top of the head then pulled his T-shirt on. "We're not done, by the way. Back to work. Let's go." Andrew clapped his hands and headed for the weights we'd abandoned for a more enjoyable workout.

The sound of his front door opening was followed by a voice. "Hey, Andrew, you here?"

It was Mike. Ten minutes earlier and our landlord would've been treated to the exact same view Nolan had had in their dorm room. I made a mental note to remind Andrew to lock the door for any future fun at Crush.

"Yup, we're here," he called back. "Me and Chelsea."

"Good." Mike speed-walked to us in his hunched, guilty-looking posture. "Glad you're both here. Listen, the buyer is coming back again tonight and he's going to be taking some measurements so I wanted to confirm you won't be here. It's gonna take a while."

My body tensed. "Hold on. The *buyer*? You sold the building?"

No, no, no. Not yet. I glanced at Andrew, but his face was un-readable.

"Okay, so I wouldn't exactly say that it's sold, but we're close." Mike checked to make sure his cigarette was still behind his ear. "But if you ask me it's as good as done."

I felt a little nauseous. A lot nauseous. But then again, Mike was always a big talker. Everything was the best, first, and most. There was a strong possibility that this "buyer" wasn't even close to signing any contracts and it was just wishful thinking on his part.

"Okay, we'll be out of here in thirty minutes," Andrew said, still deploying his poker face.

"And I'm done for the day," I added, even though the idea of a stranger nosing around in my building made me queasy.

"What's the process going to be?" Andrew asked, taking a few steps closer to Mike, who backed up to keep the buffer between them. "And do you know what they want to do with the building?"

I could tell that he was lying before he opened his mouth. "Nope, not yet. No idea."

"You need to keep us informed," Andrew said. "It's only fair, considering my entire business is hinging on who buys the building."

Mike went into shifty eye overdrive, looking everywhere but at us and shuffling his feet. "You got it. When I know, you'll know."

"Appreciate it." There was zero appreciation in Andrew's voice.

"Anyway, gotta head out," Mike said as he practically ran toward the door. "More later."

Andrew and I watched him speed-hunch his way out until the door slammed behind him.

"Fuck."

"But maybe the new owner will be better? More responsive?" We both knew that trading up from Mike was unlikely, given the way he did business. All he cared about was the dollar signs; it didn't matter who or what bought the building.

Andrew leaned down to tighten the clips on the bar I was supposed to be lifting. "Well, that would be good for you, but it won't apply to me."

I fought against a quicksand sensation. "Why? What do you mean?"

"I found a place."

Andrew didn't look happy about it, but why would he be? Not only was he ripping up the roots of his new business, he was also putting himself in his father's crosshairs. It wasn't my fight, but why did I suddenly feel like I was partly responsible for his decision?

"But wait a sec," I said, trying to get him to look at me. "Don't you want to wait to find out what the buyer wants to do?"

He shook his head. "No point. New landlords always raise the rent, which means mine will probably go up in the next few months, if they even let me stay. I didn't budget for an increase until the end of year one. Things are going well, but it's tight right now, especially because I have to relocate."

He was retreating from me and I knew better than to push, but I couldn't help it. I needed more information from him, so I could understand what he was up against.

"Where is the new space?"

"Other side of town. Smaller spot, used to be a little garage. It's a mess right now, but I'll make it work."

"Were you going to tell me?"

He stopped fussing with the weights to finally look at me. "I mean, yeah, eventually. But I was sort of avoiding thinking about it until I had to. I guess it's time."

The words were right there at the tip of my tongue. I wanted to tell him to hold on a little longer, to wait until I could make peace with the gift that felt like anything but. The fact that the thought had even crossed my mind was progress. I was inching my way toward feeling okay with something I never thought I could. But I wasn't *ready* ready.

"Enough talking," he said, pointing to the bar at my feet. "You're here to work. Let's go."

I grabbed on to the weight and when I tried to hoist it, it definitely felt like a "drag" and not a "pull."

chapter thirty-five

"May your days be merry, and *bright*..."

Sam sang along to the music piped in at the Wismer Pond and skated in a graceful backward circle around me, ending with a spin.

"Ooh, show me how to do that," Carly said to Sam. "I can only do a half-turn."

It was an epic gathering of the clans for a night of holiday skating, with Carly and Joe and Sam and Nolan meeting for the first time. Andrew and I were the only ones who knew both sides of the friend groups, but as expected, it was a perfect night so far. They'd all heard about each other forever and it made sense that the people I loved would all love one another. It felt like the right idea to take advantage of the holiday vibes at the pond for their first introduction, before the McGee family shipped off for Long Island and then back to Japan.

Sam and Carly worked on their spins together while I absorbed the magic of the moment. Even though Nolan and I had grown up skating at the pond it felt like I was seeing it for the first time. All the trees surrounding it were decorated with multicolored lights, the big-bulb 1950s type, and the little rental shack was dressed up to look like gingerbread. The crowd was displaying a variety of skating abilities, from people falling on their butts in ways that almost guaranteed morning-after back pain, to kids using PVC skating trainers to help them stay upright, to rowdy teens careening through the other skaters, to show-offs doing fancy stuff in the center of the ice. Everyone in my little group seemed to be passable to good at skating, with one giant, adorably tentative exception.

Andrew was a glacier in a parka on the other side of the pond, with his toe pick dug into the ice so deeply I worried that we might see water. Nolan was toning down his hockey skills to coach Andrew on the basics while Joe cheered him on, effectively edging me out of the lesson. Andrew looked like he couldn't understand why his body was betraying him, and the truth was I couldn't figure it out either. He was sporty and strong, and shockingly graceful, so why was he so tentative on the ice?

Carly and Sam skated over and caught me watching Andrew.

"You know this is like Joe's dream come true," Carly said. "You and Andrew hanging out. He said he predicted it at the Fall Fest."

"We're not hanging out, we're 'having fun,'" I corrected as I skated backward.

"What's the difference?" Sam asked.

"We didn't define anything." I did reverse crossovers and tried not to catch my rear skate on my front. "Remember? It's casual."

"Is that still okay with you?" Sam asked in her penetrating way, trying to keep pace with me as I picked up speed.

"Sure, yeah."

Sam and Carly skated behind me in tandem like they were doing Olympic pairs interrogation.

"Hm, I'm not convinced," Sam said, looking over at Carly for confirmation.

"Same. I'm thinking she wants parameters. A timeline. Maybe contracts and blood samples."

Sam laughed so hard she tripped. "Exactly."

"Okay, hold on a second, I'm not *that* bad."

"We're not saying it's bad. There's nothing wrong with wanting clarity."

Of course, Sam was right. I *did* want clarity and I'd do my best to get it. Eventually. But there was so much going on with the holidays and the building changes, it just didn't feel right to bring up the What-are-we-to-each-other? conversation. Of course, it wasn't just that. A part of me was nervous to broach it with Andrew and have him tell me that "fun" was exactly what it sounded like. No commitments, take it or leave it. It was easier keeping the exact definition unknown for now and enjoying it for what it was.

Incredible sex with an incredibly sexy man.

Even though our conversation about Zadie still had me a little off-kilter.

"Couples skate," a voice said over the sound system as "Rockin' around the Christmas Tree" ended. "Please clear the ice for a couples-only skate, folks. Groups of two."

Carly skated off to find Joe, leaving me with Sam. "Been meaning to ask, how are things between you and Nolan?"

She tucked her arm in mine so we'd qualify for the couples skate as "Christmas Time Is Here" started playing.

"Better. We talked, fought, made up. We needed this break.

He's been taking care of Mia more than usual while we're here and he gets it now. We're going to be making some changes once we get back."

I glanced over at her and squeezed her arm. "I was worried."

"Don't be, we're okay. Worry about yourself and the big guy."

Nolan sped over from where he'd been watching us and fell in line beside Sam. "May I cut in?"

"Please do. I'm going to try to get that wallflower out here." I glided away to where Andrew was trying to play it cool and did a simple spin in front of him.

"You're *really* good." He was looking at me like I'd just done a triple axel.

I waved off the compliment. "Let's get out there—you've got two songs before the hordes head back."

"I'm not sure you want the responsibility of trying to hold me up. It could get ugly. We both might break something."

"We have to at least try." I moved toward him and grasped both of his hands. "Trust me."

Andrew took a few halting steps toward me and immediately started flailing like a cartoon character running in place. I moved a little closer to him and he finally found his footing.

"*How* is this fun?"

I laughed at his pained expression. "Let me drive. You just keep your legs still and I'll pull you."

He clung to my hands and I started backing up slowly, doing easy S curves that enabled me to get our momentum going.

"I look stupid," Andrew said, glancing around at the other graceful couples around us.

"Stop. But maybe straighten your legs a little? You look like you're sitting on a toilet. Use those quads."

He laughed and stood up a little taller. "Throwing anatomy at me, I like that!"

I glanced over my shoulder to make sure the space behind me was clear and sped up a little.

"Whoa, whoa!" Andrew squatted again.

Once we were going fast enough I let go of him for a second then swung around so that I was beside him, holding him up by his one beefy arm. Andrew looked down at me and smiled and I swear it was the most beautiful thing I'd ever seen. There was joy on his face, mixed with a smidge of fear, given the way I was picking up speed, but in that sparkly moment it felt like every single thing was right in my world. There was no better feeling than being tucked against Andrew, gliding across the ice to the sound of "Happy Xmas (War Is Over)."

"Hey," he said, squeezing me. I looked up. "This is fun."

I hugged his arm back. "The funnest."

I felt him relax and attempt a wobbly push-off with one skate.

"There you go!" I cheered. "You figured it out, you're skating!"

He tried to hide a proud smile. "I did a little research before coming tonight since I've never skated. Did some reading, watched some videos."

"Aw, that's so cute."

"How is doing research cute?" Andrew asked as he fell out of rhythm for a second.

I adjusted my grip on him. "I guess I never considered you the research type. You're more of a 'just do it' guy."

"Huh."

I didn't like the sound of the single syllable. I glanced up to find that Andrew was focused on the ice in front of him, like he was worried there might be unexpected divots or speed bumps.

"That came out wrong," I said quickly as I tucked his arm tighter against my side. "I meant that you sort of bulldoze through life, you know? You don't let anything slow you down. Onward!"

His frown deepened and I felt a little queasy as I realized that I wasn't making it any better.

"Does that make sense?" I asked tentatively.

"Sure. Yeah."

I could feel his body bracing as he attempted to get his non-dominant foot to move. He was just about to make it happen when John and Yoko finished singing and the announcer came over the speakers again.

"Group skate. Everyone back on the ice. Group skate."

Andrew's eyes went wide. *"Teenagers."*

I chuckled at his terror. "They're a menace. I'll have you know that your buddy Nolan used to be one of them back in the day. But yeah, we should probably take a break."

I was starting to move us toward the edge when a pack of boys hurled themselves back on the ice, hunkered down like speed skaters. I felt Andrew overcompensating as they came closer, shuffling faster but seemingly moving backward at the same time.

We were nearly there when a rogue skater zipped by us, catching us both off guard. The skater's speed and the way he zigzagged in front of us were enough to shift Andrew off-balance, sending his feet shooting out from under him. He went airborne and seemed to hang there for a few seconds before crashing to the ice in a coccyx-bruising thud, pulling me down on top of him like I was riding him.

Andrew didn't move while I quickly climbed off of him so we

didn't look like ice skating porn. We wound up sitting on the ice hip to hip, facing each other. The only way to finish the perfect holiday movie moment would've been a we're-so-freaking-cute-and-adorable kiss.

Instead, Andrew patted my arm and then wobbled to a shaky stand without so much as a smile.

chapter thirty-six

The late afternoon sky looked like an overstuffed down pillow, all but guaranteeing more snow. I was celebrating a major win with Pat and the goats before the storm came.

"It's a Christmas miracle," Pat exclaimed.

She had her hand in a fist held out to the side of her body at waist height and the Mean Girls were taking turns bumping it with their noses in exchange for treats. The simple targeting exercise not only showed that they were starting to trust her but meant that we could now start doing some more advanced training, like teaching them to go to "stations" in the pen and coming when called. Soon after, we could merge the Mean Girls and the originals in the same pen, and all would be right in goat-land.

"Thistle won't stop," Pat laughed as the goat bumped her fist over and over.

"I love an eager student."

A few wet snowflakes fell, the kind that would turn the landscape muddy instead of a pretty white.

"So it begins," Pat said, pointing up at the sky with one hand while continuing to feed treats with the other. "We should finish up for today. The forecast says it's going to be a white Christmas."

I gave Darling one last scratch under the chin, then followed Pat out of the pen. "Snow every day this week. Going to make holiday travel a mess."

We headed for the house side by side.

"We're staying local," Pat said. "You?"

"Same. A quiet day at my mom's house with my sister and brother-in-law."

I realized that Andrew and I hadn't discussed how Christmas was going to play out. But then again, I had no idea if our concept of fun included any of the major holidays.

"Andrew invited us over to his house for Christmas Eve, then we're supposed to go to my brother's house in New Jersey on Christmas Day. It's nice to hand off the hosting duties after Thanksgiving. That takes a lot out of me."

We both went quiet at the mention of Thanksgiving. It was hard not to think about how the celebration of family had gone spectacularly off the rails in front of everyone. Of course, the day held other significance to me, but Pat didn't know about that part.

"It was bad, wasn't it?" she asked plainly. She didn't have to explain what she meant.

"It was a blip in an otherwise wonderful day."

Pat shook her head, frowning. "He's been quiet. Have you noticed?"

I couldn't let on how much I knew about the reasons for Andrew being less Andrew lately. Everything was connected, and to talk about one thread would start to unravel the rest of it. I wasn't sure how much he'd told his mom, or even if she knew that we were more than just neighbors, and I wasn't about to be the one who spilled the news about any of it.

"I'm sure it's entrepreneur stress," I answered vaguely.

She pursed her lips and nodded. "Maybe. He's been avoiding coming over and Gerard is too proud to reach out for help on all of his projects around here. It's never been quite this tense."

I blinked at her, wishing I could explain what Andrew was grappling with.

"That's not your concern," she finally said. "Wait here, I have something for you."

Pat jogged up the front steps to the house and left me to wonder what form of payment she'd come up with this time. I'd stopped taking her checks after the first session so she'd resorted to finding other ways to compensate me, from knitting a pair of fingerless gloves in a cheerful pink that allowed me to work with the goats but still keep my hands warm, to a bookmark laminated with pressed flowers from her garden. This time, she came out carrying a cookie tin.

"Merry Christmas! These are Spitzbube, Kipfeln, and Pfeffernüsse," she said as she handed it to me. "I went a little overboard in the kitchen this year."

I popped off the cover to find a treasure trove of powdered-sugar-dusted half-moons, scalloped cookies with circles of jam in the middle, and polished white mounds.

"My mother's recipes, straight from Hannover."

"They're beautiful, thank you!" I was reminded of the last German cookie I'd come in contact with that was still a mystery. I'd forgotten to get a translation since the frosting had crumbled off and I couldn't remember how the phrase was spelled. "Andrew mentioned that you speak German. Could you translate something for me?"

"Of course."

"My pronunciation is terrible but I, uh, I saw a big ginger-bread cookie at the German Christmas market that said 'fur mane skats.'"

She frowned for a moment, then her face lit up as she figured out what I was trying to say. "Oh, you mean *für mein Schatz*. That means 'for my sweetheart,' but in our house we translate it a little differently. *Schatz* also means treasure."

Sweetheart? *Treasure?* I'd expected it to mean something like "happy holidays." I didn't want to read too much into a message on a cookie, but it was almost impossible to resist the happy, fizzy feelings generated from Andrew calling me his treasure via a baked good. Although things had felt different since our night on the ice. A little less connected, a half step backward toward what we used to be.

My phone rang and I was glad to have a reason to stop over-analyzing what was going on.

"It's my landlord. Our landlord," I said after I pulled it from my pocket. "I'm going to head out, but we'll talk soon. And thanks for the cookies!" She waved at me as I walked to my car. "Hi, Mike," I answered. "What's wrong?"

"Not a thing. Just figured I'd tell you what's going on with the building. The people looking at it just told me what they're planning to do with the place."

I slid into my car and my heartbeat sped to a gallop as I waited for him to keep talking. "Okay?"

"Yeah, they want to open one of those indoor trampoline parks. For kids, you know? Birthday parties and crap like that."

I swallowed hard. They wanted the entire building, my space included.

"Is it a done deal?" My hand felt clammy against the phone. I sat in my car because I didn't trust myself to drive and talk at the same time.

Mike breathed hard like he was jogging, but since that was impossible I chalked it up to his smoking-induced COPD. "Not yet. They gotta do more shit on their end with the banks, but we're getting closer."

"Did you talk to Andrew yet?"

He grunted. "Not yet—could you let him know? I gotta run."

I knew it was because Mike was afraid that Andrew was going to call him on being a crappy landlord and not warning him about the possible sale of the building before he signed the lease.

I finally turned on my car. "Yeah. I'll tell him."

"Okay, see ya."

The snow was anything but pretty as I headed down the Gibsons' driveway in the encroaching darkness. It was the kind that came flying at the windshield and made it feel like I was driving through a meteor storm. I needed to focus, but I could feel myself zoning out as I headed home.

I never expected that the building would go to someone who wanted to take the whole thing over. Maybe I'd kept my head in the sand about it, but seriously, who would really want a basic bitch building on the outskirts of town, with a parking lot small enough to spark turf wars between tenants?

I sat at a stop sign for far too long until I finally admitted it to myself.

Who would want it? Me. *I* wanted it.

I drove blindly through increasingly crappy weather, barely registering where I was as I finally surrendered to the sticky, complicated thoughts required to make things right. I did an incredibly stupid, middle-of-the-road U-turn, then tempted fate even more by reaching for my phone as I drove. Luckily I seemed to be the only idiot on the road as I hit speed dial. I crossed my fingers as it rang.

"Hello?"

I smiled at the question in her voice. Every caller was still a mystery thanks to the ancient landline she still used.

"Mom, is it okay if I come over now? I need to talk to you about something."

chapter thirty-seven

D ude was on a twenty-foot-long line, proving that he could do incredibly speedy recalls even when surrounded by distractions like piles of deer poop and squirrel-filled trees. Andrew and I were holding our training session in the fields behind his house, and I was thankful that we had his most excellent dog to focus on instead of the weird tension that had been growing between us ever since the night we went skating. He'd met me at the door with the briefest of kisses, but then again we had to jump apart because Dude started playing tug-of-war with my coat pocket. I chalked up the tension to his nerves about the future of Crush, which made me even happier about what I was going to tell him.

"Time to do some leash walking now," I called to Andrew. "We've only done street walking—let's put him to the test out here where there's no clear path."

"Okay." He unclipped the six-foot leash from across his chest and traded it out for the long line. Dude looked like he was having the time of his life in the three inches of fresh powder, but happily ran back to Andrew when he did the "come" hand signal. It was the perfect weather for an outside session, a surprisingly temperate post-snow day when the sun lit up the landscape and warmed the air enough to encourage unzipped jackets and hats askew.

I met Andrew and Dude at the edge of the woods. "Is it okay to walk in these fields? Is it public land?"

He shrugged. "No one's had a problem with it yet. And I'm more of an ask-forgiveness kind of guy."

I punched him on the shoulder gently, mainly because I just needed an excuse to touch him. "That tracks. Let's start off with you walking Dude, so I can check your progress."

"We've been practicing, I think you're going to be impressed."

In truth I was having a hard time focusing on the work. I wanted to blurt out my good news, but I couldn't get past the nerdy pull to honor their lesson first.

I fell behind Andrew and Dude and watched as the high-energy adolescent transformed into an attentive student. Dude kept pace with Andrew and every time he looked up, Andrew marked the behavior with the hand signal and a treat.

"Wow, you *have* been practicing. Looking great!"

After a while I jogged to catch up and Dude gave a little hop when I reached them.

"We're still works in progress. Walking him in town is pretty tough, but in low-traffic zones we're doing okay."

I gave him a few pointers about the speed of his treat delivery and other little polishing techniques and we fell into a quiet rhythm, with just the sound of the snow crunching beneath our boots and Dude's panting echoing around us. It was a Christmas card landscape, the perfect setting for the moment we were about to share.

I looked up at Andrew and felt the usual shock to the system at how things had changed between us. I still wasn't used to being able to openly admire him, although what I was doing was closer to gawking. He'd finally surrendered to the elements and was wearing a knit cap *and* jacket, though it was unzipped to reveal a worn black T-shirt. He'd let his stubble grow into the beginnings of a beard again, and all I could do was imagine how it would feel rubbing against me.

He glanced down at me. "What?"

I was sure he could tell that something was up because I couldn't stop smiling at him. "I have news. Really good news."

I'd kept the trampoline update to myself since I'd found out about it two days prior, and I was sure that Mike hadn't told him either. I didn't want to worry Andrew unnecessarily since I knew that I could provide a solution for both of us.

As soon as I'd hung up from the call from Mike everything started to fall into place. After bottling thoughts of my dad for too long I'd allowed myself to envision what he would've said to me if I'd presented him with the scenario. I could almost see his half grin and twinkly eyes as he said, "No-brainer, sweetie. You *have* to do it." It felt not only like he'd given me his blessing during that snowy drive, but like he would've been pissed at me if I didn't go for it.

Andrew raised an eyebrow. "Clearly. You look like you're about to explode from whatever it is."

I'd tried to come up with a clever way to tell him, but in the heat of the moment none of them seemed right, so I led with the simple fact that was about to change everything for both of us.

"I'm buying the building."

He came to an abrupt stop, then turned to me. "What?"

Of course he was confused; his furrowed expression made complete sense. I'd never even hinted that it was a possibility for me. I took a breath before launching into the details, watching him carefully so I could see when his dubious expression shifted to happiness. "Those people who've been looking at the building wanted to turn it into a trampoline park, which meant we'd both get tossed out. So I made Mike a better offer."

He still looked like I was speaking another language. "But . . . *how*?"

The shift to happiness was coming, I just needed to explain a little more. Even still, my mouth felt dry as he stared me down.

"Let's keep walking." I needed a little more time to collect my thoughts in order to talk through the part that had kept me from the decision for so long.

Dude walked beside us as if he could tell that we needed to focus on something other than his manners. He even managed to ignore the pair of cardinals that tempted fate in the snow a few feet in front of us.

"Chelsea, I'm *really* confused."

"I know. It's totally unexpected, and that's on me."

Another brief silence as he waited for me to make sense of it all.

"How long has this been in the works?" Andrew asked. It sounded defensive, a jab. "Like, how long have you known that it was even an option for you?"

The edge to his voice sent my hackles up. "It's complicated, Andrew. The only reason I'm able to do this is because someone I loved is no longer here. I wasn't even comfortable thinking about it until now." I watched him out of the corner of my eye, wary.

"Ah, okay." His mouth went tight as he nodded. "Understood. So this money is from your father."

"Yeah, it is." My chest constricted and it came out in a pained exhale. I'd primed myself to stay strong, but it wasn't as easy as I'd imagined it would be, especially because Andrew was tromping along beside me frowning instead of responding the way I'd choreographed in my head.

"So basically, you've known that you could buy the building from the minute Mike put it up for sale."

A dull pain started to throb behind my eyes as I watched him scowl. "Well, technically yes."

"And you never once thought about mentioning it to me?"

I started to stutter a response, but he kept going.

"This decision concerns me too, you know. You let me run all over town trying to find a new space while all along you had this Uno Reverse Card in your back pocket?"

"Hold on," I said, my voice rising due to the mix of panic and anger surging through me. "Are you actually getting upset with me because I was having a hard time accepting my dead father's life insurance money?" Saying it that way left a coppery after-taste in my mouth, like I'd bitten down on my tongue, but I had to put it plainly, so he could hear how awful he sounded.

"For fuck's sake, Chelsea, that's not at all what I'm saying, and I'm insulted you'd even suggest it."

"Well, *what*, then?"

Andrew let out a frustrated sigh and hung his head. "I know it was probably a hard thing for you to work through." His voice went quieter, and he paused for a long time, still looking at his feet as he walked. "I thought we could be open with each other. I was, with you. But you watched while I wasted my time trying to figure everything out. You knew that there's a lot more to this business for me than just making a living. I let you in; you didn't do the same for me. We could've talked about it, about *him*. Isn't that what people in a relationship do?"

I felt raw from being forced to defend myself about something so tender and I snapped back at him quickly. "We're *not* in a relationship. Remember? We're just having fun. Big difference."

The sound that ripped out of him could've been categorized as a laugh if there was any joy in it. "Right, of course. How could I have forgotten that? Because the high-and-mighty Chelsea Higgins would never get involved with someone like me for anything more than fucking." Another mirthless laugh. "Maybe that's why Zadie and I were so good together. My heart actually mattered to her."

My jaw dropped open. He knew exactly how to wound me. "Of *course* you bring her up now. Perfect. Thanks for reminding me that I'll always be in her shadow, Andrew. I mean, look at me. I'm not exactly your type. You've made that perfectly clear since the day I met you."

The woods went quiet around us and the silence hung there while we breathed angry clouds at each other. My blood felt half-frozen and sluggish in my veins, like if I were to try to walk away I might fall to my knees in the snow and not be able to get up.

"It's no wonder my dad likes you."

The way he said it made it clear that it wasn't a compliment, so I braced myself for what was coming next.

"Neither one of you has ever believed in me."

chapter thirty-eight

"You need this, lean up," my mom said as she shoved a pillow behind my back.

I knew there was no use arguing with her because sympathy bedding distribution was nonnegotiable. She was on a mission to comfort me, so she insisted on too many pillows tucked under my arms, back, and neck, and topped it off with layers of blankets over my legs.

It was three days before Christmas and my newfound holiday spirit had shriveled up and died after I'd walked away from Andrew in the field. My mom had forced me to come over for soup and sympathy, which was why I was the one curled up on the couch and my hugely pregnant sister was placing a serving tray of food on my lap. For the first time ever Taylor looked fully pregnant. Not a cute girl with an adorable bump, but an uncomfortable woman with swollen feet and a belly big enough to give her wind drag.

"Thanks, but I'm not hungry," I said. Edith put her paws up on the couch next to me and gave me her sweetest begging look while Birdie watched from her spot by the fireplace.

Taylor settled in a chair across from me, lit by the Christmas tree. "A few bites. I made it myself."

I looked down at the bowl of tomato soup and frowned.

"Oh, come on." She threatened to throw a pillow at me. "It's really good. I've been learning lots of tricks from Mom."

Edith glanced over her shoulder and realized that Taylor's lap was available. She'd been especially attentive to Taylor and I assumed it was because my sister's belly probably felt like a giant hot water bottle. Taylor let out a groan of exertion as she leaned down to pick up the puppy, who quickly settled in next to her.

A text notification sounded off from my phone.

"Him again?" Taylor asked.

My heart lurched reflexively as I leaned over and grabbed my phone off the coffee table. "Yeah."

"What does it say?"

"Same thing, I don't even have to read past the first line. He wants to talk. Probably says he's sorry." I shrugged even though I still had to fight off hope when he reached out. This was the fourth time.

I felt weary and fluish, but the thing that had me laid out was missing Andrew. Part of me wanted to call him back and let him talk, but then I'd remember the things he'd said in the field and the ache would morph and tinge with anger, paralyzing me. All of the old hurts that we'd buried so that we could have fun were always right there below the surface, like land mines ready to detonate. I'd cried about what we'd had and lost until my eyes were almost swollen shut. But deep down I think I knew that somehow I'd end up here.

"Why don't you put him out of his misery, Chels? You can't keep ghosting him."

My mom walked in the room carrying a few more wrapped presents and slid them under the tree. "What's 'ghosting'?"

"It's when you act like an asshole to someone you used to care about," Taylor said.

"*Taylor*," my mom scolded. "Language."

I managed a smile. My dad always had the worst potty mouth and Taylor was the one who'd inherited it. My mom sat in the other chair across from where I was reclining and I knew it was time for their special kind of familial beatdown.

"Why won't you at least talk to him?" she asked.

I stirred the soup, which did actually smell delicious. "No point. Us being together always felt like an experiment, and now we know that it wasn't meant to be. We tried, we failed. Twice. We're too different. Plus, he was an absolute jerk about me buying the building."

When I leaned back and closed my eyes I could see Andrew telling me that he was still moving Crush, that it was too late for him to back out of the new lease. That if I'd been honest with him from the outset he could've avoided the whole mess. It was like he didn't even want to try to see my perspective, that coming to terms with my inheritance wasn't just about my worries about being his landlord. He'd had the nerve to ask me if it was enough to buy the building outright, or if I'd still need to finance it. As much as I hated getting into the specifics, I wanted him to know that it wasn't like I was sitting on a million-dollar payout. I was still going to have to work just as hard to keep Frolic profitable, especially now that I was going to be responsible for so much more than just my own business.

I wasn't sure what had shifted in him since he'd stormed away that day, but the Andrew that kept reaching out to me was contrite, like he'd realized how hurtful he'd been. Not that it mattered now. We weren't even going to be neighbors and we wouldn't have to go back to pretending to be nice.

"Really bad timing for a breakup," Taylor said as she stroked Edith, dumping salt in my wound.

"I wouldn't even call it a breakup," I replied as I tossed my spoon on the tray. "We weren't serious, we were just having fun."

"Well, that's how all the great relationships begin, my dear," my mom replied. "You start off enjoying each other's company, until one day you can't bear the thought of being without that person." Her eyes welled and she pulled out the tissue tucked in the sleeve of her navy cardigan.

"Mom..." Taylor's voice cracked. She leaned over and grabbed her hand.

I was trapped on the couch, pinned beneath an avalanche of blankets and an overfilled bowl of soup. But for the first time I didn't want to run away from what was happening. I watched my sister and my mom share their grief and felt ... present. The pain rolling around inside of me that had always sent me off-kilter was still there, but instead of running from it I allowed myself to feel it. I didn't fight off the tears pooling in my eyes. They flowed down my cheeks silently, and when Mom glanced over at me her face transformed. Sadness, understanding, a smile of remembrance, all in the span of seconds. There was no need for words, she saw the shift within me happen. Birdie pulled herself from her warm spot by the fire and ambled over to me, pressing her body against the couch so she could offer me a soft distraction.

I sniffled and cleared my throat so that I could speak without my voice shaking. "Remember the year Dad made us wear those ridiculous striped pajama sets for our Christmas card photo?"

"Oh yes." My mom started laughing as she dabbed her eyes. "We bought them in the summer, but then you had a growth spurt, plus that unfortunate haircut, and it looked like a neighbor boy had snuck into the photo."

Taylor cackled with delight at the memory, even though her cheeks were still wet. "Your pajamas were so short. You were wearing *clamdiggers*."

"Like I had a choice. Dad insisted on those stupid things!"

"Remember the year he put up all those white lights outside without any of us knowing, and he woke us up at midnight to show us, right as the snow started falling?" My mom stared at the Christmas tree with a wistful expression.

"Yeah, but someone was too grumpy to get out of bed."

"I know, I know," Taylor said sheepishly. "I was sixteen and an absolute dick. I'll be the first one to admit it." Her hands flew to her stomach. "Woopsie, someone is acting up."

Edith jumped and stared at her belly too, and we all held our breath as we waited for Taylor to say something.

"Your *faces*!" She laughed at us. "I still have two and a half weeks, and if history repeats itself I'll go exactly on my due date, just like Mom did with both of us. Calm down, this is a New Year baby, not a Christmas baby."

I moved the tray from my lap to the coffee table in front of me and Taylor scoffed. "Sorry, no appetite."

"Chels, honey," my mom said softly as she studied me. "You really liked him, didn't you? And I think he liked you too. I saw the way he looked at you that night I helped you decorate."

I struggled against the tidal wave of sadness I'd been fight-

ing off since I got home. Missing my dad, hating myself for missing Andrew, and doing my best to keep it together so I wouldn't
ruin another Christmas by being miserable. "I'll be fine. I told
you, it wasn't even real."

Could they see through me? That not only had it felt realer
than anything I'd known, but that Andrew had been taking up
space in my brain for longer than I was willing to admit to anyone?

"I don't buy it," Taylor said as she rubbed her stomach. "This
feels different."

I didn't answer and the room went quiet except for the sound-
track we'd listened to every year, from Thanksgiving through
Christmas, George Winston's *December*. The song playing was
"Joy," but my heart was feeling anything but. I bit the inside of
my cheek to keep from tearing up at the happiest point of the
song, the repeated crescendo of notes toward the end that always made me think of doing twirls on the ice.

Mom got up to clear away the now cold soup and Taylor hoisted
herself to follow behind her, bickering about if they should put
it back in the pot or throw it out. I reached for my phone to finally read what Andrew had sent.

> I don't know how many ways I can tell you that
> I'm sorry. Can we please talk? Don't let this be
> like after the night on the boat. Please at least
> answer me.

I froze.
What did he mean, *after the night on the boat*?

chapter thirty-nine

Babies don't care about due dates, which was why William Higgins Engelman decided to make his appearance on December twenty-fifth at 10:26 a.m. It was the second holiday turned upside down thanks to my sister, but I couldn't think of a better reason for me to be heading back to my apartment alone on a snowy Christmas afternoon. I'd spent most of the day at the hospital with Mom, Ryan, and his parents, crying happy tears about our perfect new family member. He was *everything*. The best Christmas present any of us could've asked for.

And the perfect legacy to carry on our father's name. William was named for the grandfather he'd never know, but would still come to love.

I dragged my fingers under my eyes as the tears started yet again. All I wanted to do was turn around and drive back to the hospital so I could stare at the baby, and then hug my sister for the miracle she'd grown. But she was tired and the only person she wanted around other than Ryan was my mom.

I decided the best way to commemorate this upside-down

day was to get outside in what was left of the daylight for a hike with Birdie and Edith. I didn't want to be in my apartment, partly because it didn't feel Christmasy, but mainly because I wanted to be somewhere where I could rejoice in the fact that the world was bigger and more beautiful than I could ever comprehend. The snow-frosted trees and hushed trails would be ours alone while the rest of the world celebrated.

Mainly, I wanted to stay busy so my brain didn't drift to thoughts of Andrew. Because I'd finally responded to his last text, to ask what he meant about the night on the boat, and never received a response.

When I arrived home I was greeted at the door by two very merry pups in need of a potty break. I hustled them outside, then ran back upstairs so I could change from my hastily thrown-on sweats to hiking gear. I made sure to stuff my pockets with tissues since I knew the combination of overwhelming emotions and beautiful views would one hundred percent lead to more tears. I was pulling on my socks when Birdie alerted to someone in the hallway, then went into full-frenzy barking when there was a knock on the door.

It could only be my mom, stopping by on the way home from the hospital. I jogged to the door, wrenched it open, and almost ran into a miniature Christmas tree being thrust at me.

Andrew.

I hadn't even dared to hope that I'd see him, which meant that my brain couldn't quite process why he was on my doorstep looking unsure. Nervous even. My moment of awe was interrupted by a cavalcade at our feet, barking at him until he reached into his pocket, pulled out a handful of treats, and then scattered them down the hall.

"That's my move," I laughed as Birdie and Edith skidded along the wood floor to collect their bounty.

"I know it is, where do you think I learned it?"

I watched the dogs sniff around for the treats. It was the perfect distraction to give me a few seconds to try to compose myself, because my entire body felt electrified with him standing so close. When I looked back at Andrew he was watching me, not with a glare, but with soft, questioning eyes, like he wasn't sure what to do next.

"I brought this for you," he said, holding the tree out to me. "I thought you needed a little holiday spirit in here."

"Andrew, thank you. It's perfect."

The little tree was heavier than I'd anticipated, in a galvanized pot and decorated with tiny white fairy lights, a few pine cones, and red berries, like he'd stumbled on it outside during a walk.

"It's a live dwarf Alberta spruce. You can plant it," he said earnestly. I was reminded of Andrew the Christmas tree expert, just one of the layers I'd discovered in the person I thought I had all figured out.

My body was yearning to touch him like we'd been apart for months. All I wanted to do was press myself against him and forget about all of the static that had been keeping us at odds. But we still had so much to sort out if we expected to make sense of what had happened between us, and what was to come next.

I finally realized that I was being a terrible hostess when he leaned against the doorframe. "Sorry, do you want to come in?"

"Vampire rules." He chuckled and pointed at the threshold. "I was waiting until I was invited."

I stepped back, and Edith slipped past me to welcome him with a few hops.

"Hey, Bug, Merry Christmas. This is for you." He reached into his back pocket and pulled out the fattest bully stick I'd ever seen, which she snatched from his hand. "Birdie? I've got one for you too."

Bird wandered over and gently accepted it with a grateful wag.

Andrew seemed unsure of himself, perhaps for the first time ever, shifting from one foot to the other in the small vestibule. "I was hoping we could talk."

"Same," I answered quickly, accidentally stepping on his words. "Let's sit."

I led him into the front room, where the oversized windows made my apartment feel like we were in a freshly shaken snow globe. The snow coming down was the pretty, melt-on-contact type that ensured perfect vibes without hazardous road conditions. The view out the windows plus the addition of the little tree on the ledge transformed my pathetic apartment into a winter wonderland.

"How did you know I'd be here?" I asked as I planted myself in the corner of my couch, a safe distance from Andrew.

A sheepish smile. "I sort of staked out your place. Sorry if that's creepy."

As if anything he did could be creepy. "But what about Christmas? Your family . . ." I trailed off, realizing how fraught the holiday would be for him now that he had the move on the horizon. My heart clenched at the thought of my role in his family tension.

"We had a nice Christmas Eve at my place last night, and

they're headed to my uncle's in a couple hours for Christmas dinner. I, uh, opted out."

"Uncle Teddy?" I asked, remembering the man who'd triggered the Thanksgiving meltdown.

His mouth went into a tight line. "Yup."

"Good call."

I'd never seen Andrew so tentative. The man who moved through the world as if it owed him something was frozen on the far end of the couch like I was a nervous rabbit in a clearing that he was afraid to startle.

"I took your advice," he began quietly. "About my dad. We talked last night."

I caught my breath. "And?"

A shift, a slight repositioning of his crossed arms as he remembered what was probably a difficult conversation. "It was good." He cleared his throat. "Really good." His voice was rough.

Relief washed over me. If nothing else came from my time with Andrew I would always have *this*. The knowledge that in a small way, I helped two people find their way back to each other.

"That makes me really happy."

The soundtrack of two dogs gnawing on bones added to the awkwardness in the room as we waited to get to the reason why he was here.

"I have some stuff I want to say. *Need* to say . . ." he finally began.

I nodded. "Okay."

His jaw flexed. "First, I'm sorry for being an asshole to you about buying the building."

"I should've told you," I said quickly. I wasn't about to ignore my part in the breakdown between us. I'd been so focused on myself that I hadn't considered how my inability to deal with my father's gift was impacting him.

"Maybe, but that's not the point. I reacted badly. There's just so much *noise* caught up in my business, you know? The dad stuff. I've got a lot to prove. And I took it out on you. I apologize."

He locked his eyes on me and I had to fight to stop my usual reaction to it. It was the Gibson Glare, but so different from what I was used to. Not judging me, but *calibrating*. Assessing how his apology was landing. Determining what to say next.

"Thank you. And I'm sorry that I wasn't more open with you. It's just that—"

"I know," he murmured. "I get it, Chelsea. And that's why I feel even worse about the way I reacted."

I glanced at my knotted hands. I could still feel him watching me, familiar as ever but different at the same time.

"There's something else we need to talk about, if we're going to figure all of this out," he said softly.

An ember started to singe inside my chest. Andrew wanted to revisit the past. It felt like we were heading in the right direction, so why would he want to pile on old hurts? But if he thought it was important enough to bring up, I had to let him work through it. I nodded and braced myself. I could tell by the way that he took a long pause before speaking that whatever was about to come out wasn't going to be easy for him.

"I have to ask why you didn't respond to me after that night on the boat."

I frowned at him. "What do you mean? *I* texted *you*, and you're the one who didn't respond."

"Chelsea, I sent you a message that night . . ." He seemed to have to force himself to keep talking. "I said . . . things. A lot of things."

"We were both drunk," I offered as an escape hatch, waving my hand to fan his discomfort away.

"I wasn't," he said quickly. "I took care of you."

He searched my face, frowning at me as I revisited my hazy memories of the night. I felt like I was downshifting, trying to slow the familiar images seared into my memory so that I could scrutinize them yet again with this new information. Now I could see Andrew, hovering near the edge of the dance floor, sitting with Nolan and the guys with his arms crossed, watching me from across the boat, but never clutching a drink.

"I woke up at the end of the cruise wearing Nolan's jacket—"

"*My* jacket," he said softly, as his expression went pained. "You don't remember me sitting with you?"

I had vague memories of someone rubbing my back, comforting me, but I'd always assumed that it was one of the other bridesmaids. "That was you?"

He nodded. "And that's when I sent you the text. While I was taking care of you." He managed a shred of a smile. "When you snuggled against me I decided that I had to let you know how I felt."

And suddenly a new version of the night started to swim into focus. My head resting not on the bench, but on a solid leg, while a hand that was way too big to be female made slow, comforting circles on my back. I now remembered feeling anchored by the sensation of that hand, even while my head couldn't stop spinning.

Nothing was making sense. Our story ended with him ignoring my confessions, not the other way around. "But I sent you a text . . ."

"I never heard a word back from you, Chelsea. I told you everything I'd been feeling, about you, about *us*, and you didn't respond." His face looked wounded as he recounted it.

I felt like my brain was tripping over itself as I tried to piece together my version of that night and what Andrew was telling me. "I sort of did the same thing in my text. And when you didn't reply . . ."

But I knew now that he understood what it felt like. A heartfelt confession to radio silence.

"I still have my message," he said. "I forced myself to read it every time I was tempted to reach out to you, to stop from embarrassing myself again. I figured you wanted nothing to do with me if you didn't respond to the things I said." He fished his phone out of his pocket, tapped the screen a few times, then reached over to hand it to me. "I wound up hating myself for sending it."

I felt like my entire body was tensed as I took the phone from him. It was a screenshot of a long message and my eyes started to swim as I tried to make sense of the first line.

"Read it out loud," he said.

My voice caught in my throat, but I forced myself to say the words.

"I think I've loved you from the first time I saw you."

Tears flooded my eyes as I looked up at him. He nodded slowly, then jutted his chin at the phone in my hand, encouraging me to keep going.

I could barely manage a whisper as I kept reading. "Have you ever noticed that I'm always watching you?" I stopped to take a deep breath, to once again reassess what I'd believed versus what I was now learning. "I try not to, but I can't help it. I want to know who's making you laugh, and what makes you happy, so I can be the one to make you feel that way. All I'm asking for is a chance, to show you how good we could be together. I never thought I'd be lucky enough to kiss you, and now that I have it's all I can think about. Everything changed tonight. You kissed me like you meant it. Tell me I'm not imagining it. Please tell me you care about me too."

I bowed my head and surrendered to the tears I'd been holding back. He loved me. His eyes were always on me because he *loved* me.

Andrew slid across the couch and wrapped me in his arms, drawing me against his chest and circling me in a tight hug. I exhaled as my body relaxed against his. He stroked my hair and pressed his lips to the top of my head.

"I thought you hated me," I whispered as hot tears slid down my cheeks. I felt his laugh rumble against the side of my body.

"I hated that I felt like I didn't have a chance with you, because there was no Kierkegaard in my backpack."

"Stop." I squeezed his arm. I didn't want to go back to thinking about all the ways we'd been wrong about each other.

He held me close until my breathing evened out.

"What did your text say?" Andrew asked softly.

I always felt a little seasick when I thought about the gibberish I'd sent him, but after hearing what he'd written I sort of wished I could remember the whole thing, gushing included. "I deleted it as soon as I got a new phone. I couldn't stand to look at it, especially after I didn't hear back from you. All I remember is the line that said, 'I wish I wasn't so obsessed with you.'"

"Obsessed? Seriously?"

I nodded against his chest. "I tried really, *really* hard to fight it."

"Why would you do that?" he murmured as he stroked my back.

I let out a long sigh.

"Because I felt like you were the sun and I was a storm cloud. I thought you were the most beautiful, joyful, shiny thing I'd ever seen. You *glowed*, Andrew. Effortlessly. You made everyone around you happy and you didn't even have to try. It was just... you." He squeezed me a little tighter. "I guess I felt like we didn't make sense together."

"Well, that's the dumbest thing I've ever heard," he grumbled.

I laughed. "Yeah, I guess you're right."

My stomach bottomed out as I thought about all the times I'd lied to myself about my feelings for Andrew. If I peeled everything back I realized that there was a little jealousy at the core of it all too. I didn't just want him, I wanted to be *like* him.

"How is it possible both messages didn't get delivered?" Andrew asked before I could get too caught up in psychoanalyzing myself.

I made a disgusted noise and pointed to my phone on the coffee table in front of me. "Android. Between the spotty service out on the water and getting a new phone the next day I think they both got lost in the vortex. The fates were against us."

He stroked my back. "And look, we still found our way back to each other."

My heart thrummed in my chest, but I still managed to let all the remaining tension in my body ebb away.

"So is that a yes?" he murmured, squeezing me a little tighter.

"What do you mean?" I looked up at him. "Yes what?"

He dropped his mouth so that it rested against my ear. "Do you care about me too?" he whispered.

"Care" didn't come close to describing how I felt. How could I put a word to the maddening, all-consuming, decade-long mess of emotions I'd felt for the man?

I dragged the back of my hand under my nose, which made the tears and snot situation I was dealing with even worse. I eased away from his chest to look into his eyes then shook my head slowly. "No, I don't care about you," I whispered back. I took a moment to collect myself before I said the words I'd always felt in my bones. "I *love* you."

His arms went even tighter around me and he buried his face against my neck. I finally allowed myself to believe it. I was drowsy from the day, but my brain kept replaying our history with the new filter he'd given me as we held each other. Looking back with it now shifted every interaction we'd ever had.

He'd loved me all along.

I sat up abruptly. "You didn't say it."

"Hm?" he asked, sounding as sleepy as I felt.

"You said you loved me in the text, but you haven't said—"

He silenced me with a kiss that erased any of my questions, then pulled away slowly, still cupping my face in his hand. His thumb stroked my cheek, drinking me in with the look I'd been so wrong about. "I love you, Chelsea Higgins. Always have, always will."

He drew me closer, then pulled the blanket off the back of the couch to cover us. Both Edith and Birdie wandered in and gave us a pleading look, glancing at the couch then up to our faces.

"Damn. I sort of wanted to celebrate with you under this blanket," Andrew said, raising an eyebrow meaningfully. "But your chaperones have other ideas."

I laughed. "They'll be asleep in a few minutes, then we can go to my room."

He patted the couch and they jumped up and settled in on either side of us. "I'll grab Dude in a bit and we can make our own holiday party."

Not the type of party I'd ever pictured him enjoying, but now that I'd come to know the real Andrew, it made perfect sense. We sat looped around one another on the couch as the snow fell outside my window and the light faded.

So *this* was Christmas. Another year over, and a new journey just beginning.

one year later

I still can't believe you talked me into throwing this party in December."

Andrew was helping me unload wine from my car in preparation for the reopening party for both the School of Frolic and Crush in our new and improved larger spaces. I'd managed to convince him to not call it the Merry Swolemas Grand Reopening. Merry Chrismutt sounded so much better, but we'd agreed to calling it a "Grand Reopening" sans puns.

"You'll thank me when it's over," he said. "Better to do it now so we can relax a little after the New Year."

I looked over at his side of the building and scowled, my breath making a cloud in the cold air. "Andrew, come on! You're parked too close to the door again. We've talked about this."

"Hey, you get special privileges when you're sleeping with the landlord. Once I get her in bed she says yes to anything I want." He winked at me as he hoisted two boxes filled with bottles.

"She begs to differ. Move your car before you forget, please."

"Yes, ma'am." He clicked his heels at me and I chased behind him for a few steps to try to kick him in the rear.

It was still hard to believe that everything had fallen into place so perfectly. Andrew had managed to charm his way out of the new lease he'd signed since the ink wasn't even dry yet, and our contractors had completed the renovation on the building in record time. We'd split Roz's old space down the middle, increasing both of our footprints. Now I had two new employees, Isabella and Jordan, a booked-to-capacity board and train day school, and a waiting list despite all the new offerings on my calendar.

Andrew's business was flourishing as well thanks to strong word-of-mouth recommendations. And more importantly, he was now training his own father after an unfortunate pond-skimming injury. Gerard made it to Crush three times a week, rain or shine.

I grabbed the remaining bottles of wine and followed behind him to the building that felt like as much of a home to both of us as the little schoolhouse we now shared with Birdie, Dude, and Edith. The outside of the building looked much the same as it had the night we'd run into each other a year prior, except the parking lot had doubled in size and there were dependable surveillance cameras in place. The raccoons were still attempting nightly garbage bin raids, but Myrtle had moved on to living a lush indoor life with my mom. The fact that the woman had managed to tame the wild cat was both a mystery and not at all surprising.

I still loved walking in the door on my side of the building. Not only because the space was gorgeous, but because it was truly mine. In a way it felt like everything I did there, every bit of forward momentum, was a tribute to my dad. He was the reason for so many of the new beginnings in our lives, from his namesake grandson to the business that was growing faster than I could keep up with. And in a roundabout way, I had him to thank for Andrew as well. It had taken me far too long to realize that the very things that used to drive me crazy about Andrew were the same things I loved about my dad. The two men would've adored each other.

"Just leave everything in the corner," I directed. "We still need to—"

"Set up the tables," Andrew finished for me. "Yup, I know. I made a checklist."

I placed my hand over my heart and fanned myself with the other. "Are you trying to seduce me, Andrew Gibson? Because it's working."

"Oh, you like that?" he teased. "Hold on, let me read you the rest of it." He pulled his phone out of his pocket and tapped the screen. "Put tablecloths on food tables," he said, lowering his voice.

"*Ooh*, yeah." I let my eyes go half-mast.

He backed up a few steps and urged me to follow him. "Lay out plastic utensils and napkins."

"Talk to me, baby."

He continued walking backward. "Put flower arrangement on table."

I froze. "Wait! Did you remember to pick it up?"

He frowned at me. "Are you seriously asking me that?"

"Sorry, sorry! Of course you did."

"If I may continue." He cleared his throat. "Hook up holiday playlist so it's on both sides of the building."

I stopped walking again. "Speaking of, you forgot to let me approve it."

"Trust me, you can't really screw up a Christmas playlist. There's, like, fifty songs to choose from and that's it."

"Just no 'Back Door Santa,' I beg of you."

"You'll have to wait and see." He raised a devilish eyebrow.

He'd led me to the door we'd put in that separated my side of the building from his. Tonight it would be a bridge between our businesses so our clients could mingle together, but normally it stayed closed and we were the only ones who used it. He opened it and walked through it.

"What's next?" I was still on my side of the building.

Andrew leaned up against the doorframe and checked his phone again, his lips moving as he read through the list. He nodded. "Oh, right. One more thing. Probably the most important item on the checklist."

He took a half step backward, then dropped to his knee.

"Hold on . . ." My heart was jackhammering in my chest as Andrew smiled up at me.

He reached into the pocket of his hybrid sweatpants, fished out a small black box, and popped it open. "It took us too long to get to this point, but now we've got forever to make up for it." His eyes locked on to mine. "Chelsea, will you marry me?"

I couldn't summon any words for a few beats from the shock and I watched his face go white. I finally nodded, big and awkward, as silent tears slid down my cheeks.

Andrew leapt up and pulled me into a hug that lifted my feet off the ground. I was laughing and crying at the same time, and I could tell by the way his breath hitched that he was feeling emotional too.

I wrapped my legs around his body as we kissed, wishing that we could lock the doors and celebrate the milestone on the mats in the corner. It finally struck me that I hadn't even looked at the ring, but it didn't matter to me. He could've given me the plastic band off the neck of a Gatorade bottle, as long as it meant that he'd never leave my side.

We'd been so many different people to each other on the journey to forever. Opposites, to enemies, to neighbors, to clients, to friends, to where we were always meant to be.

Soulmates, leashed together for life.

acknowledgments

Have you ever met a goat?

If you haven't I highly recommend it, because the reality is even better than the cute stuff you see on social media. Thanks to Narrow Way Farm I got to hang with a pack of them during my research phase, from babies to grand dames, and there wasn't one Mean Girl among them. I left the farm trying to figure out how I could incorporate a few goats into my dog-centric, suburban life because they are just that cool. Somehow, someday, I'll be a crazy goat lady. Until then, big thanks to Abby O'Keeffe of Narrow Way for allowing me to get my fix and for answering all of my weird questions about goat behavior.

I had another life-changing research session as I prepared for this book; a conversation with personal trainer Cameron Crosley. He was kind enough to take time out of his incredibly busy schedule to answer my questions, and as we talked I found myself thinking, "This guy really knows his stuff. Maybe I need a personal trainer?" And here we are, nearly a year later and Cam is still making me hoist heavy stuff every week. Thanks for giving me a glimpse into the mind of a trainer, and for kicking my ass in the gym.

As always, endless thanks go to the people I'm lucky enough to work with. Eternal gratitude to my agent, Kevan Lyon, for her clarity, wisdom and author-taming skills. Thanks to the outstanding Berkley team, especially my incredible editor, Kate Seaver, who is equal parts surgeon and cheerleader. My publicity team, including Bridget O'Toole, Dache' Rogers, and Catherine Barra—thank you for your creativity, and for your patience when my pre-launch nerves get the best of me. And Amanda Mauer—thanks for staying on top of absolutely everything!

Lots of love to my local favorite indie bookstores, the Doylestown Bookshop and the Newtown Bookshop, for supporting my writing career since day one. It's wonderful to walk into the shops and feel like I'm home.

To my family and friends, thanks for rolling with the highs and lows that are a part of the writing and publishing process... if you've ever gotten a stressed-out call or text from me consider yourself included, and adored.

Of course, my bottomless gratitude goes to you, the person holding this book. A million thanks for reading, reviewing, and recommending!

And finally, all of my love and appreciation to my funny little family; Millie, Olive, and Thomas, the best CPD couch crew in the world!

unleashed holiday

VICTORIA SCHADE

READERS GUIDE

questions for discussion

1. Puppyhood ain't easy. Were you surprised to learn that dog pro Chelsea was reluctant to adopt a puppy? Do you agree that the potty training/teething/manners training stages are a test of your sanity, or are you 100% Team Puppy?

2. Chelsea claims that she has nothing in common with Andrew. Do you think they're more similar than they realize, or is this a case of opposites attract?

3. There's quite a bit of rescuing going on in *Unleashed Holiday*, both canine and human. How many instances can you come up with?

4. How does Chelsea's reinvented Thanksgiving change her relationship with Andrew?

5. The building means more to Chelsea and Andrew than just real estate. Why do you think that's the case?

6. How does Chelsea's relationship with Andrew's mom impact her perception of him? Do you think the story would've

turned out differently if Chelsea hadn't worked with the goats?

7. *Unleashed Holiday* includes Halloween, Thanksgiving, and Christmas, each with traditions both old and new. If you could take part in one of the holiday experiences from the book (like the Howl-o-Ween party, or the Fall Festival) which would it be and why?

8. Both Chelsea and Andrew have complicated family issues to work through, and both have uncomfortable run-ins with family members as they try to process those issues. Have you ever had a family gathering go off the rails because of old drama?

9. Which dog from the story felt the most like your own pet; brilliant and incorrigible Edith the Boston Terrier puppy, sweet and loving mixed breed senior Birdie, or nonstop goofball Dude the deaf boxer?

10. Bonus question: Did you pick up on any of the Easter eggs that reference Victoria's prior books?

Author photo by Gabriela Barrantes Photography

Victoria Schade is a dog trainer and speaker who serves as a dog resource for the media and has worked both in front of and behind the camera on Animal Planet, as a cohost on the program *Faithful Friends*, and as a trainer and wrangler on the channel's popular Puppy Bowl specials. She lives in Pennsylvania with her husband, her dogs Millie and Olive, and the occasional foster pup.

VISIT VICTORIA SCHADE ONLINE

VictoriaSchade.com

VictoriaSchadeAuthor

VictoriaSchade

Victoria_Schade

Ready to find
your next great read?

Let us help.

Visit prh.com/nextread

Penguin
Random
House